DÉJÀ VU

Books by Fern Michaels:

Sins of the Flesh
Sins of Omission
Return to Sender
Mr. and Miss Anonymous
Up Close and Personal
Fool Me Once
Picture Perfect
About Face
The Future Scrolls
Kentucky Sunrise
Kentucky Heat
Kentucky Rich
Plain Jane
Charming Lily
What You Wish For
The Guest List
Listen to Your Heart
Celebration
Yesterday
Finders Keepers
Annie's Rainbow
Sara's Song
Vegas Sunrise
Vegas Heat
Vegas Rich
Whitefire
Wish List
Dear Emily

The Godmothers Series

Exclusive
The Scoop

The Sisterhood Novels:

Déjà Vu
Cross Roads
Game Over
Deadly Deals
Vanishing Act
Razor Sharp
Under the Radar
Final Justice
Collateral Damage
Fast Track
Hokus Pokus
Hide and Seek
Free Fall
Lethal Justice
Sweet Revenge
The Jury
Vendetta
Payback
Weekend Warriors

Anthologies:

Holiday Magic
Snow Angels
Silver Bells
Comfort and Joy
Sugar and Spice
Let It Snow
A Gift of Joy
Five Golden Rings
Deck the Halls
Jingle All the Way

FERN MICHAELS

DÉJÀ VU

KENSINGTON PUBLISHING CORP.
http://www.kensingtonbooks.com

KENSINGTON BOOKS are published by

Kensington Publishing Corp.
119 West 40th Street
New York, NY 10018

Library of Congress Control Number: 2010930789

ISBN-13: 978-0-7582-4693-6
ISBN-10: 0-7582-4693-5

First Hardcover Printing: October 2010
10   9   8   7   6   5   4   3   2   1

Printed in the United States of America

DÉJÀ VU

Prologue

Maggie Spritzer entered her office, turned on the lights, closed the door, kicked off her high heels, tossed her backpack in a chair, and sat down behind her desk. She wiggled her feet into a pair of scuffed sneakers without heels and settled down to do what she had done at 5:45 in the morning every day since becoming the EIC—read the current edition of the *Post* just as it hit the streets.

She could have read or skimmed through the online edition, but she was a newspaper person with every bone in her body. She was one of those people who needed to hold the paper in her hands and get black newsprint on her fingers. She was also the kind of person who would *never, ever* read a book on a Kindle or any of those other electronic devices. In her opinion, there was something bordering on the sacrilegious about doing that.

As she scanned the front page, her left hand was fumbling in the bag of sugary donuts she'd stopped to purchase on her way to the office. As her eyes followed the printed columns, her right hand was removing the lid of one of the two coffees she'd purchased at the donut shop.

Speed reader that she was, Maggie ripped through the paper, then went back and started over. The second time, she picked out a column, a tidbit, or a story that had caught her eye on the first go-round.

An hour from now, if given a quiz, Maggie would ace it, right down to the page and size of the article she was being quizzed on. "It's why they pay me the big bucks," she muttered to herself.

She frowned when she saw it on the Police Beat page. She read through the two-inch notice, then read it a second time. She saw notices like this every day. Why was this one bothering her? It was not until the third time she read it that she made the connection. Upscale medical building torched. Four offices burned beyond repair. Everything destroyed, including the medical files of the patients in each of the offices. Dermatology, OB-GYN, Plastic Surgery, Podiatry. Okayyy.

Building owned by the four doctors, who had been partners since 1983. Thriving practices. So what was it that was bothering her? She read the names of the doctors again and again, then one final time before it jumped out at her. Dr. Laura Valentine. "Yesssss!" Julia Webster, one of the original vigilantes, had worked with Dr. Valentine. Julia had been a well-known plastic surgeon before her death.

The fire marshal was going to hold a press conference later that afternoon. Maggie made a mental note to tune in.

Maggie stared down at the address, her mind racing. She swept everything aside, turned on her computer, and hit the Google search button. She typed in Julia Webster's name and waited. She read slowly, then clicked link after link until she had the full story on Julia Webster. Tears burned her eyes at what she remembered that had never been printed.

Scissors in hand, Maggie went back to the paper. She clipped the article on the fire, feeling sure that it meant something. What, she didn't know. Yet. But the prestigious address in Georgetown was now engraved in her brain. Sooner or later, she'd figure it out. She always did.

Maggie peeled the skin off a banana and sat back in her swivel chair as she wondered how long it would take before she figured it out.

She bolted upright in the chair. *Backup!* Surely the doctors had a backup system in place in case something like this happened. Computers crashed. Viruses appeared out of nowhere. And then there was the patient confidentiality problem to deal with. About a year ago, Ted had done a lengthy article on how businesses used outside backup systems just in case something like the fire happened. But if memory served her right, it was mostly small businesses and not medical offices because of the patient-doctor confidentiality thing. In the unlikely event the doctors didn't have outside backup, it might mean they had their own personal software in place if something just like this took place.

Julia Webster.

Chapter 1

He was a kind man with kind eyes and ever so professional in his sterile white coat, a stethoscope hanging out of his pocket. His battered medical bag spoke of years of use. His name was Alfred Montrose, and he was president Martine Connor's personal physician.

There was no formality in Connor's private quarters. They were doctor and patient, who were also old friends. "The good news, Marti, is you're going to live. The bad news is you are going to be a lot more miserable than you are right now for the next three or four days. I don't like that you're running a fever of 103, but it's to be expected when you get the flu. Yes, I know, you never get sick, but you're sick now, so suck it up. Lots of chicken soup, gallons of liquids, and bed rest. Let the vice president and your chief of staff take over for a few days. Both seem fairly competent. They are, aren't they?" Montrose asked, a tinge of anxiety in his voice.

The president nodded. "Do the media have me dead and buried?"

Montrose laughed. "What I heard on the drive over here was that you had taken to your bed with some mysterious ailment. I suppose they'll grill me when I leave here. Half your staff has it, Marti. I know it's springtime, but these things don't really go by the month of the year. They hit when they hit, and when they do, they spread like wildfire. Just because you're the president doesn't mean you are immune to catching a bug or two along the way."

"No magic cures?" the president croaked.

"Nary a one, Madam President, other than a hot toddy. A cup of tea, honey, lemon, and cognac. Easy on the tea and heavy on the cognac. Makes you sweat out all the toxins. I don't usually recommend this, because my patients want to go to the drugstore and pay outrageous sums of money for a bottle of pills."

The president nodded. "I'll give it a shot. When I was a little girl, my mother used to grease our chests with something called Musterole and wrap a warm towel around us. Then she'd string a bag of garlic around our necks. We used to get better right away. At least I think we did."

"That's because you weren't able to stand the smell, so in spite of everything, you healed yourself. Been there and survived. So, do we understand each other, Marti? Bed rest, liquids, and more bed rest."

"Yes, I understand. Thanks, Al."

Alfred Montrose looked around as he packed up his medical bag. "Isn't there some way you could . . . make this room more . . . personal?"

The president sighed. "I'm just temporary, Al. Family pictures, green plants, knickknacks, is that what you mean? What's the point?"

"Sometimes the familiar is the best medicine of all. But if this works for you, then that's all that matters."

"When are you going to ask me, Al?"

Montrose struggled to look nonplussed. "Ask you what?"

"About my engagement? To Hank Jellicoe? Don't you want to chastise me for my lousy choices in men? You were never bashful before I moved in here."

Montrose removed his glasses and slipped them into his pocket. "I assumed your engagement was off. Even I know there are some things that are too personal and private to talk about. You are the president now, Marti, and I didn't want to overstep my boundaries. As for Mr. Jellicoe, how could you know what the man was all about? People tend to let us see only the best side of them, tell us what we want to hear. It's always been that way. We all make poor choices from time to time. They say the trick is to learn from those mistakes."

"I guess I didn't read that part of the rule. My track record with men is beyond lousy. It would appear I don't learn from my mistakes. I knew there was something wrong, Al. I let it slide. Henry was so . . . in control . . . so with the program, I'm still having trouble accepting it all. What do you think I should do with the ring? I'm asking friend to friend."

Montrose chuckled. "That's all above my pay grade. You want an answer, I see. Well, then, I think I'd put it in a box and write on the lid, 'This belongs to someone I used to know,' and let it go. One day you'll know what to do with it. Is it valuable?" he asked curiously.

The president tried to laugh and ended up coughing. "I suppose it could feed a third-world country for a little while. You know what, Al? I'm not even sure if it's real. I'm beginning to have my doubts. It looks real, but I'm no authority on diamonds. Just for the hell of it, would you mind getting it appraised for me?"

"Sure. I can do it when I leave here. I'll bring it with me tonight when I come back to check on you."

"Is that necessary? You coming back to check on me?"

the president asked as she rummaged in her night table drawer for the ring she'd wrapped in a wad of tissues. She tossed it to him.

"No, it's not necessary, but it's the way things work around here. If they could, they'd have me babysitting you and reading you bedtime stories. Try and behave yourself, Madam President," Montrose joked.

When the door closed behind the doctor, Martine Connor yanked at one of her pillows and started punching it with the little strength she had. Then she started to cry. Eventually, she cried herself to sleep, her dreams filled with her one-of-a-kind memories of Hank Jellicoe. When she woke two hours later, her pillow wet with her tears, she punched at it again and again, then she got up and pulled on a ratty robe from her college days. It felt like an old friend as she wrapped herself in it. If there was one thing she needed at that moment, it was an old friend. She slipped her feet into fuzzy-bear slippers and made her way to the kitchen, where she poured herself a glass of apple juice and drank it down in two long gulps. Then she made herself a cup of hot tea and followed the doctor's order, light on the tea and heavy on the cognac.

The president reached for a box of tissues as she made her way to the living room, where she stretched out on a chocolate-colored sofa. She gulped at the hot drink and somehow managed to finish it. After she pulled up a bright purple afghan her secretary had given her for Christmas the first year of her presidency, she clicked on the television and proceeded to channel surf as tears rolled down her cheeks. If the world could only see how unpresidential she looked right now.

The president reached behind her for the pillows and fluffed them up. Within seconds, she was exhausted from the effort. She leaned back into the nest she'd made for herself and closed her watery eyes. Eventually, she dozed off as the twenty-four-hour newscasters felt compelled to drone on and on about nothing because it was a slow news day. As she drifted into a deep sleep, she started to dream, one wild dream after another, until she woke drenched in sweat. She didn't have to touch her forehead with the underside of her arm, the way her mother used to do when she came down with a bad cold, to know her fever was gone.

The president wiped at her forehead, face, and neck with a handful of tissues. Maybe she wasn't going to die after all. She picked up the remote control and clicked until she hit the USA Network to watch a rerun of *NCIS*. She wished, and not for the first time, that she had someone on her staff like Mark Harmon. She did love Leroy Jethro Gibbs's wicked smile. She wondered what would happen if she invited the entire cast and crew to the White House for dinner. Maybe she would do just that before the new season started in September. The more she thought about it, the better she liked the idea. And that idea brought another one swimming to the surface.

The president leaned back into her nest and let her mind race. Her idea was so over the top, so outside the box, she knew she could make it work. And if she couldn't make it work, she seriously did not belong in her job. She smiled as her mind continued to race one way, then another. Within minutes, she had herself so psyched that she wobbled out to the kitchen to make another toddy. If one had worked so quickly, a second one should be the magic bullet. Maybe she could sweat out more toxins, and by tomorrow, she'd be almost totally recovered. She would definitely have to be at the top of her game to put this particular plan into action.

Martine dozed and woke, dozed and woke until she

woke from a light sleep to see her doctor standing over her. She smiled when he reached down to touch her forehead. Alfred was definitely old school. "I'm feeling much better, and the underside of my arm told me earlier, after the first toddy, actually, that my fever had broken. Would that be your assessment, Alfred?"

"It would, and you are right on the money, but you aren't out of the woods, Marti. I'm still confining you to quarters. You can do what you have to do from here." Ten minutes later, Montrose was done peering down her throat, done with checking her blood pressure and reading her pulse. He listened to her heart and lungs and made some notes. When he was finished, he reached into his pocket and withdrew the bunched-up tissues that held Marti's engagement ring. He held it out to Marti, who reached for it with a trembling hand.

"I'm sorry, Marti. The jeweler said it was a high-grade diamonique. He said they're big sellers on the home shopping networks and that they look more real than a real diamond. The value he put on it is fourteen hundred dollars. I wrapped the jeweler's report around the ring."

Marti made a very unladylike sound and muttered something that made her doctor grin outright.

It was dark out when Martine woke again. She lay quietly, a little disoriented from her deep sleep. Once again, she was drenched in sweat. She looked around, aware that it was totally dark outside. Inside, the only light in the room came from the television set, which she had put on mute before she fell asleep. She wished, and not for the first time, that she had gotten a dog when she moved into the White House. Someone, she couldn't remember who, had talked her out of it. Right now, right this minute, she wished she had a warm body comforting her, even if it was a dog. It was sad to remember how many things she'd been talked out of. Well, that wasn't going to happen again.

Martine wiggled, stretched, and realized she felt a lot better than when Alfred had first arrived. Must have been the hot *tea*. She reached up and turned the lamp on. Still another rerun of *NCIS* was playing. Must be some kind of marathon today, she decided.

Because she felt so good emotionally, Martine headed off to her bathroom, where she showered and washed her hair. Alfred hadn't said anything about not doing it, so she wasn't disobeying doctor's orders. Powdered, perfumed, and dressed in a clean nightgown and her ratty robe, she made her way back to the sofa and curled up again. She spent the rest of the evening dozing and watching the *NCIS* marathon.

This time, her dreams were pleasant; she was running through a field of flowers, with a magnificent golden retriever at her side. She knew she was dreaming because no faceless person with a gun would chase a woman and her dog through a field of flowers.

Satisfied that she was on the road to recovery, Martine made a cup of plain tea with honey and lemon and carried it over to the sofa. She folded up the purple afghan and draped it over the back of the couch. Warm afghans were for sick people. As far as she was concerned, she was no longer sick, just under the weather. She did her best to concentrate on the late news. She wasn't the least bit surprised to find out she was the lead news at the top of the hour. She grimaced when the anchor and crew wished her a speedy recovery.

Martine couldn't believe how excited she was at the plan swirling around inside her head. Satisfied that with a little tweaking she could make it work, she let her mind wander to other things, like her small family. Such as it was. The day she'd taken the oath of office, her sister, Agnes, had kissed her good-bye, wished her good luck, and said she didn't want to be part of Washington's fishbowl. Agnes had signed up for Doctors Without Borders, and that was the last Martine had heard of her. God alone knew where Aggie was. Then there was Alvin, her brother, who had virtually said the same thing, although he'd whispered in her ear that he was proud of her. He'd mumbled something vague about going to build bridges in India somewhere. So much for family. Now, if she had a dog, she would have a family, someone to celebrate the holidays with. Someone to talk to, someone who wouldn't argue with her, someone who, she hoped, would listen attentively and not pass judgment. She could frolic and play with him when she went to Camp David. He or she could sleep at the foot of her bed. Maybe she'd let him or her sleep in the Lincoln Bedroom. Yessiree, very soon she was going to have a family if she didn't chicken out. She could hardly wait.

Three cups of tea and two glasses of orange juice later, Martine looked at the clock. Her PDB would be arriving along with her chief of staff any minute. The president's daily brief always arrived just as the sun was coming up. She was still wearing her ratty old-friend robe and her fuzzy-bear slippers.

When the COS arrived, they got right down to presidential business, which lasted all of fifteen minutes. The COS then inquired about the president's health and asked if she had any specific instructions for him.

"Actually, I do have something you can do for me if you can somehow do it without a media blitz. Can you get me a dog? A big one. One that needs a home, a rescue if possible. A shepherd or maybe a golden retriever. Gender isn't important, but I think I lean more toward a female. Can you do it?"

The COS looked stunned at the request, but he rose to the occasion. "Do I have a time limit, Madam President?"

Martine squared her shoulders. "Today will be just fine," she responded in her best I-am-the-president voice. The COS blinked, mumbled something about wishing her a good day, and left with the PDB.

Martine found herself giggling when the door closed behind the COS. World affairs would be taking a backseat at least for as long as it took the COS to delegate her request to others. Satisfied that she had started her day on a roll, she picked up her phone and asked her secretary to come to her quarters. Plans were only as good as the follow-through. She needed help with what needed to be done. In order to get any, she had to start in her own backyard.

Martine settled deeper into the chocolate sofa and flipped through the channels till she found the Home Shopping Network. She narrowed her eyes to slits as she stared at the array of jewelry being hawked. Sooner or later they would show something diamonique.

Chapter 2

Charles Martin had set up a buffet on the terrace at Pinewood. "It would be a shame to eat indoors and miss all this beautiful sunshine on such a glorious day," he'd said. The Sisters had agreed.

Sunday these days was dinner at Pinewood. It was the Sisters' way of staying in touch after a week of getting on with their lives. Or as Annie put it, there will be no more separations in *this family*. Everyone agreed, so it was dinner at Pinewood every Sunday, and each of them looked forward to it because when dinner was over, the table cleared, they sat around and hashed and rehashed and speculated on what the future was going to hold for all of them. Today was no exception.

"And there still has been no word on Hank Jellicoe," Alexis said. "I don't know why, but I find that hard to believe. The man gets away from some of the most experienced, the most knowledgeable guys in the spook business and hasn't been seen or heard from since. *Un-be-lievable!*"

"There are a lot of red faces on the other side of the world," Nikki said. "I think we made the right decision when we turned down the Big Five's request to find him. I also think we were right when we told them that sooner or later *Hank will find us* and to save their money. It's nice to know, though, that they wired half our fee into our secret account in case we changed our minds. Speaking of minds, I think we blew theirs when we had Lizzie return our fee. I guess it's safe to say we built a little goodwill by doing that. And not one of the five rescinded our immunity contracts. Lizzie said that was a good thing, and it is."

"I have some news," Annie said, a smug expression on her face.

"And that would be . . . what, dear?" Myra asked.

"Fergus Duffy from Scotland Yard called me early this morning. Me! He asked me to have dinner with him the day after tomorrow. Why are you all looking at me like that? I am not in mourning over Fish. Just like Isabelle is not in mourning over Stu Franklin. What? What? Do you think no man would want me after . . . after Fish?"

"But . . ." Nellie sputtered.

"But what, Nellie?" Annie bristled. "Are you trying to say something here, like maybe I'm not attractive to men of a certain age? Some men prefer *experienced* women, did you ever think of that?"

"That's not what I meant, Countess de Silva, and you know it. What I meant . . . mean is, why now? It's been almost eight months since you all signed off on your deal with the Big Five. What is Fergus Duffy doing here in Washington? He is here, right? Or are you jetting off to some wild and woolly place for this surprise dinner?" Nellie said, refusing to give Annie an edge.

"I hate a wiseass, Nellie. All he said was he was going out to *the farm* at Langley. Seems there is some kind of powwow going on at the CIA, and they called him in. I'm going. But I don't have a thing to wear."

"I'll lend you my pearls," Myra volunteered.

"I never wore that dress I bought in Neiman Marcus, it's yours," Maggie said. "But those rhinestone boots won't cut it with that dress."

"I have a beautiful pair of slut shoes if you can walk in them," Alexis offered.

Jack Emery looked around at the men seated at the table. He rolled his eyes, a signal they should retire to the garden while the ladies got down to the real business at hand, high fashion and a thousand and one ways to reduce Fergus Duffy to mincemeat.

"Oh, good, they're gone," Nikki said. "What else did Fergus say, Annie?"

"That he wants to talk to me. I don't think it's a date date, if you know what I mean. I think he has some questions about Fish and Stu, and he thinks I can fill in the blanks."

"Do you *know* anything you haven't shared, Annie?" Myra demanded.

"No. Listen, I had . . . have a hard time coming to terms knowing the man I slept with was a cold-blooded killer. I can't make that go away. Nor can Isabelle. You were all with me when we ransacked Fish's house out in the desert. We found everything there was to find. The same goes for the penthouse at Babylon, which, by the way, now belongs totally to me because of our key-man agreement. I didn't even know Fish had a will until Cosmo Cricket came up with it.

"Just because he left everything to me doesn't mean I *know* anything. I plan to donate all of his holdings to charity when I get around to it. Isabelle said she's going to do the same thing with Stu's monies. I convinced her to keep a portion of it to start up her new business. She graciously agreed to accept it. Babylon is different, that was a business deal. So if Fergus Duffy's intention is to pick my brain, he's going to come up empty-handed."

"I think he's smitten with you, Annie." Yoko giggled. "I have a stunning jade bracelet that would look lovely on your arm."

"Where are you going for dinner, did he say?" Kathryn asked.

Annie grimaced. "Well, he did say . . . more or less . . . and when I wasn't overly enthusiastic, he said perhaps I should pick the place. He's got that thick Scottish brogue, and it's hard to follow him sometimes."

"Where did he suggest you go?" Kathryn asked.

"*Chick-fil-A*. They have some kind of chicken he likes." Annie's voice was so defensive sounding, the girls went off into peals of laughter.

Down below in the garden where the men were smoking their cigars, they stopped in midpuff.

"I feel sorry for old Fergus," Jack said.

"Maybe we should do a little discreet tailing the night of the date?" Bert suggested. "You know, just to keep up on what's going on. We all know the girls don't share *everything*, much as we lie to ourselves and say they do. It's every man for himself when it comes to gathering information where they're concerned."

"Who are you kidding?" Elias said. "Fergus Duffy travels with a security team just like our Secret Service, and you won't get anywhere near him. Forget it! Then again, Annie might take it upon herself to shoot your dick off for interfering. I'm just saying," Elias twinkled.

"Point taken," Bert said.

"You think Annie will be packing some heat Tuesday night?" Ted asked with a straight face. "She's been like a wet hornet since . . . you know . . . Fish, and how that all went down."

Harry barked a sound that was supposed to be a laugh. "Who do you think would have the guts to frisk Annie? A pat-down? And get away with it?"

Jack blew a perfect smoke ring. "As always, Mr. Wong, you are on the money."

Back up on the deck, the fashion discussion was winding down, with Annie saying she'd accept any and all offers even if she ended up looking like a rummage sale gone wild.

"Anyone want more coffee?" Kathryn asked, getting up from the table.

"Absolutely I would like more coffee; and bring that bottle of brandy in the cabinet. We need a little excitement here," Annie replied.

"I'll help," Yoko said, getting up to follow Kathryn into the kitchen.

The minute the kitchen door closed, Annie leaned forward. "Listen up, girls. I have this fabulous idea. Kathryn's upcoming fortieth birthday. Five weeks from today. I want to throw her a surprise birthday party at Babylon. I'll close the joint, and we can have ourselves a *real* party. What do you think? Don't let on, it has to be a surprise. I can have her haul our slots in for repair and bring a new batch. She'll never be the wiser. Is this a plan or what?"

"That's right up there with going out to dinner with the head of Scotland Yard to Chick-fil-A," Nikki observed, laughing. "Count me and Jack in."

"I'm going to invite everyone I can think of," Annie said. "There's Rena Gold out in the desert with Paula Woodley. Maggie, I'm sure you'd like to invite your new best friend Emma Doty and her friends and that person with the strange name, Abner Tookus. Then there's Pearl and a few of her closest . . . allies. Lizzie and Cosmo, of course. We'll make a real party of it. Maybe Joseph would like to bring his family. While the hotel has excellent security, I'm also thinking I'd like Mr. Snowden helping us out. As an added precaution."

"You're willing to close the casino on a weekend?" Isabelle asked in awe. "You'll lose a fortune, Annie."

"No, dear, I will be deducting it from Fish's side of the ledger. I'm thinking I'll even empty out the hotel. We'll need the rooms. Not all of them, but why not? That way, we'll have *total* privacy."

"I think it's a wonderful idea, Annie. You can count on Charles and me. It will do him good to get away from here for a few days."

"The best part will be the whole strip wondering what I'm up to. We need a theme, though."

Alexis cleared her throat, a signal that Kathryn and Yoko were on the way with the coffee and brandy.

The conversation quickly switched to other matters as Myra poured coffee.

"So, girls, how is life in town these days?" Myra asked as she watched Annie pour brandy into each coffee cup.

"Jack and I are managing, "Nikki said." Since he and Bert made the decision to take over Lizzie's office, things are a lot better. But it's just temporary. Basically, they're closing up shop, clearing the decks, so to speak. He still complains that he's not a defense attorney, but he is, and he's a good one. I'm back with my firm, and it's all working out. More or less."

"I'm back on the road a few days a week," Kathryn said. "Bert and I agreed to each keep separate residences, at least for a while. We still have some issues to work through, but we're getting there. I think. He doesn't think like I do, however."

Annie saw her opening and jumped right in. "Kathryn, who do I have to call to get some of our slots picked up and taken in for repair? We have an order for fifty new ones. Do you want the job?"

"Well, yeah, Annie, I'd love to haul your machines. I'll give you the number later. Tell the dispatcher you want me doing the hauling. Are you going to Vegas?"

"I am sometime in the next week or so. There are a lot of legal ends that have to be tied down," Annie said vaguely.

"Sounds good," Kathryn said. She reached down to pat Murphy on the head.

"Yoko, how are things with you and Harry?" Myra asked.

"Harry is very busy. He likes it when his classes are full. I'm working back at my old nursery. My people took very good care of the business in my absence. I have no complaints."

"Joe wants to get married, and I don't," Alexis blurted. "I do love him, but that piece of paper bothers me. I'm willing to live together, but Joseph said no. He said he's tired of living in sin, and his mother doesn't approve of such things. So, I stay in my little house, and he stays in his apartment, but somehow or other we manage to hook up six days a week. I'm the new office manager at Lizzie's firm. Jack and Bert are working me to death. The pay and benefits are really good. The plan is for me to transfer over to Nikki's firm once they close down Lizzie's office."

The girls hooted to show what they thought of that and offered a ton of advice, none of it good for Jack and Bert.

"I really don't have a story," Isabelle said, "other than I've sworn off men. I opened a small office downtown. I used some of Stu's money to fund the start-up. I'm keeping enough of it in reserve to help me pay the rent for two years, because that's how long I had to sign the lease for. I plan to donate the rest to worthy charities. I have three clients. Small jobs, but I have to start somewhere. I bought a ramshackle house on Connecticut Avenue that's a work in progress. I rescued two cats from the SPCA, Lily and Lennie. And I got a fish tank. I haven't gotten any fish yet. Like I said, small steps."

Maggie held up her left hand, her emerald-cut diamond engagement ring sparkling in the sunlight. "Ted and I are happier than two pigs in a mudslide. We might get married someday, then again, we might not. Time will tell."

"Elias and I are very contented. Well, he is; he sleeps most of the time. I do my thing with the shopping channel, he feeds all the cats and oils the lawn mower for the gardener. My new hips are working out well. I've been able to ride as of last month. Not much, but it's a start. Like Isabelle said, small steps," Nellie said.

"Charles and I just putter around. We have the dogs now, and with Annie here, it's wonderful. So, what we're all saying is we are reasonably happy and content, at least for now, is that it?"

The Sisters jumped in with, well, there's happy and there is happy and similar remarks ending with yes, they were all reasonably content.

"What we're really saying without saying it is, we're missing the adrenaline rush," Annie said.

"We're still on the Big Five's payroll, and we have all that glorious immunity that we can activate anytime we want," Myra said slyly.

Annie chewed on her lower lip. "That only applies to Henry, call me Hank, Jellicoe. Do you girls really think he's going to come after us? By the way, last night I had a dream that there was a line of people outside Myra's gate begging us to help them. We were getting ready to vote on it when I woke up. Maybe it wasn't a dream but a nightmare," Annie said fretfully.

The Sisters as one said there was no doubt in their

minds that Hank Jellicoe, even though he was on the run, would somehow, some way, come after them.

"I heard Global was being sold off, division by division," Kathryn said. "It was on the news last week. That means to me that Jellicoe has no one to call on to help him. We took all his money, so he has to scavenge for funds. I'm sure he's got safe houses all over the world he can hide out in until things cool down. The man could be anywhere. For all we know, he could be living down the road from Myra, and we'd never know it. As far as the public goes, he's already just a memory. I don't know what his priority is in the spook world. My gut tells me he is not at the top of anyone's list but ours. I could be wrong, but I don't think so."

"Did you see his face when Nikki said, 'Hello, Mr. Graverson' back there on Dolphin Drive? It was so priceless I don't think I'll ever forget it," Isabelle said. "He literally didn't bat an eye when Kathryn crashed her truck through his house, and he didn't seem surprised to see us all come off the Jet Skis at his dock. Nope, it was that we knew who he really was. In a million years he never thought we'd find that out, and we wouldn't have except for Emma Doty," Isabelle said.

"He also didn't figure that you and Annie would incapacitate Fish and Stu as quickly as you did," Myra said. "He was counting on them to keep him safe. What a silly, stupid man he is."

"Ah, here come the boys," Maggie said. "Do we need more coffee? Dessert?"

"I'll have another piece of that banana pineapple upside-down cake," Elias said.

"No, he won't. He'll have a sugar-free mint," Nellie said.

To Annie's dismay, the conversation returned to her

date with Fergus Duffy. She turned a bright pink as everyone chimed in at once to offer additional advice. When she had had enough teasing, Annie held up both hands, a signal that all conversation should cease.

"Listen up, all of you. I think I can handle Fergus Duffy all by myself. If I need any of you, you're just a phone call away. Are we all clear on this?"

"Yes, ma'am, we are clear on that," Harry Wong said.

Chapter 3

Myra set the paper aside when she heard the sliding door to the terrace open. She looked up, her eyes full of questions. "You're late today, Annie."

Annie sat down, reached up to tilt the sun umbrella over the table, and smiled. "I've been on the phone all morning. I looked out the window earlier but didn't see you. We need to talk, Myra. Where's Charles?" she said, picking up a small tuna sandwich.

Myra shrugged. "In the war room I guess. I spent the morning out in the barn with the vet. Dogs are all fine, and we managed to corral a lot of the barn cats and give them their shots. It was a busy morning. What do you want to talk about, Annie?"

Annie gulped at her glass of ice tea. "This and that, more that than this. What's going on in the world?" she said, pointing to the paper.

"Well, it seems the president got a clean bill of health. She had the flu. The White House issued a statement saying she has returned to her full-time schedule. And she got a dog. A girl dog, and she named it Cleo. Also, dog gifts have been flooding into the White House. The dog is a German shepherd rescue, more or less, and she said she's going to train it herself. The dog is trained, but she's going to train it to live in the White House. Don't look at me like that, I'm just repeating what I heard on the news." Myra sniffed to show what she thought of that statement. "Other than that, the world is pretty much the same as it was yesterday when the paper arrived. What do you want to talk about, Annie?" she asked a second time.

Annie finished her glass of ice tea and poured another. She leaned across the table, and said, "I want to talk about my *date* tomorrow. If you believe for one minute Fergus whatever his last name is is interested in me, I have a couple of bridges I can sell you. Besides, he's not my type, and I know I'm not his type. I played along the other day with the girls because it seemed like the thing to do at the time.

"By the way, Myra, did you happen to notice anything in today's edition that said the president was hosting some kind of meeting with some of those loony-tune guys who head up all those alphabet agencies?"

Myra bit down on her lower lip. Her hand automatically went to the strand of pearls at her neck, a sign that she was under stress. "I guess I missed that, Annie. Did you read the paper online?"

"I did. Today at four o'clock. Too late for lunch, too early for dinner. A quick in and out, possibly a thirty-minute meeting to discuss . . . *something*."

Myra gripped the pearls. "What do you think that something is? Do you know something, Annie?"

"For heaven's sake, Myra, how could I *know* anything? After all, 1600 Pennsylvania Avenue is chock-full of secrets. When they put it in the paper, it is no longer secret. I did call Maggie, who put Ted and Joseph on it. She was just as suspicious as I was, more so with Fergus wanting to have dinner with me. She's going to have Ted and Joseph show up where we have dinner and they'll run the picture in the Life section of the paper. Something is going on, or else something is in the works. I feel it. Hell, Myra, I can *smell* it."

"I wish you'd stop talking in riddles, Annie. What? Are you sure you just aren't jittery about your dinner date? White House business is not our business. We're done with all of that."

"No, we are not done with that, Myra, and you damn well know it. We aren't done with *that* until Hank Jellicoe is caught."

"Well, dear, according to Charles, that is not going to happen. He said Hank is too smart. He said the only way Hank will get caught is if Hank wants to get caught. Period. End of Hank Jellicoe."

Annie laughed, a strange sound that held no merriment. "And you *believe* that? From here on in, Myra, I'm going to pretend I don't even know you."

Myra had the good grace to look chagrined.

Annie relented. "It's okay, Myra. Sometimes you just can't fix stupid. I'm not saying you're stupid, but I am saying you need to be more alert, more with it, as the girls say. We don't want them coming down on us for being old with antiquated thinking, now, do we?"

"God forgive me, and God forgive me for being stupid," Myra said with a bite to her voice. She stared across the meadow of green grass as Lady and her pups, who were on the verge of leaving puppyhood behind, romped and played.

"As long as one of us has her wits about her, we'll be okay. By the way, after dinner with Fergus tomorrow, I am taking the red-eye."

"You're leaving me here alone!" There was such outrage in Myra's voice, Annie blinked, then blinked again.

"Whoa, there, Myra. I don't live here, I'm your guest.
It's time for me to leave. I have to start thinking about
putting down roots someplace. Since I turned my planta-
tion over to Joseph and his family, I'm more or less root-
less. Oh, yes, I have that penthouse in Vegas, but it doesn't
feel like home. I want someplace where I can make a mess,
putter around, get some dogs and cats of my own. Maybe
someplace in the desert. You could come with me, you
know. That's if Charles will let you come. I do have to
plan Kathryn's party and could use some help. I could get
one of those party planners, but then it becomes imper-
sonal, if you know what I mean."

"I know what you mean, but what did you mean when
you said if Charles will *let* me go with you?"

Annie smiled, and said sweetly, "Just what I said. You
are married, Myra. You always check with Charles before
you do anything. I'm just saying . . ."

"Well, you can stop saying whatever it is you aren't saying. I can do whatever I want, and Charles would never
stop me. Shame on you, Annie, for even thinking I don't
have a mind of my own. I will be happy to accompany you
to Las Vegas. And, no, I do not have to *ask* Charles, but I
will *tell* him I'm going. It's the right thing to do. Now," she
said briskly, "tell me what we're really going to be doing
besides arranging Kathryn's fortieth birthday party."

Well, that worked rather nicely. Annie smiled.

Myra stared across the table at her old friend. "You
tricked me. Dammit, am I that gullible?"

"You said it, I didn't." Annie laughed. "I'm so glad you
decided to go with me to Vegas."

Myra snorted. "Why do you keep looking at your watch?"

"Because . . ." Annie said dramatically, "Nellie called me a little while ago and said she's coming over. She sounded in a snit over something. Maybe something went awry with Elias. I have to say she sounded upset. Nellie rarely gets upset, and right now she seems to be late."

"No, I'm not late, your watch is fast. I let myself in, ladies. Some watchdog you have there, Myra. The five of them didn't even pick up my scent," retired federal judge Nellie Easter said as she plopped down on one of the deck chairs. She winced, then squirmed till she got comfortable. "My hips are telling me it's going to rain before the end of the day."

Myra and Annie looked upward at the clear blue sky. According to Nellie, her new hips were never wrong.

"So, what brings you over here in the middle of the day?" Myra asked as she poured ice tea into a frosty glass she pulled out of the minicooler at her feet. "The sandwiches are tuna or salmon. Help yourself."

"Elias. Elias is what brought me over here."

Myra risked a glance at Annie, who rolled her eyes and looked smug.

"He's been acting very secretive the past few days. And this morning he said he had to go into town. We all know Elias does not go into town unless it is to go to someone's funeral, and there are no funerals going on. I checked. He even took that crazy phone he uses into the bathroom when he took a shower. But I outfoxed him. I turned the hot water up and steamed up the bathroom and sneaked in. I checked his phone, and he's been getting calls from blocked numbers. Quite a few of them, and one of them came from the White House. He's done with all that. Or he said he was. Now I'm not so sure. I think we should have someone follow him when he leaves the farm. Do you think Maggie could arrange . . . a . . . tail?"

Annie's expression clearly said it all as far as Myra could see. "Funny you should mention that, Nellie. Annie and I were just talking about how strange we think things are at the moment. Annie's got herself convinced her date tomorrow evening with Fergus . . . for some reason neither of us can remember his last name, is about more than dinner."

"Duffy. His last name is Duffy," Nellie volunteered. "You can't go out to dinner with someone whose last name you don't know. It just isn't done, Annie. Remember now, his name is Duffy. I also think Myra is right, Annie, and I mean no offense. Why were you singled out, and what is he doing here in the States anyway? He's from Scotland Yard."

"You sure know how to make a girl feel good about herself, Nellie," Annie grumbled.

"The president was sick, the flu or something like the flu, according to the paper, and I am thinking she had about ten days to sit up there in the presidential quarters. I bet she did a lot of thinking while she was recuperating. And time to think about Hank Jellicoe and that crazy engagement she had going on back when she granted our pardons. I think Annie is right; something is going on or will be soon. Now that you tell us Elias as former director of the FBI is getting calls from the White House, I think Annie's instincts are right. Something is about to happen," Myra said.

"But the big question is . . . is it any of our business? Does it involve us? We aren't the vigilantes anymore," Annie said. "We've been reduced to planning birthday parties for entertainment."

"We will always be the vigilantes. If not physically, at least in spirit," Myra said, her tone haughty and defiant.

Annie sighed happily. "I love it when you talk like that,

Myra. It gives me hope. Of what, I have no clue. So where does all of that leave us?"

"Right where we were before Nellie arrived, except you have to call Maggie to put a tail on Elias."

Myra turned to Nellie, and asked, "How alert is Elias these days?"

"I don't think he thinks I know anything. He's been retired from the FBI for quite a while now. I don't think he's on high alert, if that's what you mean. I don't think it will occur to him that someone might be following him. I haven't done anything out of the ordinary to make him suspicious. I always go riding around this time of day if I'm up to it. I can tell you this, though, I know Elias, and he was *not* happy with whatever it is he's going to be doing at four o'clock. What really made him unhappy is that he has to wear a suit and tie. I saw his outfit hanging on the bedroom door, his best suit. He also polished his wing tips. And he washed his car this morning. That alone tells me he's going to the White House. You know, spit and polish. Look your best, that kind of thing."

"So, what you're saying is, this is something new. Elias doesn't get called on for consultations or anything like that?" Annie asked.

"Not since we've been married. At least that I know of. Elias shares most things, and the fact that he didn't share what this is about really does concern me. I don't want the administration dragging him into something he doesn't want any part of. And trust me, he was like a wet hornet when all this went down. He does not want to be part of it."

"I'll call Maggie and alert her now. I left my phone in the house. Now, don't you two talk about me while I'm gone," Annie called over her shoulder.

"I hate to tell you this, but you aren't that interesting, dear," Myra said.

"Oh, yeah, well, chew on this one. Who is it that has a dinner date with Fergus Duffy? Aha! Beat it to death, Myra."

"She does have a point, Myra," Nellie said. "By the way, I hate ice tea. Don't you have anything stronger, like maybe bourbon?"

"I do, but you're driving and the sun is hot and, no, I'm not going to be responsible for your falling off your horse on the way home. Drink the ice tea and pretend it's bourbon," Myra shot back.

Nellie sighed and leaned back in her deck chair. "I heard yesterday that the Needleman estate is putting the farm up for sale. I hope we like the new owners, whoever they may turn out to be. We certainly wouldn't want strangers knowing our business, Myra. Maybe you should make an offer, or perhaps Annie would be interested. That way, we'd have a lock on the two-thousand-plus acres and all the privacy we could ever want."

Myra's mind raced. The perfect solution for Annie. "Do you know the asking price?"

"Actually I do know. They lowered it from thirty-seven million to thirty-six million. I didn't even know it was for sale until Elias came home from the barbershop and told me. In this economy, according to Elias's barber, thirty-five million should do it. The estate is eager to sell."

"Annieeeee!" Myra bellowed, excitement ringing in her voice. Annie came on the run.

"What? My God, Myra, that scream would wake the dead! What's wrong?"

Myra told her. She wound down with, "You said you wanted roots. Well, the soil on that farm is about as rich as you can get to put down some good, strong, healthy roots. The house itself is a real hot mess and will need a lot of work, but that's a job for Isabelle. It's been sitting empty for about seven years now, so that should tell you something. We'll be neighbors. The three of us. It doesn't get any better than that. Buy it, Annie. Please."

"Okay," Annie said agreeably, "but what exactly am I buying, ladies?"

"Three hundred and fifty acres of prime Virginia real estate. That's how many acres are on the Needleman parcel. The layout is pretty much the same as my place here and Nellie's farm, though mine is considerably larger. It will need a lot of work, but like I said, Isabelle is your girl. Oh, Annie, this is your chance to put down those roots and still be close to me and Nellie, not to mention all the girls. It's the perfect solution. But you have to be happy with the purchase. I know you're into bright lights and glitz and glamour, but this could be your nest to come home to when you're . . . you know . . . burned out from that busy life."

"Okay, I'll call Conrad and tell him to do it. He's my business manager," Annie said for Nellie's benefit. "Do you know the name of the realtor?"

"Alice Orman, Adventure Travel. It's right on Main Street in town."

"Okay, I'm going to do it. By the way, how much is it?"

"Well the barber said it was reduced from thirty-seven million to thirty-six but he, the barber, thinks you can get it for thirty-five. I'd offer thirty-four five and offer a cash deal, no mortgage. The barber said the estate is eager to sell, and in this economy they might jump at a cash sale."

"I'll have to buy it through one of my holding companies. If they find out I'm the buyer, the price will double or triple. People think I'm made of money and stupid at the same time."

"That should work," Myra said happily. "You might want to stop by the barbershop and offer the barber a finder's fee or whatever it is they give someone who turns you on to a property."

"I do love the way you spend my money, Myra." As she punched in her business manager's phone number, Annie said, "Maggie's on it. A tail will pick up Elias at the gas station. She's going to have Joseph do it. She said he is exceptional at tailing cars. She's going to have Ted positioned somewhere farther on to pick him up the closer he gets to town. She's on that, too, and that's all we have to worry about." Annie turned her back and spoke quickly to the person on the other end of her cell phone. She was beaming when she hung up.

"I do think, ladies, I may very well be your new neighbor very shortly."

Myra and Nellie jumped right in with suggestions.

"A sunroom for the morning sun where you can have your coffee."

"The library has to be redone, and I think mahogany would be great."

"Super-duper state-of-the-art kitchen that will make Charles drool."

"One of those really modern bathrooms with thirty-seven jets to pound your body!"

"A real veranda with a lot of Southern rocking chairs."

And on and on it went until Annie's cell rang. She was grinning from ear to ear when she said, "The estate accepted my offer for thirty-four five. In thirty days, I will be your new neighbor!"

"All rightttt! Myra, what does this call for?" Nellie asked.

"Mr. Kentucky himself. Coming right up," Myra said as she headed for the kitchen and the bourbon. "Should we include Charles in this little celebration?"

"Let's not," Nellie said cheerfully.

"Okay," Myra said just as cheerfully.

Within minutes the celebration party was on.

When all three cell phones rang, one after the other, four hours later, there was no one coherent or who cared enough to answer them except Charles, who had just come out to the terrace to ask what the ladies would like for dinner. Lady and her pups were lying on the deck, whimpering and whining at these strange goings-on. Charles picked up the phone, clicked it on, and heard Maggie giving him a breathless update. He listened, frowned, and told her to keep calling with updates, as Myra, Annie, and Nellie were indisposed.

"You mean they're snookered? What are they celebrating?"

"God alone knows. Do you want to tell me why you're tailing Elias? No, this is not need to know, Maggie. I *do* need to know, and I need to know *now*!"

Chapter 4

Maggie Spritzer slowly took the skin off a banana, then leaned back in her comfortable chair. She was wearing what she called her granny glasses. She peered over the top of them as she glared at her star reporter, a.k.a. her fiancé, and his partner, her star photographer. She chomped down on the banana and motioned for the duo to take a seat.

"I'm not going to like this, am I?" Ted grumbled.

"Probably not, but ask me if I care. A job is a job, you take the good with the bad. Actually, I'm going to give you a choice, so think carefully before you answer me. That goes for you, too, Espinosa."

"I live to serve you, Mighty EIC," Espinosa said, waving his arm to indicate he was totally at her disposal.

"Suck up!" Ted hissed.

Maggie waited as she worked on the banana. When she was satisfied she had both men's complete attention, she said, "This is your choice. Saint Anthony's is having their Christmas-in-July bazaar this afternoon. They expect a tremendous turnout. They have a lady attending who makes purses out of candy wrappers. The newest rage, I'm told. She's donating over five hundred of the purses to the bazaar. The church is going to use the proceeds from the affair to send the inner-city kids to camp next summer. A profile of the donor would be great. Now, if you two don't want to cover the bazaar, I understand, so that's why I'm giving you a choice here. Your second choice is to tail Elias Cummings. He should be leaving the farm around two-thirty if Nellie's intel is on the money, and I see no reason it wouldn't be since she's married to the man. Espinosa, you pick him up as soon as he hits the highway after he leaves the farm. Ted, you pick him up as soon as he hits the District."

Maggie tossed the banana skin into her trash basket and broke open a package of Oreos. "So, what's it going to be, the bazaar or the tail job?"

"That's a no-brainer, Maggie. You gonna tell us why we're tailing one of our own? Don't try pulling that NTK on us because if it was need to know, you wouldn't be sending us out to do this job. What the hell is going on?" Ted demanded.

Maggie pretended to think about the question. She shrugged. Annie hadn't said she couldn't clue in her people, and besides, if she couldn't trust Ted and Espinosa, whom could she trust?

"It seems Elias has been acting very secretive of late. Nellie says he tells her *everything*, that they have no secrets from each other. Unlike some people I know," Maggie said, fixing her steely gaze on her fiancé. Nellie managed to check Elias's phone on the sly, and it seems the White House has been calling. Yesterday, or maybe it was this morning, Nellie said he got out his best suit, the one he wears to funerals; he polished his wing tips, got a haircut, and picked out a power tie. All he would tell her was he had a meeting today at four o'clock. You are tailing him so I can report to Annie, who will then report to Nellie, her husband's whereabouts. I don't think I need to remind you that the Countess de Silva owns this paper. We do what we're told. Joyfully, willingly, and we smile while we're doing it. Any questions?"

"More a comment than a question," Ted said bravely. "Elias was the director of the FBI before Bert took over. I'm sure he's been called to the White House so they could . . . you know, maybe pick his brain, some forgotten case the Bureau worked on, and they want clarification, that kind of thing."

Maggie finished off the Oreos and yanked at a bag of pretzels from the overflowing goodies drawer in her desk. "Ya think, Ted?"

Espinosa decided it was time to weigh in. "Shame on you, Ted. Everyone knows Maggie is the one who does the thinking. We're here to serve, to do her bidding, and we *never* ask questions. Is there a bonus involved in this?"

"No, there is not. The two of you are still standing here. Move! Go! Call in every thirty minutes or text me. If you're late, you work the bazaar tomorrow since it's a two-day affair."

Phone in hand, Maggie called Annie. "We're good to go."

Outside, in the summer sunshine, Ted looked at Espinosa and snarled. "What the hell was that all about? I don't like this. If I thought for a minute it was just Nellie getting her bloomers in a knot, I wouldn't have a problem tailing Elias. This ain't some domestic issue. You agree or disagree, Espinosa?"

Espinosa looked down at his watch. "We have two hours till we have to leave. We can either go to an early lunch or do what you're thinking, which is to head over to

Lizzie's office to see Jack and Bert. Five bucks says they are not in the loop on this. We better call Harry, too, and tell him to meet us there. You call him, Ted."

"I'm not calling him, you call him. That crazy bastard can send death vibes through the phone, and I want to stay alive so I can spy on Elias Cummings as per my assignment. Do it, Espinosa." When Espinosa didn't pull out his BlackBerry, Ted said, "Look, you don't have to have a running dialogue with him. State the facts and hang up. As long as we tell him what's going on, we're in the clear, and he won't kill us. He just gets pissy when he's excluded. So! Will you do it already?"

Espinosa hopped from one foot to the other as he toyed with his BlackBerry. "I have a better idea, Ted. I'll text him!"

"Listen, you dumb shit, Harry does not text. We're lucky he answers the phone, and he might not answer, and you can leave a voice mail. You're wasting time."

Ted didn't realize he was holding his breath until Espinosa blurted out his message, which had to mean Harry was live on the other end. "Well?"

"He didn't say a word. You heard my end of the conversation. Now what?"

"Now we hail a cab and head over to Lizzie's office. I still can't believe Bert and Jack are working there. I know it's just temporary until Lizzie can transfer everything over to Nikki's firm, but it still isn't working for me."

"I wonder what Alexis will do when the office shuts down for good," Espinosa said fretfully.

"Do I have to do all your thinking? She'll go to work for Nikki, or else she'll open her own business. She's got a good business head on her shoulders. You're still smarting over the fact that she won't marry you, eh? You know that living-in-sin shit you keep talking about is a real turnoff to women. You know that, right, Espinosa?"

"I don't want to talk about it, Ted, so stop sticking your nose in my personal life."

"Cranky today, aren't we? Alexis is a fine woman, but then you already know that. I don't know what she sees in you to begin with. Be a shame if she bails on you for your puritanical attitude. Get it through your head, some women just do not want to get married. Look how Maggie is dragging her feet. Not that I mind. Kathryn made it very clear to Bert she won't marry him. That should tell you something. All I'm saying, Espinosa, is this—don't do something stupid like give Alexis an ultimatum. Well, we're here!" Ted said cheerfully, as the cab pulled to the curb. He tossed some bills over the top of the seat, grabbed a receipt that he would fill in later, and exited the cab.

"Follow me," Ted said.

"Why should I?" Espinosa snarled.

"Because if you don't, I'm ratting you out to Maggie."

"You are dumber than I thought. Maggie is not supposed to know we're here."

"There is that," Ted said agreeably, as both men went off into peals of laughter.

Alexis Thorne looked up and smiled when she saw Ted and Espinosa enter the office. "How nice to see you two. Did you come to take me to lunch?"

"Nope. We need to see Bert and Jack. Are they free?"

Alexis laughed, a delightful musical sound that rendered Espinosa witless. Ted had to drag him down the hall to Jack's and Bert's offices. They turned when they heard Alexis squeal Harry's name. For some crazy reason, Ted flattened himself against one wall while Espinosa did the same thing on the opposite wall. Harry laughed, an evil sound, as he danced past them straight into Jack's office.

Jack looked up, a confused look on his face. "What did I forget?"

"Nothing," Ted said. We come bearing news. Of course it goes without saying we are not supposed to be here, and for God's sake, don't tell Maggie or our asses are grass. She'll fire us in a New York minute. We literally took our lives in hand by coming here."

"Bert!" Jack bellowed. "Get in here! We have company!"

"Looks like old home week." Bert grinned as he came through the door. "What's up? Were we supposed to do lunch or something?"

Everyone took a seat in Lizzie's luxurious office. Jack pressed a button to ask for coffee and sweet rolls. "Unless you guys want to go to lunch?"

"Coffee's fine. We don't have all that much time before we have to head out on Maggie's orders. It goes without saying, we are not supposed to be here. Maggie will hand us our heads if she finds out. Capisce?"

Jack looked at Bert. Bert looked at Jack. Harry tilted his head to the side, his eyes dreamy and unfocused.

His eyes on Harry, Ted rushed to tell his story. When he was finished, Harry relaxed and slouched down in his chair. "It means something, but we don't know what. Whatever *it* is, it concerns the girls. Just the fact that Elias is keeping it all secret from Nellie is all they need to know. Their imaginations are running wild, ditto for Maggie, and that's why we have to tail him this afternoon. We came here for your input and to spring you on this nice sunny day. We could use some help, and by help I mean . . . we're going to be busy. Maggie would like to know who else is going to this little meeting at the White House. She didn't say she wanted to know, but I'm anticipating her asking, and God help me if I don't have the answer. We thought you two could sort of spot for us. Don't forget that Fergus Duffy, the guy from Scotland Yard, is here in town."

Jack looked up, a frown building on his face. He was about to question Ted when a motherly looking woman wearing shell-rimmed glasses entered the room carrying a tray with coffee and pastries. "It's okay, Melissa, we can pour our own coffee. Will you tell Alexis on your way out to hold all of Bert's and my calls?"

"Sure thing, Mr. Emery."

When the door closed behind Melissa, Jack leaned forward. "Yeah, things are slow here. Bert and I can do that. The Secret Service hates us, you know that, right? If they get downwind of the fact that we're spying on the White House, they'll fry our asses. Just so you know, Ted."

"So don't get caught. Our job is just to tail Elias to see if he really is going to the White House. That's it. The rest of it, that's just the icing on the cake. Maggie did say the girls are extremely worried," Ted said, lying through his teeth. "Especially Nellie."

Bert cleared his throat. "She should be worried. If I tell you guys something, will you swear on Myra's and Annie's lives that you won't repeat it? Especially you, Ted. Maggie can drag anything out of you, so tell me now if you think you can't keep your lip zipped."

"I swear. Okay? She can only do that sometimes," he added defensively.

Harry took a moment to turn completely around in his chair. He locked his gaze on Ted. "Bert has it all wrong. *You* swear on *me*, Robinson. That goes for you, too, Espinosa."

"Yeah, yeah, I get it. I swear on you, Harry."

"Oh, yeah, me too, Harry. I mean it. We both swear on you."

Harry smiled.

"Okay, here goes. Remember now, this is just among us. About four months ago, Elias came to me and asked me to go to the doctor with him. Seems he had some tests done, and he wanted someone with him when he got the results. I was that someone. Elias has been more than a mentor to me, he's been like a father. I'm not telling you something you don't already know. I went with him. Elias has the onset of Alzheimer's. He doesn't want Nellie or anyone to know. He's fine right now, but he does have little lapses in memory, nothing serious at the moment. Like he forgets where he put something or thinks he did something when he didn't do it. He's on some meds now, which he keeps in the car so Nellie won't see them. My point is, whatever reason he was called to the White House, Elias has enough brains not to take anything on. I don't know how he'll get out of it, but I know he won't commit to anything. That's it. All of you, stop looking at me like that. This is not something any of us can fix for him. He's got great doctors. I'll be watching over him, and I'd like you guys to do the same as much as you can.

"Yeah, yeah, I know, Nellie should be told, but I promised, and I intend to honor that promise until such time as I have to break it. You guys would do the same thing if you were in my place, so stop looking at me like I'm some two-horned creature from outer space. I want your promise to help me keep my promise." Four heads bobbed up and down.

"Considering Elias's condition, I know that secret or not, Elias will tell me what went on at the meeting today if it comes off. When that happens, we'll act on the information. Until that happens, we go about our business. Do you all agree?" Again, four heads bobbed up and down.

Jack took a deep breath. "What's Harry's assignment?" Jack asked with a devilish glint in his eye.

Still in his ass-kissing mood, Ted said, "How should I know? He's good at everything. What do you guys think he should do. We called him to keep him in the loop. We have to stick together. Wait a minute, can Alexis hear any of this, because if she can, we are dead in the water, gentlemen."

"What kind of office do you think this is?" Jack asked indignantly.

"It's Lizzie Fox's office. And you don't think this place is wired for *everything*!" Ted said in disgust. "Right now she's probably on the phone with the girls. We didn't have an appointment. We just showed up. That in itself is suspicious, don't you think? Oh, shit, now it's going to get back to Maggie. We screwed up, Espinosa."

"What's with that *we* stuff. This was your idea."

Bert grinned. "Relax. Lizzie made Alexis sign a confidentiality contract when she hired her. She can't talk about anything that goes on here. That means she can't say *bubkes* about anyone who walks through those doors. I was with Lizzie when she explained it all to Alexis. She understood. Lizzie went to great lengths to explain how she could go to jail. Alexis understood that also."

"And you think that will stop her from talking to the girls. I-don't-think-so! She's a goddamn vigilante, and we all know where their loyalties lie—with each other. Sorry, Espinosa, but it's the truth," Ted said.

"Ask yourself who Alexis fears the most—us, the girls, or Lizzie? Lizzie wouldn't bat an eye if she had to turn her in. Alexis knows that. Plus, the girls, especially Nikki, understand that confidentiality part. She wouldn't forgive Alexis, and I also think she'd head her off at the pass if she thought Alexis was going to divulge confidential information. And she'd convince the others to do the same. Believe it or not, those women have rules and ethics that have gotten them where they are. We might not agree with them, but that's not our problem. We're safe," Bert said.

"From your lips to God's ears," Espinosa mumbled.

"Time to make a plan, boys," Jack said.

"We're screwed for sure if we have to go with one of *your* plans," Ted said, getting up to stretch his legs. "Let's hear it!"

Jack sniffed. "I didn't say I was going to make a plan, I said it's time to make a plan, that means all of us have input. Your problem, Ted, is that you're afraid of Maggie. You need to think on your own. You have to learn how to act independent of Maggie. We're here for you, aren't we, Harry?"

Harry looked over at Ted. "Uh-huh."

"Yeah, sure, whatever. So, let's hear your contribution to our plan, and it better not have anything to do with pumpkins," Ted said ominously.

Chapter 5

Bert looked around the office as though he hoped for an idea to land square in his lap. He shrugged and waved toward Jack when there was no lightning bolt. "So, articulate, Mr. Emery. What kind of plan?"

Jack looked around at the skeptical faces staring at him. He, too, shrugged. "I guess we just go for a walk around the White House and watch to see who shows up. It's not exactly a plan, more like surveillance in my opinion. And, guys, we aren't even sure that Elias is going to the White House. Nellie just *thinks* that's where he was going because of the suit and polished shoes. I'm thinking we should be in position about three-thirty. If there is a meeting, no one wants to be late. Scratch that to three-fifteen, forty-five minutes prior to the meeting. They have to sign in, get rid of the junk they're carrying, be escorted to an anteroom, where they wait for the president to see them. Actually, a full hour is probably more like it. Harry can do a few spins on his Ducati, and Bert and I can alternate going round and round while we all keep our cell phones turned on for easy communication. Ted will be the one who knows first where Elias is headed. If it even looks like he's headed for the White House, we get in position and start our surveillance. That's my input. You guys got anything to add, feel free to share it with us right now."

Ted stuffed a pastry into his mouth and mumbled something that sounded like, "That works for me, stupid as it sounds." He licked his fingers and reached for another gooey bun, thinking, if Maggie were here, the pastries would be gone in the blink of an eye. He ate a third one, telling himself it was for Maggie.

"Yeah," Espinosa said.

"Once we confirm that a meeting is actually going on and identify the attendees, what's the next step?" Bert asked.

No one had an answer to the question.

"When are you guys outta here and what are you going to do when you close down the office?" Espinosa asked.

"Two weeks, give or take," Jack said. "Most of the cases and files have already been transferred to Nikki's firm. Bert and I are just cleaning up a few pro bono cases Lizzie had on her calendar. It's a good thing. I wasn't cut out to be a defense attorney or a corporate attorney or any other kind of attorney except a prosecutor. Bert said he feels the same way. But to answer your question, I don't know what the hell I'm going to do. My old boss is trying to win me back but . . . I don't know, it isn't feeling right." He looked over at Bert to see what he was going to say.

Bert threw his hands in the air. "I'm in the same place Jack is. After being director of the FBI, then going through that nightmare with Jellicoe . . . I'm kind of up in the air about which direction I want to go in. We've got nest eggs now, thanks to Lizzie. When I make my decision, I want it to be the right one this time around. You know how it goes, by the time you hit forty, you want to be settled for the long haul."

Harry startled everyone by saying, "That's about the most intelligent thing I've heard since we arrived."

"Well, thank you, Harry Wong," Bert and Jack said in unison.

"Who's moving into these digs once you clear things out?" Espinosa asked.

"Another small law firm. Two lawyers—brothers, actually. Nice guys. They bought all the furniture, even the pictures on the walls. All they have to do is move in. Actually, they're taking over Lizzie's lease, which still has four years to run. That's Lizzie, hedging her bets in case she ever wants to come back," Jack said.

"Well, as far as I can tell, guys, we're done here. Espinosa and I better get on the road," Ted said as he reached for the last pastry on the plate. "Thanks for the eats. Lunch would have been better, but beggars can't be choosers." He gathered up the backpack he was never without and headed for the door, Espinosa in his wake.

"Starting at two-thirty, call, and we'll arrange an open line," Jack said.

"You got it!"

When the door closed behind Ted and Espinosa, Harry bounced out of his chair. "Something's wrong here."

"No shit!" Jack said.

"There's always something wrong," Bert said. "You got any clues, any insight to what that might be, Harry?"

"Well, for starters, what business is it of ours where Elias goes? So we're doing Nellie a favor by spying on him. That's it. So what? We don't even know if anyone else is going to the White House. Ted said it himself, that he wanted to know *in case*, the operative words here are, *in case*, Maggie asked who else was there. This does not smell or feel like a mission to me, and furthermore, the girls are out of business, so the point is moot," Harry said.

"Son of a bitch!" Jack said, ticking off his fingers, "you just said eighty-seven words all in one breath. Way to go, Harry!"

"Eat shit, Jack."

"Boys! Boys! Enough with the compliments. There is that little matter of . . . Annie and her date with Fergus Duffy. That's important, but I don't know why. Maybe because the guy never met her. Don't give me any of that shit that he saw a picture of her and he's lusting after her. I suppose he could be lusting after her money. Don't get me wrong here, there's nothing wrong with Annie in the looks department, and she does have a winning personality. What I'm saying is, why Annie?"

"Maybe because Myra is married and the others are too young for him. Fergus Duffy is an old geezer. I'm thinking that might be the fly in the ointment in what's going on or at the very least motivating the girls to help Nellie. Always bear in mind the girls only tell us what they want us to know. Always, always, remember that," Jack said ominously.

"They miss the action, the adrenaline rush," Harry said.

"Harry, you are absolutely amazing today. I cannot believe how astute you are. You're absolutely right on that, too. To be honest with you, I kind of miss it myself. This," he said, waving his arms about, "is about as exciting as watching paint dry."

"You are a witty man, Jack Emery." Bert guffawed.

Harry wisely remained silent.

"Hey, Bert, I have an idea. You still have contacts at the Bureau. How about giving one of them a call and see if you can find out if the director has a four o'clock meeting at the White House today," Jack said.

Bert thought about the request and shrugged. "I can try, but that doesn't mean my guy will even know, and even if he does know, he might not share his info with me. We're talking FBI here, and the FBI does not have loose lips. He might have to do some hand-wringing and get back to me. It could be a hard sell, and I am persona non grata, as we all know."

"You won't know unless you try, so just do it," Jack said.

Bert did it. Harry and Jack listened to what Jack later described as Bert's version of sweet talking. The sweet talking consisted of the promise of two tickets to the first Redskins game, dinner at Wasabi for two, and sixteen gallons of free gas.

"Well, boys," Bert said as he powered down his cell phone, "I think I got more than I bargained for. My buddy just told me that Director Yantzy is indeed headed to the White House, and he is royally pissed—the director, not my guy—because . . . he is going to have to see Calvin Span, the director of the CIA, at the same meeting along with, are you ready for this one? Donald Frank, Secretary of Homeland Security. John Yantzy hates Calvin Span the way I hate rattlesnakes.

"By the way, I was sort of hoping Span wasn't going to return to the CIA after his open-heart surgery back before we joined up with Jellicoe. When they appointed Karen Star as his temporary replacement, I cheered her on. Langley loved her as much as they hated Span, but I see now he's back in the saddle. He should have stepped down for good. I wish they'd boot his ass to the curb. So, there you have it. What say you all? Harry is so right, I'm smelling something here."

"And he just gave that all up with all those promises you made," Harry scoffed.

"Well, yeah. He did say everyone in the Bureau heard the director bellowing about the meeting, and he didn't think it was a secret, so he told me. It's so wonderful to have friends in high places. We have to divvy up on the promises I made. Three ways, boys, five hundred each should do it! Remember this—I am only as good as the promises I make and the promises I keep. Shell it out and smile while you're doing it."

Jack and Harry handed over the money. Bert pocketed it gleefully as Jack immediately started to text Ted to bring him up to speed.

"Wonder who else is in town that we don't know about, aside from Fergus Duffy," Bert mused more to himself than to anyone else.

"Maggie might know. I can't remember who the *Post*'s White House reporter is because they rotate them from time to time. Shoot, we should have thought to ask Ted. Now, if we were astrologers, we could figure out if the confluence of the planets is merging with the stars and what the outlook will be for this afternoon." Jack grinned from ear to ear at the stupid look on Harry's face.

"You know, Jack, these little White House tête-à-têtes are nothing unusual. I used to have to go there at least once a month. The president just wants to be brought up to speed, then she dresses everyone down and everyone moves on till the next time. I do have to admit, though, that most of those meetings were with the locals."

Jack finished his text and looked up. "Explain Elias going to the meeting."

"That's just it, I can't. I can't explain Fergus Duffy, either, assuming he's attending the meeting," Bert grumbled.

Jack looked down at his BlackBerry and the incoming text from Maggie. "Alan Freeman is the *Post* White House reporter on rotation. They had a briefing at eleven o'clock this morning. Something about an energy bill, something about a diplomat in Pakistan, and the White House sprinkler system is on the fritz. The dog is doing great and is at the president's side at all times. That's it, boys."

"Now what?" Harry asked irritably.

"Let's head out. We'll tell Alexis we're going to lunch. I suggest a hot dog from one of the street vendors. I think better when my stomach isn't rumbling," Bert said.

"Harry, you got your sprouts and seeds with you?" Jack needled.

Harry pulled a plastic bag out of his trouser pocket to show that he did indeed have all the luncheon nourishment he would need. "If your arteries explode, I will leave you right where you fall."

"Oooh, like one little hot dog is going to do that! Get real!" Jack said, dancing out of Harry's way.

Harry stopped in the middle of the lobby. He held up his hand to get both Bert's and Jack's attention. "Just stop and think about what you already ate this week. Steak, fries, hot dogs the other day, burgers, and cheese. Egg muffins every morning. All that sugar in those soft drinks you guzzle. Ah, I hear it now, do you hear it? Click, click, click."

"I don't hear anything," Bert said uneasily.

"I don't hear anything, either," Jack said.

"That's because they're your arteries clicking shut. We all know my hearing is extraordinary compared to yours."

"You are so full of it, your eyes are turning brown," Jack sputtered.

"Better my eyes turning brown than my arteries exploding," Harry said, pushing at the revolving door.

"Maybe we should head to that fruit bar on the corner and get one of those ultrasmoothies instead of the hot dog," Bert said.

"If we do that, he wins."

"Yeah, but he's right. We do eat a lot of crap. Kathryn is always on my case about it. She eats healthy, unlike us. I'm getting the smoothie."

Jack was relieved that the decision to wuss out in front of Harry was taken out of his hands. So Harry was one up on him today. But in a good kind of way.

While the trio waited for their smoothies to go through the blending process, Elias Cummings was tooling along listening to the stereo system in his car, his mind on other things. But he wasn't so preoccupied that he didn't see the black Saturn peel out of the gas station as he drove by. Because he was tall, he didn't have to move his head at all to take a quick glance in his rearview mirror. He had a tail. He almost laughed out loud. And the tail had a name: Joseph Espinosa. He wondered whom he should thank later on. Nellie? The girls? More than likely that pest Ted Robinson, who—in his opinion—was the nosiest reporter he'd ever met. Maggie Spritzer's right hand.

Just because Elias was retired, out to pasture, so to speak, didn't mean he'd forgotten the tricks of the trade. He knew he could lose Espinosa if he wanted to, but sometimes it paid to play the game. What was that old saying? Just because there's snow on the roof doesn't mean there's no fire in the chimney. Yeah, yeah, that was it. Old dogs not knowing any new tricks. A load of crap if he ever heard one. Still, did he want to play the game? No, not really. Let Espinosa follow him. He wouldn't be privy to anything that happened once Elias reached his destination, so in the end it really didn't matter. All they—and there was a *they,* he was sure of it—would end up with was a report on his travel itinerary.

Now, if it was back in the day when he himself did surveillance, he'd have arranged for a second tail the minute he hit the District. Maybe even a third tail. Ted Robinson would pick him up in the District, then Jack, Harry, or Bert would stick with him till he got to his destination.

Elias felt pleased with himself. So much for memory

loss. Well, he wasn't going *there,* he didn't want to think about *that.*

This whole thing was beyond stupid in his opinion. He was retired. These last years he'd gone out of his way to ignore anything and everything that pertained to his old profession. Helping Bert out on occasion when he was director was a pleasure because Bert was like a son to him. And to be honest, Bert always arrived at the right decision even before he asked for his input. Elias had been just a sounding board. A confidence builder for want of a better term. Screw it all. Maybe he should just turn around and go home.

Elias felt his mind start to wander to why he even agreed to make this trip to the White House. The old, tired argument—the president is my commander in chief—wasn't working for him right now. His foot tapped the brake when a maroon SUV in front of him put on its brakes. Great! Just what he needed, a traffic jam. Before he knew it, traffic was moving again, and he was back to thinking about turning around and going back home.

But . . . he'd never turned his back on the Bureau or his commander in chief in the past. He was proud of his dedication to the Bureau. What could it hurt to sit in on a meeting and listen. He'd always been a good listener.

Elias looked in his rearview mirror. There was Espinosa, three cars behind him. Well, he would be entering the District in about two minutes if the traffic kept moving. Then he'd know if he had a second tail. He laughed when he envisioned telling Nellie all about this little trip. Sooner or later, no matter how he tried, he knew she'd worm it all out of him. One way or the other. And to tell the truth, he'd be glad to share what this was all about. He hated secrets. Really, really hated secrets.

Chapter 6

Martine Connor gulped at the last of her cold coffee, draining the cup. She glanced out the window to see that it was what she would have called a glorious day in her other life. Life in the White House was different. Living here she had no time to enjoy glorious days. When she did find a few minutes during the day that she could call her own, she was too wired to do more than sit down and close her eyes. Never mind spending the time looking out a window to see if it was a glorious day or not. Vaguely, she remembered someone saying something about rain later in the day. Well, since it was coming up on four o'clock, and the sky still appeared to be cloudless, that had to mean it wouldn't rain till later or the weatherman was wrong, which was often the case.

When the knock sounded on the door, the president's new best friend, Cleo, bolted upright and waited for her brand-new owner to give her a command.

Cleo, a retired K-9 dog, had adapted to her new owner and her surroundings within hours. The bonding was almost instantaneous. She nudged the president's leg gently, the signal indicating that they should move toward the door. The president's hand dropped to the shepherd's head. "Okay, girl, time to sally forth. Your handler told me you were top dog when it came to judging people. I'm relying on you to do just that when we get into the room." The huge dog looked upward as though she were listening and assessing her new owner's words. "I'm counting on you, Cleo. I'll be making decisions based on what you do."

And if this ever gets out, they'll lock me up and throw away the key. It's kind of like making decisions based on fortune tellers and the stars the way the press said Nancy Reagan did.

As they walked down the hallway, the president kept up a low-voiced running dialogue with the dog at her side. Twice, the dog slowed and looked up at her and again seemed to be assessing her words.

The president smiled and continued smiling when she recalled the conversation she'd had with Cleo's handler. "I can't explain it, Madam President," he'd said when he got over his stage fright at speaking with the president of the United States, "but Cleo can anticipate, she seems to know what I'm thinking before I do. A half dozen times she stopped me from doing something I thought was right at the time. During her time of duty, she was always number one in the field trials. She never screwed up . . . ah . . . sorry, she never fouled up once. I just want you to know, Madam President, I did everything I could think of to keep that dog, but I'm going overseas, and they said no. She did her tour and deserves to be retired. That dog will give up her life for you if it ever comes to that, and I sure hope it doesn't. Ah, could I ask a favor, Madam President?" And of course she'd said yes.

"Don't let her forget me. When I get back, can I come to

see her?" Again, she'd responded affirmatively, with a lump in her throat.

The president stopped outside the door of the meeting room. She bent over and whispered to the big dog. "Make Gus proud of you now, Cleo." The big dog raised her head, and President Connor was 100 percent certain that the shepherd smiled at her. "Good girl! Remember now, these guys are not exactly *the enemy,* but I sure as hell don't like them."

Cleo used her snout to edge the president backward. "I get it," she whispered, "you always go first. Okay, I won't make that mistake again."

President Connor almost laughed out loud when she saw her guests freeze in place when Cleo marched into the room. Whatever they were expecting, Cleo definitely was not it.

"Gentlemen, I'd like to introduce Cleo to all of you." As the president made the introduction, she had to wonder if Cleo would remember the long heart-to-heart talk they'd had earlier about the individuals she was introducing. "We're not going to bother with protocol today since this is just a little informal gathering. Cleo, this is Director Span of the CIA. Director Yantzy of the FBI, and Secretary Frank of the Department of Homeland Security. This last gentleman is the former director of the FBI, Elias Cummings."

Her gaze guileless, the president watched as Cleo's tail dropped between her legs, and her ears flattened against her head as she walked in front of the standing men. She didn't do anything obvious like sniff their shoes, but she did look up at them as she walked along. When she came to Elias she did sniff, her tail wagged, and her ears went to full attention. She offered a paw, which Elias took.

"You remember me, don't you?" Elias said, stooping

down. Cleo barked again. "I personally pinned a medal on this little lady when she came back from her first tour of duty in Iraq. She did a second tour if I'm not mistaken. The *Post* did a long article on her and her fellow K-9s. Sergeant Sullivan . . ."

"Is on his way to Afghanistan. They retired Cleo, and she's mine now," the president said.

Elias ruffled the dog's ears and grinned.

The president motioned for the dog to walk with her to the head of the table that had been set up. "Take a seat, gentlemen. This won't take long. Anyone for coffee or a soft drink?" A steward in a pristine white chef's coat stood ready to serve. "Coffee for everyone," the president said as she withdrew a chew bone from her pocket and handed it to Cleo.

"I want to thank all of you for coming on such short notice. I know how busy you are even though it's summer. I never did believe the myth that nothing goes on in the summer in Washington."

A smattering of small talk ensued until the server quietly closed the door behind him, at which point the president barked an order in a voice none of them had ever heard. "I want a yes-or-no answer to this question. I don't want excuses because there is no excuse I will tolerate. Let's be clear on that right now. Director Span, have you made any progress in tracking down Mr. Jellicoe?"

"No, Madam President."

"Mr. Yantzy?"

"No, Madam President."

"Mr. Frank?"

"No, Madam President."

"It's been a while, gentlemen. I'm finding it very difficult to understand why the three of you and your agencies have been so unsuccessful. It can't be for lack of manpower. I give you everything you ask for. Especially you, Director Span. Sometimes I wondered who was running the CIA, you or Mr. Jellicoe. Which means he knows all your secrets. And all the secrets of the Agency. Do not try to tell me he doesn't know them. The whole world knows he knows. And I want a full briefing on our agents that were killed. He's popping them off, one by one, to show you he can. This is on your doorstep, Director Span. I mean a *full* briefing. As for you, Director Yantzy, this might be a good time for you to say whatever you have to say."

"Madam President, I can truthfully say Mr. Jellicoe knows nothing of the inner workings at the Bureau. I never liked the man, and I make no bones about it. I've said on more than one occasion that the CIA was too loose where he was concerned. It was my belief then and it still is my belief that Hank Jellicoe told the CIA what to do, not the other way around. I'll go to my grave saying and believing that."

"Hold on here, Yantzy!" Span bellowed. "You clods over there at the Bureau don't know your asses from your elbows. You're the goddamn laughingstock of this town."

"That will be enough of *that,* Director Span! I will not tolerate anything but civility in this room. Children squabble, grown men discuss issues and negotiate. Director Frank, do you have anything to add?"

"Only that I agree with Director Yantzy. I have tried repeatedly to get information from the CIA, and none has been forthcoming. They do not share anything with the Bureau and Homeland Security. Our hands are tied, Madam President. I have our best agents on Jellicoe, as does Director Yantzy. The man has gone to ground. I for one have asked repeatedly for intel on those six brave agents. Nothing has been forthcoming. I agree with Director

Yantzy's assessment of Jellicoe and the CIA. The whole damn world knows he was at the helm and Span was his yes-man."

"You burned Jellicoe, Span," Yantzy said. "Did you really think he'd take that lying down? The guy is an expert at black ops, covert ops, and all other kinds of ops. Once you burned him and left him out in the cold, he went to ground just the way Frank said. Now he's going to burn other agents, and I'm not taking the fall for you and your ego."

"Once again, I agree with Director Yantzy," Frank said.

"I think we all know what happened, gentlemen. You have left me no other choice; so listen closely to what I am about to tell you. I am giving you thirty days. T-h-i-r-t-y days to track down and capture Mr. Jellicoe. If on the thirty-first day that has not happened, I will expect your resignations on my desk at first light. Now, I suggest you all go somewhere and have a talk and agree to agree and start from there. That means whatever agency asks the other for something, it is to be given what it needs. All three of you can call here twenty-four seven to apprise me of failure or success on any agency's part. Thirty days, not one second longer."

Elias Cummings looked around at his colleagues, wondering what the hell he was doing sitting here. The three directors looked like they were wondering the same thing but wisely refrained from asking.

The president solved the problem by saying, "Mr. Cummings, I'm sure you are puzzled as to why I invited you to this meeting. Suffice it to say I had a reason. Mitch Riley, your predecessor, who belonged to the previous administration, if I recall correctly, kept dossiers on just about everyone in the world, including Henry Jellicoe. My memory is telling me that Mr. Riley's wife turned those files over when the special agents arrested him. Do you happen to know who has those files at this point in time, Mr. Cummings?"

Nellie was going to love this. Elias cleared his throat, aware of the eyes on him. Was that a smile tugging at the corners of the president's mouth? It sure looked like a smile to him. "Actually, Madam President, I know who had them at the time. I can't be certain of their whereabouts at this moment in time, however."

"Do you recall seeing those files, reading them?"

"Yes, Madam President. However, I was not allowed to copy them. I have to admit I was impressed with the thoroughness of each and every one of those dossiers. I do remember a file on Mr. Jellicoe and it was *thick,* twice the size of the other dossiers. I remember thinking at the time that Riley put J. Edgar to shame with the thoroughness of the material he obtained. It was downright scary as I recall."

Director Yantzy stood up and bellowed, "What the hell do you mean you weren't allowed to copy those files? They are FBI property! I should have them. What? What? You let some creep bamboozle you? That creep let you look at them, then walked off with them, and you didn't arrest that person! I don't believe I'm hearing what I'm hearing."

Elias shrugged. "You weren't there at the time, Director Yantzy. I had no other choice."

"Everyone has choices, even a director of the FBI. Who the hell has those files? I want a name, and I damn well want it now. If you don't give it up, I'll damn well arrest you myself, right here and now, for obstructing justice."

"Stop blustering, Director Yantzy. You are not going to arrest anyone. If you try, then I will have to give Mr. Cummings immunity. Stop grandstanding. Mr. Cummings, tell us who had those files."

"The vigilantes."

Cleo barked at the loud declaration. The president smiled.

A chorus of "Oh, shit!" echoed around the room.

Span stood up and bellowed that he was going to haul in each and every one of the vigilantes and sweat them till they gave up the files.

"Those files belong to the FBI, and you are not going to sweat anyone on our behalf," Yantzy bellowed in return, his face brick red. He also reminded Span that the CIA had no jurisdiction within the United States and that any attempt on its part to engage in the sort of illegal behavior he had just spoken of would lead to the arrest of any member of the CIA involved, up to and including the director.

"No one is going to arrest or sweat anyone. The vigilantes now have full immunity, along with their pardons, from all of their ... ah ... ventures. I personally guaranteed that in writing before setting up this meeting. My name and seal is on every single piece of paper granting them that immunity. Having said that, you are free to contact Lizzie Fox, who represented the vigilantes. If you want to go a few rounds with her, feel free. I want to warn all of you right now, if I hear so much as a squeak that any of you or your agents or anyone representing your agents or your respective agencies goes after those women, I will personally see to it that you will begin to serve your golden years in a federal penitentiary.

"I think we're finished here, gentlemen. Remember, thirty days. Oh, one other thing." Suddenly, the president had the full attention of everyone in the room, even Cleo. "You are not to harass, call, write, or in any way bother

Mr. Cummings. He has told us all he knows. I am giving him full immunity as of ten minutes ago."

The president stood up, and motioned to Cleo, who looked up at her and tilted her head like she was trying to tell her something. Because she didn't know what to do, the president nodded as Cleo trotted around the table to where Elias Cummings was seated. She offered up her paw and barked.

Elias leaned over, took the big dog's paw in his hand, and shook it. He whispered, "You take good care of that lady, you hear?"

"Woof."

The moment the shepherd was at her side, the president turned, and said, "Thank you for coming, gentlemen. Someone will be here shortly to escort you out of the building."

The moment the door closed behind the president the language turned ripe and foul. All eyes were on Elias Cummings, who simply stared at the three angry men. "This room is bugged, you all know that, right?" Elias laughed at the instant silence that suddenly surrounded him.

Just as the door opened, Elias decided he wanted to have the last word. "You three remind me of the Three Stooges. Not only do you look like them, you act like them."

"Oh, yeah, and who the hell do you think you are?" Span hissed.

"I'm the guy that dog liked." Elias laughed, a great booming sound that echoed around the room. "I wish you could see how stupid the three of you look right now. You don't get it, do you? Well, when you have nothing to do, think on it, maybe something will come to you."

"What the hell is that supposed to mean, Cummings?"

Span snarled as they made their way out of the White House.

"You're supposed to be the best of the best in this damn wacky city. Figure it out."

"Crazy old coot!" Yantzy growled.

"Yeah, but this crazy old coot has full immunity and you Three Stooges only have thirty days!"

"Son of a bitch!" Frank bellowed just as a Secret Service agent clamped his hand over his upper arm.

"A problem, *SIR?*"

"Not at all. I'm just a bit wired. Coming here to this prestigious address makes me go haywire. No problem at all."

The moment Elias settled himself in his car, he whipped out his cell phone, powered up, and called Bert. "I know you're all tailing me. Meeting is over. Meet me at the Dog and Duck and bring the boys. I have a story to tell you that will curl your hair. By the way, I'm buying. We could even do dinner if you're all up to it." He powered down, shoved the gearshift into first, and sailed out of the lot. He was laughing so hard he could hardly catch his breath. Damn, maybe this retirement gig wasn't going to be so bad after all.

Chapter 7

Director Yantzy looked up at Director Span. He had to admit, he looked pretty damn good for a guy who'd just recovered from serious heart surgery. He was lean, athletic, with a full head of hair, unless they were plugs. Yantzy knew that the CIA chief wore contacts because he could see his reflection in the glassy orbs. He was dressed in a nice summer suit that probably cost more than Yantzy made in a couple of months. Rumor had it that his wife had money. Obviously, they shared it. And Span drove a hundred-thousand-dollar Range Rover while he himself tooled around in a nondescript Bureau vehicle.

"I guess we better do what the lady ordered," Span said tightly.

"Don't you mean the president? Are you suggesting the three of us go for a drink or coffee?"

"Count me out," Frank said. "I'm coaching a Little League game at six, and I have to get on the road. I'm in no mood for the blame game. The two of you know where I stand on Hank Jellicoe." Without another word, the Secretary of Homeland Security headed toward his car, a maroon Ford Taurus that looked like it had some heavy-duty mileage on it.

Span shrugged. "Looks like it's just you and me, Yantzy. I'm up for a cup of coffee. Let's do the Dog and Duck. It's just down the block. My agents tell me it's a decent place to eat. Peculiar that Cummings bolted so quickly. Guess *she* put your ass in a sling, eh? You look like you're smarting a bit."

Yantzy drew himself up to his full height, which was six two, and snarled over his shoulder, "I'd rather be smarting than have six men's deaths on my conscience!"

Span had no comment as he made his way to his Range Rover and climbed in. "Son of a fucking bitch!" Like he really needed that shit right then. He drove carelessly as he made his way to the parking lot of the Dog and Duck. The only reason he was even bothering to go to some half-assed little meeting was that he knew he was being watched.

Twenty minutes later, having parked his Rover himself rather than allowing some lame-brained valet to do so, Span got out of the vehicle and made his way to the entrance, where Yantzy was waiting for him. They hissed and snarled at each other in low tones, but their expressions left no doubt to anyone who was watching them that both men preferred to be somewhere other than that particular watering hole.

Inside, seated in a dark leather booth, Yantzy gave his order to a waitress dressed in yellow boots that obviously had something to do with a duck. "A double order of spring rolls with the mango sauce and a glass of ice tea."

"Sir?"

"I'll have a salmon burger with no condiments and a house salad. Mineral water, please."

Span decided to go first and open the dialogue. "Look, regardless of what you think of the Agency and me personally, I want you to know I am doing everything possible, just as my agents are, to bring in Jellicoe. If you think I'm blowing off my agents' deaths, think again. They're with me night and day, and before you can ask, no, I am not sleeping.

"You're right, we burned the bastard. We had to. Did I think he was so over the edge he would start killing my agents? The answer is no, and I have to live with that. We'll get him, but I don't know if it will be within the thirty-day timetable."

"Well, that was informative, Span. How the hell did you let that guy get such a foothold in your Agency, anyway?"

Span reached for his mineral water. "I inherited the son of a bitch from my predecessor. Just the way the president inherited him, and the Bureau inherited him. There's something personal in the president's directive. I think she wants to hang him out to dry for what he did to her. I'm not saying she doesn't want him brought to justice for what he's done. I'm saying she has a personal agenda where Hank Jellicoe is concerned."

Yantzy dug in his heels. "I'm not buying that! For Christ's sake, Span, will you get real here? The president is beyond that kind of petty crap. I never even believed she was engaged to begin with. That's something the media came up with on a slow news day."

"I'm not saying you have to buy it. I stated my personal opinion. But let's get back to Jellicoe and how he wormed his way into the Agency. I compiled a rather thick dossier, and as a show of good faith, I'll messenger it to your office first thing in the morning. It details his life from the day he started his own business. He worked around the clock, did favors, ingratiated himself with anyone who could help him. It didn't take that long because the man always delivered on whatever he promised.

"He could cut corners, make things happen that we couldn't do because our hands were tied legally. I think it's called plausible deniability. It worked for him, for the Agency, for the president, and he's been through four presidents. Likewise three directors, not counting me, at the CIA. As long as the job got done, whatever that job was, everyone was happy. Including me. He was the Pentagon's Golden Boy. He got every lucrative contract there was and then some. I'm laying it out for you and not making excuses."

Yantzy looked down at his steaming spring rolls, and then across at Span. "Okay, I can accept that. I'll look forward to receiving the file tomorrow. How thick is thick?"

Span grimaced. " 'Thick' is a word. Pounds is more like it. I'm talking *boxes*. Six, to be exact. And let me tell you right here and now, we missed the name change. Not me and my agents, the first set missed it back in the day. We had no idea Jellicoe's real birth name was Andrew Graverson. So you can hang that one on me if you want. My guys or I should have caught it, but we didn't."

Yantzy said, "Shit happens. I've made my own mistakes where Jellicoe's concerned. Let's just call a truce here, okay, Span? Let's put our heads together and come up with a plan before we find ourselves in the unemployment line. I, for one, happen to like my job, and obviously you like yours since you had a pass after your surgery and didn't take it but elected to return to head up the Agency. I consider Jellicoe your headache, not mine. He comes under your purview. The Bureau will help if need be. Thirty days isn't very long. Don Frank is not going to be any help at all. He's too busy covering his own ass to worry about yours or mine."

Span poked at his salmon burger. He'd only eaten half of it even though it was good. After his surgery he'd made a pact with himself, and that was to never clean his plate and always walk away a little hungry, and it was working for him. His doctors had told him a little more than a month ago that he was in the best physical shape since his midtwenties, and he intended to stay that way. A pity those damn doctors didn't evaluate his mental state. He looked around, his eyes going to the mirrored wall. His eyes popped so wide Yantzy looked up, then into the mirror to see what he was seeing, which was Elias Cummings offering up a sloppy salute of sorts.

"Fuck!" Span said under his breath, his lips barely moving.

Yantzy pushed his plate of spring rolls to the center of the table. "The Big Five!"

"And all of them are *untouchable.*"

"What the hell are you talking about, untouchable? How do you figure?"

"It's your turn to get real here. Emery is married to one of the vigilantes, Nikki Quinn.

"Navarro, my predecessor at the FBI, is keeping company with another one of the vigilantes, Kathryn Lucas. That photographer, Espinosa, is tied to still another vigilante, Alexis Thorne. And Robinson is engaged to the editor in chief of the *Post.* That guy Wong, Jesus, he's a one-man fucking army and he trains my agents, yours, too, and all of law enforcement. He's also married to another of the vigilantes, Yoko Akia. Any further questions, Yantzy?"

Yantzy dabbed at his mouth with a napkin. "I imagine by now Cummings has informed the little group all about our *informal* meeting at the White House. Informal meaning Robinson can relate whatever Cummings is telling him to his girlfriend, who is the editor in chief of the *Post,* and we'll be reading about it tomorrow with our morning coffee. I sure as hell would like to know who owns that rag."

"Scuttlebutt has it Countess de Silva owns it, but like I said, it's just scuttlebutt. Ownership is buried so deep a proctologist couldn't find it on his best day. We're going to look like assholes tomorrow once the paper hits the street. Speaking of that rag . . . don't you find it just a little strange that the *Post* always got there first when it was something about the vigilantes? The *Post* always got it right, like they had an inside track. Spritzer is a personal friend of Lizzie Fox, that hotshot attorney who represents the vigilantes. Spritzer is engaged to Robinson. Robinson is partners with Espinosa and the two of them are best buds with Emery, Navarro, and Wong. The whole goddamn thing is incestuous. So, in summary, yes, I think there is a good chance the scuttlebutt is true and de Silva now owns the *Post*. Now do you understand the meaning of *untouchable*?"

Yantzy flinched and nodded as he plopped down two twenty-dollar bills and shoved back his chair. "If we ever do this again, you're paying, Span." Standing, he turned to look at the chattering group and the array of beer bottles lined up like soldiers sitting on the table. All five men waved cheerily as the director of the CIA and the director of the FBI stomped out of the Dog and Duck, but not before Espinosa got his pictures, which were already on their way to Maggie.

"Do you think it was something we did?" Bert cracked.

"We did wave. Maybe there is some kind of Agency rule saying that's not allowed." Jack guffawed.

"I got their pictures," Espinosa said proudly.

"Maggie's going to love you. Did you upload them to her?" Ted asked.

"I did! And her text says, 'What else?' She wants to see us like *now.*"

"Are any of you interested in their conversation?" Harry asked.

"Now that would be nice. They were like two scalded cats, in my opinion. And they didn't finish their food. Oh, Jesus, I forgot, you can read lips. What? C'mon, Harry, what'd they say?" Jack almost shouted but caught himself in time and lowered his voice.

All five men leaned into the table. "They said we are *untouchable*!"

"No shit!" Bert said in awe. "What else did they say?"

Harry told them, enjoying the stupid looks on their faces.

Eyes wide, jaws dropping, the boys listened as they absorbed Harry's tale.

Jack bowed his head. "Oh, wise one, I will never ever, as in ever, doubt you again. Harry, I am so impressed, I can't find the words to tell you."

"Eat shit, Jack. It always comes down to brains and brawn, and I got them both. God must have gone to lunch when it was your turn in that department."

"You can't hurt my feelings, Harry, because I know you love me like I was your own brother." He made a kissing sound with his lips.

Harry reached across the table and tweaked Jack's ear. Jack went to sleep. "Anyone else want to take on my prowess? Ha! I didn't think so."

"How . . . how long is he going to . . . you know . . . sleep?" Espinosa asked uneasily.

"How long do you want him to sleep?" Harry asked.

"Till we're out of here, and he gets stuck with the bill." Ted laughed as he leaned as far back in his chair as he could get so Harry couldn't reach him.

"Okay," Harry said agreeably. "He might not like it when he finds out it was your suggestion."

"There is that. Okay, wake him up, and I'll use my expense account. Maggie will be happy to okay it." He flagged down the waitress in the yellow boots and handed her his credit card. When she returned, he signed with a flourish and was on his feet a second later. Jack woke up in time to wave good-bye.

"You put me out, didn't you, you son of a bitch! Just for that, I'm telling Yoko . . ."

". . . Nothing. Don't you feel wide-eyed and alert, ready to take on the world? In other words, refreshed and your thinking is clear and pure? I just let you take a little power nap."

"Well, now that you mention it, yeah, I do feel like I could kick your ass all the way to Baltimore and back."

"In your dreams." Harry cackled.

"Yeah, in my dreams," Jack said.

"It's late, boys. Time for me to head home," Elias said. "Don't look at me like that. I only had one glass of beer, and I just had two cups of very strong black coffee. You boys lined up all those soldiers, so I suggest you all take a taxi home. Nellie's going to be wondering what happened to me."

"Who you kidding, Elias? She already knows everything that happened, just like the girls already know. If Maggie knows, they know. You're right about the taxi, though. I can pick up my car in the morning. Harry, you want to go with me, or I can drop you off."

"I drank tea. Not only are you stupid, you are not observant. You and Bert drank all that beer."

"Oh, my goodness gracious," Jack said.

"Damn," Bert said.

"Good night, boys," Elias said as he made his way to

the door. "This place really hops," he muttered to himself." I wonder if Nellie would like to come here sometime." He scratched that thought immediately. Nellie did not like noise, nor did Nellie like bars and raucous laughter.

Right now he wasn't even sure if Nellie liked him. Oh, well, tomorrow was another day.

Chapter 8

It was just turning dark when Elias Cummings drove through the electronic gate at Myra's home. He was here to pick up his new bride. He grinned because that was how he still thought of Nellie—as his new bride even though they'd been married for four years. New because every day he learned something new about her or something new she hadn't told him or something so new he got heart palpitations.

Charles met him at the kitchen door, a silly look on his face. Elias winced. Charles clapped him on the back and said cheerfully, "The ladies are on the terrace, and they are feeling no pain."

"You mean they're drunk?"

"I think they're feeling . . . different than when they woke up this morning. But yes, if you want to be succinct, the ladies are drunk. I think they're celebrating something or other that I am not privy to at the moment. I did hear about your meeting this afternoon. Dare I ask how it all went?"

Elias stared at Charles, a dumbfounded look on his

face. "Are you telling me you don't know? I thought all of Washington knew by now."

"Sometimes, Elias, the girls think of me as the Evil Stepfather and don't tell me what I *need* to know. By the way, I stabled Nellie's horse. We'll take her home tomorrow morning if that's all right with you. How about a drink?"

"Yes, how about one?" Elias quickly rattled off the details of the White House meeting and the aftermath at the Dog and Duck, where Harry read Span and Yantzy's lips, and Espinosa snapped pictures that would be on the front page of the *Post* in the morning. "Washington will be buzzing for a week over that one."

"*Untouchable!* I can't wait to read tomorrow's paper. How very interesting. I think you just answered my question as to what the ladies are celebrating out there on the terrace. From their point of view, I'm thinking they think . . . Oh, I don't know what I'm thinking. A very heady experience for them, to be sure. I can hear Myra now—'untouchable' is such a lovely word."

Elias laughed as he reached for the drink Charles handed him. "This looks like lemonade," he said suspiciously. "I thought you said a *drink*."

"It is lemonade, and you're driving Nellie home. A drink is a drink. It's tart and yet sweet and tangy. I make good lemonade, if I do say so myself."

Elias ignored the light banter. "What do you think this all means as far as the girls go, Charles? Does it mean they can go back to doing what they used to do and get away with it? That's what 'untouchable' means to me. Who in the damn hell has Mitch Riley's dossiers?"

Charles swirled the ice cubes in his glass. He liked the tinkling sound they made for some reason. "Elias, think about what you just asked me. Do you *really* want to know where those dossiers are for certain, or would you just rather . . . speculate? What you don't know can't hurt you. Did Span and Yantzy say *you* were *untouchable?*"

"Now that you mention it, Charles, no, they didn't. Pretend I never asked the question. Well, thanks for the drink. I guess I better gather up my bride and take her home. Thanks for taking care of the horse."

Fifteen minutes of long good-byes left the ladies on the terrace by themselves. Charles walked out, carrying a fresh pot of coffee on a tray.

"Oh, no, Charles, it's too late for coffee. I'll be up all night peeing," Annie said.

"That's so . . . unthoughtful of you, Charles. Is that a word? You need to take Annie's needs into consideration," Myra singsonged.

"I made it, you drink it, then you go to bed," Charles said, authority ringing in his voice.

"Well, if you insist, pour away, Charles," Annie sniffed.

"Yes, dear, pour us coffee. It was nice of you to think of us at this hour. Why aren't you inside working?"

"I was wondering if you'd care to tell me what it was that you ladies were celebrating before Elias came to pick up Nellie."

"Oh, pish and posh. Did I say that right, Myra? You already know, so don't pretend you don't," Annie grumbled.

"I think so, dear. People don't say that anymore, though. I think they're a little more explosive, like Kathryn is when she tells us to get out of her face or to get over it, something like that. So what did you think? *Do* think . . . whatever," Myra said.

Charles sat down and looked at the two women. "Elias asked me where Mitchell Riley's files are. It seems Director Span and Director Yantzy would like to have a look at them."

Annie and Myra both bolted upright at the same moment. "What . . . what did you tell him?" both women asked simultaneously.

"I told him what he didn't know couldn't hurt him. We all agreed that those files are never to see the light of day again. They're safe. He was okay with that."

"Are you sure, Charles?" Myra asked, her hands clutching the pearls at her neck.

"Is there a file on Hank Jellicoe?" Annie asked. "How is it we never thought of that or missed it, Myra?"

"I don't know, dear. Sloppiness on our part, I guess. That isn't saying much for either one of us."

"I don't think it was apparent to the girls, either, so don't go putting all the blame on the two of us. Charles, did you think about it?" Annie demanded.

"No, I didn't. You're off the hook. But you better believe I will be looking into it rather quickly."

"Do you think there might be something in his file that will be a clue as to where he is right now?"

"Myra, I don't know. What I do know is Riley was every bit as good as Hoover at gathering information. My personal opinion is that Hank Jellicoe is close, very close. Everyone thinks he's skipped the country, and he could very well have done that; he's got contacts all over the world, safe houses, identity documents, all fake of course, stashes of money. He could be anywhere in the world. But I think he's right here in this country, and that takes him away from the CIA.

"If he's here, he belongs to the FBI. He'd get a perverse kind of pleasure being somewhere so close we'd never think to look here. He could be living on Dupont Circle or in Georgetown for all we know. The man is a chameleon. He knows how to blend in, assume a new identity, then live that identity."

"Are you going to share that file with all of us? Seven

sets of eyes might pick up something you aren't seeing."
Annie asked.

"Of course. I welcome all the help I can get. Thirty days
to bring him in is not a big window of time. Even for the
CIA and the FBI using all the manpower they have. It isn't
going to work."

"Then what will happen?"

"If the president stays true to her word and follows
through, she will nominate new directors; it's that simple.
If I were to take a wild guess, I'd say she'll go with Karen
Star, the woman who was acting director while Span was
recovering from heart surgery. As to Yantzy, if it turns out
Jellicoe is here in the States hiding out, he'd probably also
be replaced by a woman, and I think it would be Olivia
Malone. First female director of the FBI. President Connor
is weeding out yet once again. Before you know it, all of
them will be gone. Yantzy should have been very careful
about turning the clock back to the good old days before
Elias, then Bert, took over. The president pretty much had
him shoved down her throat after Bert left, and now is her
time to get rid of him and put in someone she wants. If she
can make it all work for her, the next election is guaranteed."

Annie looked over at Myra and smiled. "When Charles
explains it like that, it really does make sense. Maybe this
has been her game plan all along. Think about it. I like
your thinking, Charles. I'm going to call Maggie in the
morning and have her write some kind of column and
mention all of this. If nothing else, it will be like a burr inside Span's and Yantzy's undies, spurring them on and at
the same time letting them know eyes are watching. But
what about Donald Frank?"

"He's already halfway out the door, according to the
press. Frank is another of those nominations she had to

make, according to her early advisors, virtually all of whom were more interested in protecting their own positions in the party than helping the first woman president to put together an administration that would successfully push her agenda. I'm sure that Connor can find some capable woman who can run that monstrosity of a department and be confirmed by the Senate. If that happens, we won't have to wait till the Fourth of July for a fireworks display."

"Then that has to mean she doesn't give two hoots about Jellicoe getting caught. She wants all three out, so she can put people whom she trusts in."

"Well, yes, in my opinion, but you're wrong about her not caring about Jellicoe; she does care. Having said that, she gave the trio an impossible timetable for accomplishing the goal. I would almost bet the rent that she's already in talks with Karen Star and Olivia Malone."

"And at the end of the thirty days, when they can't produce Hank Jellicoe, she just announces the resignations and has the new appointments ready to go?" Myra said, her mind racing.

"And . . . that is when she makes contact with the vigilantes," Charles said. "Don't you ladies get it? Connor is not dumb. She gave all of you full immunity; she's got new people in place, people loyal to her, then you girls bring in Hank Jellicoe, and the next four years are guaranteed. Win-win for Martine Connor."

"Oh, my God!" Annie said.

"Absolutely brilliant," Myra said.

"I think so," Charles drawled.

"The president must think very highly of the vigilantes' capabilities," Annie said thoughtfully. "We're as much in the dark right now as those three men. I wonder why she thinks we can do what they can't."

"Maybe because we're women, and we take no prisoners?" Myra smiled. "If you had to put your money on them or us, whom would you bet on?"

"Well, us, of course," Annie said. "I just had another thought. I think we need to have Maggie get in touch with her friend Emma Doty again. She might remember something else she hasn't told us. Charles, why didn't Jellicoe ever get married?"

Charles blinked. "He was married once. It didn't work out. Lord, it seems like a hundred years ago. His wife was very young at the time; they had a little girl, as I recall. She didn't like his lifestyle. When I went to see him at his compound last year in Pennsylvania, I tried asking him about her, but he chopped me off at the knees. I did hear once, years and years ago, that she was put into the Witness Protection Program. It was a rumor. I don't know how she could have arranged for something like that for herself and daughter, because it wasn't like Hank was involved in something illegal. It was a marital dispute, but she was afraid of him. I do know that from that point on, Hank never spoke about his wife or daughter; it's like they never existed. He's good at doing things like that. Hank didn't like that she left him, and it got nasty. Other than being dumped by the Pentagon, that was the only time I know of that Hank Jellicoe came up on the short end of the stick."

"That's something we didn't know before," Annie said. "There might be something there we can sink our teeth into. Do you know her name? How old do you think the daughter would be today?"

"No, I can't remember her name; he just referred to her as his wife. If I did know it, I've forgotten it. I'm thinking the daughter would be near forty, possibly a little older, maybe a little younger. Don't even go there; that was way before Hank became so successful. They have nothing to do with his life, and why disrupt those lives even if you could find them?"

"But, Charles, what if suddenly, considering the circumstances he now finds himself in, Hank starts searching for them? What does he have to lose? He'll use anyone he can to stay ahead of the game."

"If he hasn't found them after all these years, he isn't going to suddenly find them now. This time, ladies, you are wrong. Let sleeping dogs lie. I think I'll retire now. It's been a very long day. Myra?"

"I'll be along in a few minutes, Charles."

The minute the kitchen door closed behind Charles, Annie leaned across the table. "Aha! Did you know that, Myra?"

"Actually, I did in a vague sort of way. Like Charles said, it was many, many years ago. To be honest, I don't know if it was Charles who told me or Hank himself; but yes, I knew. I never attached any real importance to it; it was a marriage that didn't work out because of his dedication and long hours in building his company. I think that's what I thought at the time. Now that I know for certain, I'll think about it and possibly remember something else."

"It's more information than we had ten minutes ago and more information than the CIA and the FBI have. I can't wait to share this information with the girls in the morning," Annie said as she got up to gather the plates and coffee tray.

Myra wrapped her arm around Annie's shoulder. "We had a good day today, my friend."

"Yes, we did, Myra, and tomorrow it's going to be even better."

Chapter 9

"This is so nice," Nikki said as she looked around the quaint little restaurant in Georgetown. "We're all together just like normal people having a girls' luncheon. We're all here but Myra and Annie, who are preparing for Annie's *big date*. I think Myra is more excited than Annie is for some reason."

The girls giggled as they flipped open the menus the waitress had handed them. Always the most verbal of the group, Kathryn closed her menu, and said, "Why do I have the feeling this is a little more than a girls' midweek luncheon?"

"Because it is," Isabelle quipped. "By the way, in case any of you are interested, I landed a *big* job yesterday. Annie is buying the Needleman farm down the road from Myra, and she wants me to redesign it with her needs in mind. It's going to take me at least a year, but she said that was okay. Yeah, yeah, I didn't go out pounding the pavement for this one, it just fell in my lap, but hey, I'll take it, nepotism aside. I can't wait to sink my teeth into a real honest-to-god project and all the nitty-gritty that goes with it."

A chorus of congratulations rang through the little restaurant as the girls high-fived one another.

The girls played catch-up until their ice tea arrived, and they gave their orders. Then they got down to business, with Maggie taking center stage. "By any chance did any of you have time to read the paper this morning?" It seemed that no one had, so Maggie whipped a copy of the *Post* out of her backpack and proceeded to enlighten all of them on what she was very proud of. "I did it on Annie's orders. She got me right before we were putting the paper to bed last night. Read it and cheer me on, ladies?"

The whoops of delight were muted but still exuberant. "The White House is going to be smarting this morning, and I bet Span and Yantzy, as well as that clod Frank, already have a bounty on your head. You scooped the other papers again. This town will be buzzing from one end to the other," Alexis said.

"I like that ticking-clock logo you have on there. You gonna run with that every day as the hours count down?" Yoko asked.

"Oh, you bet I am. Ted dropped a hint to one of his colleagues at a rival paper at my suggestion, and he should be here shortly to somehow just manage to take a picture of this table or as we exit when we're done. I'm putting myself front and center. I'm not sure whether it's a good idea or not, but my gut tells me to run with it."

"Shows them you've chosen up sides, and you'll take the hit if there is one headed your way. Good going, Maggie," Nikki said. The others agreed.

Kathryn broke off a chunk of crusty bread on her plate, buttered it, then popped it in her mouth. When she finished chewing, she had a dour look, and her tone was just as dour. "They're going to say you're one of *us* now. Even though there is no *us* any longer. Being free agents can still taint you, Maggie."

"Yeah, there is that," Maggie said. "I'm sort of thinking I fall into the category of *untouchable* right now. Who in their right mind is going to take on the *Post*? The only people we, or I should say *I*, have to be concerned about is the court of public opinion. Everyone is fed up with this damn Alphabet City and those cockamamie agencies that are supposed to be taking care of all of us and watching out for us. Ha! We can do better with our eyes closed, and as you all well know, the pen is mightier than the sword."

The women laughed. "She does have a point," Yoko observed.

"Myra called a meeting tomorrow evening out at the farm. Charles is going to barbecue, and he's promised to have some reading material to go over," Nikki said, barely able to contain her excitement. "And the icing on that particular cake will be we get to see Annie's face when she tells us all about her date tonight. I for one can't wait to hear how that goes. Ooops, wait a minute here. I thought Annie and Myra were taking the red-eye tonight after the big date. Did they postpone their trip? Obviously they did if they invited us to dinner tomorrow. What's up with all of that?"

Panic in her eyes, Alexis leaned forward, and whispered, "Nikki, aside, does this mean we're back in business? But I thought . . ."

"What it means is we're consultants. Of a sort. That's how we have to look at it. No one said we're going to do anything. Reading whatever Charles wants us to read doesn't mean we're back in business. I do miss it, I have to admit. Be honest, the rest of you do, too," Nikki said.

"I can't argue with you there," Isabelle agreed. "Here comes our food."

The luncheon talk consisted of listening to Isabelle's plans for the renovation of Annie's newest acquisition with input from the girls that she considered helpful but saying their input was not exactly what she had in mind.

The easy banter continued right up until the coffee and chocolate mousse arrived, along with a chubby reporter from the *News,* who looked like he'd just stopped in for some takeout.

Maggie, who professed to have eyes in the back of her head and hearing that was equaled only by Harry Wong's, waited until she heard the tiniest of clicks before she hopped off her chair and confronted the startled reporter. She snatched the camera, dropped it on the floor, stomped on it, and said, "Oops!"

The reporter started to curse loudly and ripely.

"None of that! This is a family restaurant. My friends and I were having a nice, peaceful luncheon until you started taking our picture. We do not like having our picture taken. You are invading our privacy. We do not like having our privacy invaded. Here," she said, rummaging in her backpack for a roll of bills. Maggie shoved them into the reporter's shirt pocket along with a burn phone Yoko had used to take a picture of all of them at the table, then gathered up the bits and pieces of the camera. "I paid for it. I own it. Now get out of here before I call someone who will make you leave." The chubby reporter scurried out the door, all eyes on him and his hasty retreat.

Maggie looked around at the wide-eyed diners and apologized for upsetting their lunch. She summed it up by saying, "I'm so sorry, but my friends and I are private people."

"Well, damn," Kathryn said. "I thought the object was to have our picture in his paper."

"I think what I just did was for theatrics. I slipped the burn phone in his pocket. Now that scuzzy paper will print all kinds of stuff and get people to wonder even more about what is going on. It seemed like a good idea at the time. This mousse is really good, don't you think?"

"Well, yeah, here, have mine." Yoko laughed.

"Maggie gobbled it down, waved for the check, and said, "Lunch is on the *Post*, ladies. This was fun. Let's do it again next week. Gotta go and see if there's some more trouble I can get into." She signed her name with a flourish, waved, and was out the door before the others could catch their breaths.

"Well, that was exciting," Nikki said as she gathered up her purse and umbrella. "See you guys tomorrow night out at the farm."

The manager of the restaurant looked at his assistant and whispered, "Are those women who just left here who I think they are?"

"Uh-huh."

A second later the manager of the restaurant was on the phone with his wife, who was the chairwoman of the District's Democratic party.

Alphabet City, also known as the nation's capital, started to buzz the moment the restaurant manager ended the phone call to his wife, which just went to prove Maggie's theory that the most powerful method of spreading gossip was by word of mouth.

Myra looked up just as she threw a stick for Lady and her pups to retrieve. The dogs bounded away as Annie walked out to the yard.

"Annie! I thought you'd be taking a bubble bath and getting ready for your big date. That doesn't mean I'm not happy to see you out here. Is something wrong? You don't look real happy right this minute."

Lady returned the stick, her pups yelping behind her. Myra threw it again, and the dogs raced off. "Let's go up on the terrace. We can have some ice tea. I was bored so that's why I'm down here with the dogs, but I think they're getting tired, which was my object when I came out here. I so wish I had half of their energy," Myra babbled as she climbed the steps to the terrace and poured tea into glasses. "Talk to me, Annie."

"I've been reading up on Scotland Yard. I tried to come up with a bio on this guy Fergus, and I'm not getting a feel for him. I need a feel for him, Myra; otherwise, this whole thing is going to be a big bust. He's got the edge. I'm an open book; he can Google me and know everything about me in minutes. I am notable, as you so often remind me."

"What exactly is it that you want to know about this man? His work ethic? His successes at the Yard? His personal life?"

"The whole ball of wax, Myra. How am I supposed to keep up a conversation if I don't know anything about him, and, for the umpteenth time, I do not think for one minute that Fergus Duffy is interested in me as a person. Socially, that is."

"Do you want to borrow my pearls, Annie?"

"For God's sake, Myra, no, I do not want to borrow your damn pearls. I have my own, thank you very much."

"Well, then, what did you come up with, dear?"

"Nothing, that's what. And by the way, it's now referred to as the New Scotland Yard. Based in England. Why is it called Scotland Yard if it's in England? It should be in Scotland, don't you think," Annie said fretfully.

"One would think. When I think of Scotland Yard, I think of Jack the Ripper. If it's in England, as you say, and I did not know that either, Annie, why do they have MI5 and MI6. I know they are on Downing Street. I had an experience there, if you recall."

"Actually, Myra, when Sir Robert Peel was Home Secretary, the first Metropolitan Police Act was passed and the MPS was established in London. They were at Number 4 Whitehall Place. The back of the location opened into a courtyard, which, as a popular anecdote would have it, had once been the site of a residence owned by the kings of Scotland or alternatively a Scottish Embassy, and was therefore known as Scotland Yard. Then in 1967 they moved to a larger and more modern headquarters building at Broadway, which is now known as New Scotland Yard. Do you think that's going to be heady dinner conversation? Oh, one other thing, do not confuse the Metropolitan Police Service with the City of London Police, which is a separate force responsible for the square mile in the City of London."

"The Brits are amazing. They have it . . . as Kathryn would say, going on.

"I wish we had some intel on why the man is here in the first place. I think this all has something to do with that meeting on the plane with Nikki, Jack, Bert, and Kathryn. I just feel it here," Annie said, pointing to her stomach. "My gut," she clarified in case Myra wasn't getting it.

"That's all you were able to come up with?" Myra asked in surprise.

"Other than the DOI has six hundred trained officers targeting surveillance and covert photography techniques. They have something called CRIMINT, which is a computer-based intelligence application that has been completed and sent to all MPS police stations. I was not impressed, Myra."

"Why not?" Myra asked.

"I was hoping for . . . you know . . . *stuff*. I printed out a lot of charts and graphs, but it was like gobbledygook to me. I'm thinking Scotland Yard is small potatoes in the covert espionage world. Almost like a stepchild. Like I said, I wasn't impressed."

"But that's okay, Annie. You are not impressed with Scotland Yard, but that doesn't mean you won't be impressed by the man Fergus. I think you might just be over-reacting right now. What is it Nikki says? Kick back and go along for the ride, and if you don't like where that ride is taking you, get out of the car. See how simple that is?"

"I'm wondering if Fergus is what they call a sleeper," Annie said, scowling. At Myra's puzzled look, she explained, "Espionage writers always use that term to describe someone of importance who they try to make into a nerdy type so no one will be the wiser. I always figure it out."

"I see," Myra said, fingering her pearls.

"You're trying to pacify me, Myra. I can read you like a book. Well, as much as I would like to sit here and continue this conversation, I just can't. I have to get ready, and I'll be heading into town during rush-hour traffic. I have to admit I am relieved that we postponed out trip to Vegas for a few days."

"Yes, Annie, with all that is going on, that was a wise decision on your part. Do you need any help, dear?"

"I think I can get dressed by myself, Myra. Just keep your cell phone on in case I need to call you."

"I will, dear. Annie, wear some of that decadent perfume I gave you at Christmastime."

Annie flipped her friend the bird and stomped into the house.

Myra looked down at Lady, who was at her feet, and said, "I do not know what to do with her. One minute she's hotter than a firecracker, and the next minute she fizzles."

Lady barked as she offered up her paw for Myra to shake. "Yes, you're right, she's a friend, so I take her with the good and the bad. How astute you are, Lady, to bring me up short like this."

"Woof."

Chapter 10

Myra turned when she heard Annie's footsteps on the tiled floor in the kitchen. "Annie! You look . . . beautiful, and you smell heavenly. Wherever did you get that dress? I love it."

"Really, Myra, you aren't just saying that?" Not bothering to wait for a reply, Annie continued, "I saw it in a boutique in Las Vegas. At the time I thought it screamed my name. So, you're saying I'm not overdone or underdone?"

"That's what I'm saying. I just love the color green in all its varying shades. How did you get that gossamer shawl to match so perfectly?"

"Dumb luck. I was at the right place at the right time when they were draping it on a model in the window. Restaurants are always so cold, or at least I think so. And shawls cover multitudes of things, like sagging upper arms. What about my hair? I didn't want to fuss with it because of the humidity, so I just pulled it back. Well, if I look okay, I guess I better be on my way. I'm going to hit rush-hour traffic once I get into the District."

"Annie, try to look like you're going to a pleasant outing of some kind. You look . . . tortured."

"It's these shoes. No, I can see you aren't buying that. What it is, Myra, is this. I like to be the aggressor because then I am in control. I arrange things, I set it up, I know the plan, so I'm in control. I have no control here. This was unexpected. Do you understand what I'm saying?"

"I do, dear, I do. The simple answer is *take* control. You are so good at that, Annie."

"Ya think?"

"Think about it. Look how you tricked me into agreeing to go to Las Vegas with you."

Myra was saved from a response when Lady sat up on her haunches and let loose with a long howl. "See! Dogs are such uncanny creatures. Lady understands and approves. Now, get going and don't speed. Maybe you should hit the bathroom before you leave."

"Myra, for God's sake, I am not a child who needs to be reminded to go to the bathroom before starting on a trip. Besides, I don't have to go."

Myra gently urged Annie through the kitchen door. "Drive carefully. If you can, call me when you take a break and let me know how it's going. I'm going to be worrying about you all night long. Don't stay out too late. I'll wait up for you."

"Myraaaaaa!"

"All right! All right! I won't wait up. Go!"

The moment Annie drove through the gates and down the long, winding road that led to the main highway, unmindful of Myra's warning not to speed, she put the pedal to the metal and roared up the road as she blasted the exquisite stereo system in her brand-new lemon yellow Porsche.

Annie tried to clear her mind, to think of pleasant things like her childhood, her early married life. When she felt a pall settle over her shoulders, she switched gears and thought about Fish and the casino. That just seemed to make her more angry, so she switched again to how she was going to arrange Kathryn's surprise birthday party. Those thoughts stayed with her until she entered the District, at which point she had to give her full attention to the road and the drivers who surrounded her. She received more than one admiring glance, which she knew was for the car and not her. White hair, wrinkles, and gnarly hands did not make for admiring glances. Yellow Porsches, now, that was something else.

Annie suddenly realized as she turned onto O Street that she hadn't given one moment's notice to her dinner evening with Fergus Duffy. She did start to think about it when she turned into a minuscule parking lot that was no bigger than the restaurant itself and turned the Porsche over to a valet attendant.

Annie looked down at the Mickey Mouse watch on her wrist with the huge numbers on it. She was right on time. Seven o'clock in her opinion was an acceptable dinnertime. If she ate later in the evening, she got gas. She'd eaten here at La Petite several times, and she was neither impressed nor unimpressed. French food was so rich she tried not to eat it on a regular basis. Maybe she'd made an unwise choice when she'd suggested it to Fergus Duffy. Maybe the chicken place was the way to go after all. Well, too late now.

Annie opened the door to the dim interior and was greeted by a host whom she knew for a fact pretended to be French but wasn't. Charles told her he was from Poughkeepsie, New York, and used to be in the roofing business.

Jerky Jacques, as she thought of him, a.k.a. name-dropper,

gushed when Annie walked over to his station to inquire about her reservation and to ask if Fergus had arrived.

"But of course, *Countess*. For you, the best table in the house, and your guest arrived just seconds ago," Jerky Jacques said in his best bogus French accent. Annie sniffed as she trailed behind another bogus Frenchman to the table where Fergus waited for her. He stood up, all six foot five of him, and smiled a very toothy smile. He waited until she was seated before he leaned across the table, and said, "I'm sorry, I'm not dressed appropriately for such a fancy restaurant. You, of course, look lovely."

"I think you look just fine," Annie said, looking at his open-necked sports shirt and creased khaki trousers. And he did look fine. Wholesome, interesting, and handsome in a rugged kind of way, and he had a full head of iron gray hair that had once been red, or at least rust-colored. She liked his brogue and said so, then belatedly thanked him for his compliment. "Just for the record, no one here is French. They're all poseurs." A devil perched itself on her shoulder as she shared Charles's information on the help at La Petite. Fergus laughed, and Annie was instantly at ease. She'd worried for nothing. This man was just a nice man, and she knew she could get through dinner and not be a nervous wreck.

The wine steward approached. Fergus waved him off. "I don't know anything about fine wines. I only drink ale. Do you drink . . . what should I call you?" he asked in a jittery voice.

"How about Annie? And you're Fergus.

"As for drinking, I do. Sometimes I drink a lot and other times not at all. I'm a happy drunk if that's what you're trying to ask me." *Oh, God, did I just say that?* Obviously she had because Fergus was laughing.

"I've been known to need help getting home a time or

two myself. I think I fall into the same category as a happy drunk. At least on those occasions."

Annie frowned as she looked around. Fergus was being a good sport, but he didn't want to be here, and she felt he was uncomfortable. "You know what, I just had an idea. Get your cell phone out and pretend you have a call. When you end the call, stand up and let's bug out of this place. We can stop by the Kickin' Chicken, grab some chicken and some ale, head for the Tidal Basin, and have a picnic at twilight, my favorite time of day. By the way, I like dark beer. Just out of curiosity, where is your security?"

"Front and back. Do you mean it?" Fergus's expression clearly showed he hoped she did.

Annie loved the way Fergus followed orders. He did exactly what she told him to do, then moved quickly to pull her chair back before she could change her mind. Five minutes and fifty dollars to Jerky Jacques later, they were out in the parking lot, and Annie was settling herself in the lemon-drop Porsche, explaining that Fergus and security should follow her.

"Why can't I ride with you?"

Why not indeed? "Climb in. I thought you had to go with your security. What are you doing here in the States anyway, or is that NTK?"

"I'm on a case that involved the CIA, but it turned domestic and is now under FBI jurisdiction. I much prefer working with your FBI rather than your CIA. The Bureau is cooperative, unlike the Agency. I can't tell you anything other than that."

"Okay, why are you here? I mean with me? What do you want from me?"

Fergus laughed. "They told me you were blunt speaking. We can discuss that later. Why don't we just talk about ordinary things. Tell me about yourself, and I'll tell you about myself."

Annie laughed, an unpleasant sound as she steered around a panel truck that was going too slow to her liking. She blasted her horn and squealed on past. "I took a defensive driving course. Charles insisted. I was the only one who passed with flying colors. You already know everything there is to know about me and don't deny it. Tell me about yourself."

"I'm three years from retirement, at which point I will return to my little village in Scotland and while away my days fishing, hunting, reading, and drinking good ale. My wife died twelve years ago. We had a wonderful life, and a day doesn't go by that I don't miss her. On our wedding day, she said to me, 'We are going to have arguments, fights, but I want your promise that when we go to bed at night we don't do that kiss-and-make-up thing. I want us to shake hands.'

"I thought all women wanted that kiss, but not my wife. She wanted my handshake because a handshake is your word that you mean what you say. It worked for us all our lives.

"My children are busy with their lives, and I see them, if I'm lucky, on holidays. But more often than not I'm working. My grandchildren are all at university, and young people are much too busy to visit grandparents. It shouldn't be that way, but it is. I think that's another way of saying I'm married to New Scotland Yard. I've worked there since I was a young pup."

Annie turned on her blinker as she nodded in understanding. "Here we are, the Kickin' Chicken! Just smell all that lovely grease! I got us here, so you can do the honors. Make sure you get plenty of napkins."

Fergus laughed. It really was a nice laugh, Annie decided. She watched as three burly men as large as oak trees got out of a rental car and followed Fergus into the chicken palace.

Fifteen minutes later, the Fergus Duffy party, as Annie thought of them, marched out of the Kickin' Chicken with six colorful bags between them and a cardboard carton that held what looked like a case of beer. The moment everything was settled in the trunk of the Porsche, Annie turned on the engine.

Annie whipped around corners, cutting off SUVs, all in the hope that the chicken would still be warm once they arrived at the Tidal Basin.

Fergus untangled himself and got out of the sports car and walked around to open the door for Annie, his security surrounding him. "Looks like a lot of other people had the same idea you did, Annie. Dinner at dusk, the stars are about to come out, there's a balmy breeze, and there is a spot with a bench right under that huge tree. Oh, dear, what about your dress?"

"This old thing! Please. The girls like to come here often. I think Maggie, she's the editor in chief at the *Post,* comes here to run. After her run, she has a double-decker ice-cream cone. She has a metabolism problem," Annie volunteered.

"Is there any truth to the rumor that you own the *Post?*"

"Absolutely none at all," Annie said cheerfully as she fished around inside the bag and triumphantly pulled out a chicken leg. "This is what I love about their chicken—it's sweet, and it actually tastes like chicken is supposed to taste. But concerning your question, I've heard that rumor myself. Where did you hear it?"

Annie munched contentedly, her legs drawn up under

her. "Chatter at the Bureau, but it was also mentioned at Langley. I didn't believe it for a minute," Fergus said, his eyes twinkling.

"Good for you, Fergus. This town, as you must know by now, is full of secrets, rumors, and dirty deeds. I don't even know why I want to live so close by. Ah, well, Las Vegas, my other sort of home, is pretty much the same. Secrets, scheming, gambling, crime, you name it."

Fergus's eyes continued to twinkle. "I'm thinking you're a woman of action. You like to be on the move, create situations if you find things too dull to your liking. How am I doing so far?"

Annie laughed as she fished around for a crisp slice of potato and popped it in her mouth. "I suppose that's one way of looking at it. As one ages, all the thrills seem to be left to the younger people. So as a senior, I like to take charge of my life and do what I want to do. I think I earned that right, and anyone who doesn't like it, well, let's just say it becomes their problem. You have to embrace life, Fergus, or it passes you by. Are you really going to be happy doing nothing when you retire?"

Fergus looked across at Annie in the gray light, and said, "Fishing, hunting, reading, and drinking ale aren't exactly nothing."

"They're deadly. Inside of a month, you'll be pulling out your hair. Trust me on that one. Now, I want to know why you called me, why we're sitting here eating greasy chicken that is delicious but not good for us, and I want to know *NOW*."

Fergus cleared his throat, dabbed at his mouth, and sat back on the bench. He crossed his legs and turned sideways to see Annie better in the early-evening light. "I chose you . . . wait, that's not a good way to start this. Years and years ago, when I first started with the Yard, I was feeling my oats, and a case was assigned to me. It wasn't a career builder by any means, just routine, but it took me to other places. That's how I met your husband. Who, by the way, I liked very much. My case involved an employee of your husband's who, along with a few of his friends, was smuggling Spanish relics. On one of your husband's boats. Your husband worked with me, young pup that I was. He helped me set a trap for the offenders, all ended well, and I got promoted.

"I remember seeing a picture of you with your husband on his desk. He said at the time you'd only been married a year. I had just gotten married myself, and we talked about finances and married life. I was struggling, and he was already a success. He told me to be patient, that my time would come. The promotion worked wonders for me and my new bride. To this day, no one has ever been more co-operative than your husband was with me that day. Things like that stick with you.

"You probably don't remember me, but on the day of the memorial service, I was there. I said many, many prayers for the souls of your husband and children.

"To make a long story short, I called you . . . because I thought you might be able to help me the way your husband did. I lost a young lad who was the age I was when I visited your husband. I trained Sean myself, and he was one of my best agents. He was like a son to me. I believe in my heart, my mind, my soul, that Hank Jellicoe is the one who had him killed. Sean walked into some kind of trap, of that I'm sure. I don't know the whys or the wherefores of it all, just that no one will ever convince me otherwise.

"This visit, this request, has nothing to do with the agreement you and the other ladies signed with my colleagues. I wanted to hire you independently of the others. By you, I mean the vigilantes. I don't even know if it's possible, that's why I came here in person. All trails led me to the CIA, then got cold. And then I picked up something that led me to the FBI. That's pretty much the sum total of it all."

"But when we were pardoned, we were not given immunity from prosecution for any future activity here in the States. If your trail is here, which means Hank Jellicoe is here somewhere, maybe as close as the other side of the Tidal Basin, the immunity you and your colleagues gave us is of no relevance. Things would be different if he were on foreign soil. Don't take what I'm saying as any kind of commitment on my part, I'm just talking out loud. What did they tell you at the Bureau that made you come to me?"

"John Yantzy told me that one of his predecessors kept a file on just about everyone in the world, much like J. Edgar Hoover did. He said the vigilantes have those files, and your president herself told him that you were off-limits." Fergus threw his hands up in the air to show he now was at an impasse. "Do you ladies have those files?"

Annie's head jerked upright. "That's NTK, Fergus Duffy," Annie said coldly.

"But . . ."

"There are no buts here, Fergus. I said it's NTK. Furthermore, assuming for one crazy, wild moment that the vigilantes did have those files, why would we trust you with them because of the FBI? Yantzy, I'm told, wants them so bad he'll do just about anything to get them. His clock is ticking, and as of this minute, he has only thirty days to come up with Hank Jellicoe or he's on the unemployment line along with Calvin Span and that dickweed from Homeland Security. Personally, I think that's a good thing. Everyone in this damn town needs to start cleaning their respective houses and start over. Young eyes, young blood, a fire burning in their bellies. That's what all those damn agencies need. When and if that happens, then you can call me. Thank you for this lovely . . . dinner. I can see myself to the car. Stay here. That's an order, Fergus Duffy. Oh, and don't forget to clean up this mess. The park police will fine you if you don't."

Three minutes later, Annie was in the yellow Porsche headed back toward the farm. She hit number 2 on her speed dial, and said, "Myra, you are not going to believe what I am about to tell you. Stop interrupting me; yes, I will drive carefully; no, I did not drink. Well, I did take a few sips, but I'm fine. Myra, shut up and listen to me before I bust wide open."

Chapter 11

Myra lowered the retractable awning on the terrace. "It's been threatening to rain all day. I'm not sure cooking out is such a good idea," she said fretfully. "The grill is protected, so I guess since everyone is expecting Charles's famous apple cider spareribs, we need to do a little rain dance to ward off the rain. Why don't you do that, Annie?" Her tone was still fretful.

"Myra, dear heart, one does a rain dance to bring *on* rain, not to ward it off. And I'm sorry to have to tell you that I don't have the faintest idea of how to do a rain dance to ward off rain. You need to come up with something better than that." Annie's tone sounded just as fretful as Myra's.

"You certainly are surly this afternoon, Annie. I would have thought that while you'd not necessarily be on top of the world, at least you'd be climbing up there after your meeting or date, whatever you want to call it, with Fergus Duffy."

"Stop right there, Myra Rutledge Martin Sutcliff! I told you how all that went down. You know what I can't get out of my mind?" Without missing a beat, she continued, "When Fergus said he and his wife used to shake hands before going to bed if one or the other was upset. Part of me thinks that's a wonderful thing, and another part of me wonders why I never did that with my husband. When he spoke of it, it seemed so perfect, and before you can ask me, no, I don't know why it bothers me. Kissing and making up is soooo . . . American, I guess."

Myra frowned. "I can see why that might bother you. Look at it this way, dear. Should you ever find yourself in that position again, you can shake hands *and* kiss each other. That way you can't go wrong."

Annie flopped down on her favorite chair. "I guess. Do you want me to turn on the grill?"

"I think Charles plans on using charcoal this evening. I saw the bag in the kitchen on my way out here. Don't we have something better to talk about? When is Fergus returning to England?"

"I don't know. I forgot to tell you, one of his security guys gave me Fergus's card as I was getting into my car and said I should call. But to answer your question, we didn't get that far, Myra, when I decided to hightail it out of there. Do we even care?"

"Let's see what the girls have to say when they get here," Myra said soothingly. "Relax, Annie. We'll talk this to death when they arrive, and I'm sure we'll come up with something that will put you in a good mood. I just hate it when you're cranky like this."

"You know what, Myra? Ask me if I care."

Lady and her pups, who were playing on the terrace, stopped tussling, their heads jerking upright. As one they started to bark. "Someone's here!" Myra said happily. She literally bounded out of her chair and raced to the kitchen.

It was uncanny, Myra thought. The girls always seemed

to arrive one after the other almost like a caravan, yet all their starting points were different, so how could that be? Since it really wasn't important in the scheme of things, she let the thought drop by the wayside and held out her arms to Kathryn, who hugged her tightly.

"Am I the first? I'm never first. Usually it's Isabelle. I like being first sometimes. I'm babbling here, Myra."

Murphy raced through the house, Lady and her pups right behind him. "Isn't it wonderful? The patter of little and big feet." Myra laughed. "Although 'patter' is too tame a word, more like stampede of the thundering herd."

"How'd Annie's date go?" Kathryn hissed.

"Oh, dear, I'm not sure. She's on the terrace waiting for all of you. I have to warn you, she's rather cranky."

"Cranky or *pissed off*? There is a difference," the ever-verbal Kathryn asked.

Myra laughed. "Take your pick, dear. Ah, here's Nikki and Jack, and I see Alexis behind them. And Maggie is just turning onto the road."

The greetings were effusive as they always were. Inside of ten minutes, everyone was on the terrace, even Charles, who looked around to see whom he could trust to carry the ribs and to follow his instructions. He finally chose Bert, who for some reason looked like he had lost his last friend. He well might have, Nikki whispered to Yoko as she watched Kathryn avoid standing anywhere near Bert.

An hour later, the mingling and the joke-telling wound down. Annie related the details of her meeting with Fergus Duffy to wide-eyed disbelief. "I told him I would talk to all of you. I don't want any of you reading something into that meeting that wasn't there."

Ted Robinson looked over at Charles, who was expertly turning a rack of ribs, and said, "Charles, if you had a mind to, you could auction off Mitch Riley's files and rake in tens of millions of dollars. Did you have a chance to go through Jellicoe's files?"

"My dear fellow, it has taken me *days* to sift and collate those files. In the kitchen you will see nine, I say *NINE* boxes of files on Henry Jellicoe. It's literally a day-by-day file on him from as far back as his early twenties. I did not read through them, I just figured out a system that would work for all of us. It would take months to go through all of those files to look for any one piece of something or other that would help us. I made it so we could divide it up by years and assign each of you a year, then you can sit down and compare whatever it is you think will be important in our quest to find Mr. Jellicoe. I understand from Harry's lip-reading that Director Span has an additional six boxes of files that he himself accumulated. I would give my right elbow to see what's in them."

"Wait a minute!" Jack all but bellowed. "Who's the client? Is this on our shores or foreign soil? Is something going on here that I don't know about?" He swung his attention to Nikki, and said, "You aren't seriously thinking of giving up your . . . your current immunity here. I know 'immunity' is not the right word, but your pardon only applies to past actions. It does not cover anything done in the United States afterward."

Nikki's face froze into a grimace. "Jack, how can looking at files affect us? We own the files; they were given to us. We can do whatever we want with them. Even the president of the United States said those files are off-limits, and so are we.

"We can read them, we can try to decipher them, we can try to find Jellicoe's wife, which is what this is all about. We are not actively out there on a mission. Think of this as a fact-finding . . . ah . . . mission. Girls?"

The Sisters weighed in, their comments echoing those

Nikki made. The boys managed to slink over to where Bert was standing. Charles, unsure what exactly was going on, removed a rack of ribs to a serving platter and did his best to move as far from the ostracized guys as possible.

The girls all started to talk at once as they tried to figure out the best way to tackle the upcoming project. "I think we should all stay and work from here. Being free agents these days will allow us to do what has to be done," Yoko said.

"What about the boys?" Isabelle asked.

The women grinned and shook their heads.

"I think we should send them home after dinner," Maggie said. "I can stay and work through the night. You have to admit they don't have our *eye* for detail, and they do tend to clutter things up."

"As usual, you're right, Maggie. I can stay through the night, too," Alexis said. The others agreed.

Ted, who was watching the women, poked Jack on the arm, and hissed, "We're outta here as soon as dinner is over. Right now, I'm not even sure I want to stay for dinner. I don't know about you guys, but this is really pissing me off. We need to revolt like *NOW!* They only want us when they want us. Those females over there have shown a total disregard for our feelings once too often. What are we, chopped liver? How many times have we stepped up to the plate and made things happen for them? Now, when it's getting interesting, they want to send us home. Well?"

"Numerous times. What will revolting do for us?" Harry asked as though he were questioning a seven-year-old.

Jack whirled around, a suspicious expression on his face. Harry rarely volunteered anything, and when he did, his voice was never gentle. Right now he was smiling, which further puzzled Jack. "What? You okay with being dismissed like . . . like . . . we're flotsam and jetsam?

Flotsam and jetsam?

"That's an interesting declaration, Jack. If anyone is interested in a suggestion, I would like to suggest we pack up our old kit bags and head back to town and forget about dining on apple cider spareribs. I'm willing to forgo the coleslaw in the hopes we can redeem our dignity."

"Oh, Harry, you are so witty this evening. And you think this is going to solve . . . what?" Jack growled.

"Not being needed. And when a request comes our way for help, which will happen very shortly, we should be busy doing other things," Harry said quietly.

"And you're also stupid this evening," Jack mumbled as he saw his buddies head toward the kitchen door amid a chorus of "Where are you guys going?" and Maggie's bellow, "Get back here, Ted, and you, too, Espinosa." Jack turned tail and hustled after his friends as he waved his hands in the air.

"Charles! What happened? Did you say something? The boys are leaving, and they look angry. Why are they angry, Charles?" Myra demanded.

"I have no idea, Myra. I knew the boys were talking among themselves, but I was so busy watching the ribs so they didn't burn that I wasn't paying attention. If you want my opinion, I believe it was something you ladies said that stirred the mass exodus. That's just a guess on my part," he added hastily.

"Bert has his jockeys in a wad," Kathryn said unkindly. "He doesn't like it that I'm going on the road once or twice a week. Right now it's a big bone of contention between the two of us. However, I don't think our little squabble had anything to do with Bert's leaving with the others."

Maggie struggled to blink back her tears. "This is really the first time Ted disobeyed me. He always listens and does what I say, but that doesn't make him a wimp, so don't think that of him. The reason he always agrees with me is because I'm always right."

"Joseph always follows Ted. They're like two peas in a pod," Alexis said.

Isabelle looked at everyone, and just said, "Men!"

Nikki wasn't quite so blasé. "Jack . . . I was watching him . . . just because I love looking at him. He even winked at me. So he was okay with whatever was going on until I saw Ted nudge him, then things changed."

"Oh, dear, who is going to eat all of this food?" Myra fretted.

"It was Harry's suggestion that they leave. I read his lips. He was most unhappy when he heard they weren't needed. For reading the files. Truthfully, I am on Harry's side. He's right when he says we only use them, meaning the boys, when we want to. Otherwise, it is like they don't belong, which is very unfair of us," Yoko said. "Harry, in case you don't already know this, can be extremely stubborn. Even with me."

"I know Harry likes flavorful food and I made the coleslaw with Jamaican Jerk since he told me that was his favorite. I made a huge bowl of it," Annie muttered. "I don't understand any of this. I thought men were above such pettiness."

The Sisters eyed the platters of food on the table. Suddenly everyone's appetite seemed to disappear.

"I think this dinner is fizzling, and it's really raining now. If it keeps up, it will soak through the awning. Perhaps we should go indoors," Myra said, just as a roll of thunder sounded overhead. The Sisters needed no further warning. Each of them grabbed a platter of food and beelined for the kitchen door. A bolt of lightning zigzagged across the sky, which had gone dark, followed by a bellow of thunder that seemed to rock the old farmhouse.

With the mad dash from the terrace, the women were soaking wet. Myra handed out tea towels before they sat down to contemplate the mound of food on the kitchen table. The dogs sniffed and pranced, uncertain of what exactly was going on. Charles pointed to the huge family room, then followed the dogs, bacon-flavored chew bones in hand. Large ones that would occupy the dogs for hours until matters in the kitchen were resolved one way or the other.

Kathryn and Maggie, whom the others often referred to as bottomless pits, which meant they would eat anything anytime, simply stared at the food platters. Isabelle reached for a rib, bit into it, and chewed. "Delicious." No one else reached for food.

"Now what?" Nikki asked.

"Mutiny is not a good thing. We need the boys," Annie said.

"What she's saying is we haven't sucked up enough where the boys are concerned," Kathryn said flatly. "I for one hate sucking up. It is not becoming or acceptable for women ever, as in ever, to have to suck up. We don't suck up to each other so why do we have to do it with them?

"Are they so insecure with their own manhood that we have to coddle them? Think about it, what are they going to do without us? Just think about that!" Her voice was even flatter now that she'd said what she had to say.

"Up till now we were in control. At least I think we were," Nikki said. "Being in total control, and I want to stress the word *total* here, has allowed us to get where we are at the moment. Yes, the boys have done everything we asked. So, why are we excluding them? Did I miss something?"

"No, you are not missing anything. We just reacted the way we always react, as a team of seven. *We* check it out, then *we* make decisions, and that's when *we* enlist their help. This is not something new. We do it this way because we're a team, we are on each other's page, so to speak. If we throw something into the mix that hasn't worked for us, even though we haven't tried that *something*, we're all smart enough to know that's not the way to go. I suppose we could have offered up an explanation, but like Kathryn said, that goes under the heading of sucking up to appease them," Yoko said.

"Very well put, dear," Myra said.

"Charles, you haven't said anything. Would you care to contribute to this conversation?" Annie asked.

"I see both sides, ladies. From your perspective it's if it ain't broke, don't fix it. The lads, on the other hand, subscribe to the notion that they are underappreciated, and there is no respect when they did in fact put their lives as well as their reputations on the line for you. Take Bert, for example. While he was the director of the FBI, ask yourselves how many times he broke the law to help all of us. That goes for Jack, too, who was an officer of the court. Harry spies on the CIA and FBI agents he trains and reports back to us. Ted and Joseph are out there beating the bushes and pushing things around to make things work for us, so Maggie can get banner headlines. Do you need any additional input?"

The Sisters looked at each other with narrowed eyes. "Charles is right," Alexis said.

Annie and Myra shrugged. "Perhaps we should have a roundtable discussion to clear the air."

It was a lifeline, and the girls as one reached for it.

"And you all think if we concede, the boys will come running back?" Isabelle asked in disbelief. "Did any of you *really* see the expression on Ted's face? I'm certainly no authority on men, but I know enough to realize it's going to take more than sucking up to get him back in the fold."

Maggie started to whimper. "I get so carried away. This is my fault. Wait a minute, no, it isn't *all* my fault. Just because I'm always right doesn't mean I should take all of the blame. It's how I get Ted to stay focused and be the best of the best. As soon as I slack off, he gets lazy and pre-occupied." She swiped at a tear trickling down from the corner of her eye.

"Men need to feel superior. Why is that? Were they born that way, or is it a learned thing?" Kathryn snarled. "Bert just hates that I drive a big rig. He doesn't think women should do things like that. He doesn't think I should sit home and knit, but he thinks I should work at my engineering degree instead of driving a truck. That's his insecurity. I can't be part of that kind of thinking."

"See! See! That's how Joseph is thinking. He wants me to marry him so we can be legal. I'm not ready to get married. That kind of thinking carries into the job place. It's not that I don't trust him to watch my back, I do. But I don't want him having doubts. We really do need to clear the air and make peace," Alexis said

"Why?" Annie said. "We aren't the vigilantes any longer. Our wings have been clipped. We aren't going on missions. All of those," she said, pointing to the boxes at the far end of the kitchen, "are just boxes of information. Even if we find something, no one in this room has made a decision as to what we'll do with that information."

Nikki shrugged. "I think we might have a problem."

All eyes turned to Charles, who threw his hands high in the air. "Don't look at me, ladies! I'm one of them. *A man!*"

"Crap!" Annie said.

Chapter 12

"Well, I guess we better get to it," Myra said, heading to the far end of the kitchen, where the boxes of files were stacked neatly. "Take your pick," she said, waving her arm with a flourish.

"Wait. Wait!" Maggie said. "Listen to me for a moment. I don't belong here with you all doing what you're going to be doing. I'm an honorary vigilante, just as the guys are honorary members. It's not that I don't want to help, I do, but my help is in other venues. The last thing I want to do is jinx all of you. Having said that, I'm going to head back to town and do some research of my own. The only problem is, I came out with Ted and Espinosa, and I have no means of transportation."

"Take my car," Alexis said, fishing the keys out of her pocket and tossing them to Maggie. "I can bum a ride with Isabelle and pick it up when I get back to town."

Maggie danced from one foot to the other. "Are you sure you guys are okay with me leaving?"

"Absolutely," they all agreed. Brief smooches and hugs followed as Maggie headed for the door, stopped, and returned and asked for an umbrella. It took Myra a good ten minutes to unearth Charles's golfing umbrella, which was as big as a sun umbrella, and handed it over.

"Be careful on the road," the women shouted, as Maggie raced across the compound, the rain and the wind buffeting the colorful orange-and-yellow umbrella. The women watched until the taillights on Alexis's car were mere specks in the darkness.

"I'd like us to sit here and have a little roundtable before we tackle the boxes," Myra said.

"I'll make fresh coffee," Annie volunteered.

"It seems right now," Isabelle said as she looked around at the table. "It should be just us. That's how we first started, then out of necessity, we had to recruit others to help us. I'm not saying I am not appreciative, because I am. But if we take a vote, I want us to stay the way we are. Somehow we have to convey that to the boys. Maggie understood, but Maggie is a *female,* so it's understood."

Nikki tugged at her earlobe as she frowned. "We aren't the vigilantes any longer. We're private citizens."

"Private citizens with an agenda," Yoko said.

"That's true," Nikki said.

Annie finished with the coffeepot and took her seat as the first drops of water dripped down into the pot. "What are we doing here? More to the point, let's assume we find something in one of those boxes. What are we going to do with that information? Are we planning on turning it over to . . . the FBI? The White House? I think we need a plan here. And what about Fergus Duffy? Do we get back to him, or do we ignore him?"

"Those are all good questions, Annie. I wish I had the answer to even just one of them," Kathryn said.

"Let's see if I can sum up our temporary predicament. Right now we're just private citizens. Once we open those boxes and, with luck, find whatever we think we need to find, is when we have to decide if we're going to step over that line *again*. Yes, we have just been granted immunity for future activity by the president of the United States, but I am quite sure that such immunity does not protect us against being arrested by local and state authorities. Even if the FBI has to leave us alone, that does not apply to breaking the laws of Virginia, Maryland, et cetera.

"I know you all feel you have a personal score to settle with Hank Jellicoe, and you want to see him pay for all that time you lived under his thumb. But I think you have to put personal issues aside and concentrate on what he's accused of doing now. If what we're hearing is true, every law-enforcement agency in the world is looking for and blaming Hank Jellicoe for the deaths of those CIA agents. Perhaps we need to use the word *allegedly* when we accuse him of murdering federal agents. And Fergus Duffy told Annie about *his* agent," Myra said. "I think that means what we're hearing is all true in regard to Hank Jellicoe."

"Technically, Hank Jellicoe is one of their own. I'm referring to the CIA. He knows their secrets. He probably anticipated all of this and is reacting like a true agent. They burned him and tossed him away. He's out there, all alone with no one he can count on to help him.

"Don't any of you watch that show on TV called *Burn Notice*? The main character in the show got burned, and he's trying to get his life together. It's not easy on the show, but he's doing it. At least that's what we're currently thinking. And yet he's still surviving out there and on his own just like the character on *Burn Notice* and on a killing spree. He's gone over the edge, and if the CIA can't find him, how are we going to find him, and if we do find him, are we prepared to cross the line?" Kathryn asked as she got up to pour the coffee.

"Do we have to make that particular decision right

now?" Nikki asked. "Why can't we go through Jellicoe's files and see if anything turns up, and if it does, that's the time when we make a decision? That works for me. What do the rest of you think?"

Yoko's exquisite features tightened. "I want to register my vote now. I am willing to cross that line to bring that man to justice."

Myra grappled with her pearls and somehow managed to say, "Duly noted, dear." She, like the others, knew that Yoko blamed Hank Jellicoe for her two miscarriages while Harry was his employee.

"Hank Jellicoe must have people somewhere helping him. I don't see how he could do what he's doing on his own with the intensive search for him that's going on," Annie said.

"Charles explained how it works to all of us, Annie. Weren't you listening when that happened?" Not bothering to wait for Annie's response, she continued on. "People, agents like Hank Jellicoe, during their active years, set up dozens of safe houses all over the world because he was a global entity. Your regulation agent has one safe house to go to for sanctuary as they don't have the financial means Hank has.

"In *Burn Notice*, the main character didn't have time to set up a safe house and the stuff that goes with it. After they burn him, he wakes up in Miami without a cent to his name, no identity, no nothing. Agents, especially deep-cover agents, never know when their cover is going to get blown. Charles is the perfect example. That means at each safe house Hank Jellicoe has a separate identity, a bank account in the name of that identity.

"In other words, a presence wherever that safe house is. That also includes a vehicle, a passport, a driver's license, credit cards, everything a covert agent needs to blend into a community to survive. If Jellicoe has safe houses all over the globe, he's as safe as he can be. He can lie low for *years*. But as Charles put it, men like Hank who are so super-charged can't lie low. They have their vendettas and their agendas, and they live to act on them. He's on the move, and he's clever," Myra said.

Annie sniffed. "I always say there is clever, then there is clever. Let me sum it up for all of you, but I know you know what I'm going to say. Henry, call me Hank, Jellicoe is a man. We are women. I think collectively, we can out-think him, and I even think we can catch him. Providing that's what we decide we want to do."

"Ah, the big decision!" Isabelle said airily as she added cream to her coffee.

"I'm having a problem with something," Kathryn said. "Listen up and think about this. Mitchell Riley supposedly compiled these files," she said, pointing to the stacked boxes. "He was director of the FBI for only a few years before he went off the rails. Then Elias took over, and when he retired, Bert became director. We are not talking a lot of years here, ten at the most. Neither Elias nor Bert had anything to do with compiling the files.

"If Riley did it on his own, he would have had to have spent every waking moment of his life working on those files, and this is just Hank Jellicoe's file. Think about all those other files, thousands of them. Where did they come from originally even though they were in Riley's possession? Who compiled them? Where are the people who compiled them? Is it even remotely possible that Riley somehow got his hands on a bootleg copy of Hoover's files that he'd compiled over his fifty years as director? Everything I ever read said those files were destroyed a long time ago, but knowing politicians and the way this town works, I think there might be a bootleg file somewhere, and maybe that's what *WE* have.

"Think about it, girls; it's the only thing that makes sense. And we never read those files. We turned them over to Charles. I don't recall his ever saying he read them, either. It's been quite a few years since that little caper, and I have this vague recollection that we all agreed we didn't have the right to read someone's file considering the way the files were collected. Do you all remember that?"

"I do remember. We said it was none of our business and that we were not the Bureau's personal police. We did agree among ourselves that those files would never see the light of day again," Nikki said.

The others mumbled and muttered to themselves as they dragged the cartons of files to the center of the floor and squatted down Indian style to go through them.

Outside, the rain came down in torrents, slashing at the windows. Thunder rolled overhead as lightning lit up the sky. The dogs, oblivious to what was going on outside, sprawled wherever there was an open space on the cool kitchen tiles.

Hours passed, with coffee and ice-tea breaks. From time to time one or the other of the Sisters would forage for something to eat in the refrigerator, taking no more than ten minutes from their work.

The clock on the microwave oven clicked over to three-thirty in the morning. "Girls, we've been at this for over eight hours. We need to take a break. Our eyes are as tired as our bodies, and we might miss something important in these files. Let's all catch a few hours' sleep and get back to it after breakfast. Eight o'clock? How does that sound?"

"Like music to my ears," Isabelle said, getting up from the floor and rubbing at her neck and shoulders. "I'd kill for a good sixty-minute neck and shoulder massage right now."

"A nice hot shower will serve the same purpose," Yoko said, heading for the back staircase that led to the second floor. "See you in the morning." The Sisters trailed behind her, leaving Annie and Myra in the kitchen alone.

"You don't look all that tired to me, Myra," Annie said, suspicion ringing in her voice. "For some reason I feel all charged up. It's almost like . . . it's there . . . right in front of us, and we aren't seeing it. Do you feel like that? What could it be, Myra? "

"I do feel like that, too, but I can't put my finger on it. I'm coffeed out. Would you like a soda, something cold?"

"You know what, Myra? I think I'll have a beer. I got cheated last night and didn't get to drink mine other than a few sips. For some reason when I'm sleeping, I always wake up at four in the morning. I don't know why that is. It doesn't matter what time I go to bed, either. I still wake up at four o'clock. Then I just doze until it's time to get out of bed. I read something about that once but can't remember what it was. Yes, yes, I'm fretting, and I don't know the why of that, either. So, do you want a beer or something else?"

Myra's mind raced. Annie was on a toot of some kind, and when that happened, it behooved her to fall in line. "A nice cold beer sounds really good so, yes, I will join you. I also wake up at four. Charles gets out of bed at four to start his day. I don't know what the significance of that is, either."

"I think it's one of those little mysteries of life that will never be solved." Annie looked around at the stacks of files scattered all over the kitchen floor. Yellow legal pads with scribbled notes were next to each Sister's stack of boxes. "I'm almost thinking this mess isn't going to be solved, either."

"Who do you suppose compiled all of this?" Myra asked, waving her arm about. I know this is the high-tech age, but I'm thinking it would take a team of specialists to accomplish what we're looking at. Which director had this done? I don't even know if it's important for us to know who did it, but it's bothering me. Everyone is spying on everyone else, which tells me there is no trust anywhere. That really bothers me, Annie."

"Ask yourself what else we don't know. The whole world knows this town is full of secrets. We'd probably curl up and die if we knew what just *some* of those secrets are," Annie groused.

"Do you think Bert or maybe Elias might have heard . . . you know, tidbits, something, maybe even just outright rumors on how this stuff went down?"

"We can ask. Nellie wakes up at four just the way we do. I'll call her to see if she can rouse Elias. I think where Bert is concerned, we should leave well enough alone and let Kathryn handle that," Annie said.

"I agree," Myra said.

Myra listened to Annie's end of the conversation with Nellie. She looked around the messy kitchen when she heard Annie invite Nellie and Elias for breakfast.

"Not to worry, she's *bringing* breakfast. Homemade coffee cake and fruit. She said that's what you do when you wake up at four in the morning—you bake. I'm learning all these new things these past few days. Shaking hands instead of kissing and making up. Now Nellie saying she makes coffee cake at four in the morning. It boggles my mind. It stopped raining a little while ago, so we can dine on the terrace. It should be dry by the time she gets here."

Myra pretended to slap at her forehead. "Task force, Annie! That's the term we're looking for. The directors must have had a task force set up to compile all this data. Probably a team of agents too old for fieldwork and just putting in their time until retirement. Whoever it was is probably retired by now. Or possibly dead. What do you think?"

"I think you might be right. But, Myra, assuming you are right, what is that going to do for us? Even if we have names, talk to those names, how are they going to help us with this?" Annie said, kicking a box she'd been working on.

"If I knew the answer to that question, we wouldn't be sitting here at four-thirty in the morning trying to figure out if it means anything. More likely than not, it means nothing. We keep saying any little thing that we don't think is important might turn out to be the smoking gun we need. I'm just saying . . ."

"The volume of these files is horrendous. Someone had a real itch on for Jellicoe to go to all this trouble. I guess that old adage of powerful people having skeletons in their closets is true. But, dammit, these files are nothing more than Jellicoe's rise to glory. I wonder if the files Director Span is turning over to Director Yantzy at the FBI are duplicates of what we have here. We don't have anything after Mitchell Riley was sent to the federal penitentiary. I wonder if that's when Span started his own file. Do you think we'll ever know, Myra?"

Myra reached for Annie's empty beer bottle, carried it along with her own into the pantry, and placed it in the recycle bin. "At the rate we're going, probably not," she tossed over her shoulder.

"Myra, think about this. Knowing what we know about Hank Jellicoe, at what age do you think he would have gotten married? If we can get a lock on that time frame," Annie said, pointing to the boxes scattered about the kitchen, "it would save us a lot of work."

"I'm guessing his early thirties. The minute he changed his name, his life as Hank Jellicoe started. I'm guessing that was either at nineteen or twenty, give or take a year or so. Give him ten years to create his new life, start his business. I don't think it would have been later than the age of thirty-three. I'm thinking the new bride would be mid-to late twenties. What do you think?"

"It makes sense. Who had that age bracket?" Annie said, dropping to her knees and looking at the dates written on the covers of the boxes in permanent black ink. "Ah, it's Nikki! She's only gotten to age twenty-nine in her notes," Annie said, holding up the yellow legal pad Nikki had written on. "This box goes up to age thirty-one. And"—she stretched her arm to look at another cover— "Alexis has age thirty-two to age thirty-seven. Her notes say she's up to age thirty-four. Look at the size of these files in Alexis's box. This box must represent the years he really hunkered down and made it all work for him."

Myra squatted down next to Annie. "Okay, let's see if he has any unexplained absences during those years. Like two weeks for a honeymoon. Back in those days, a honeymoon was definitely a priority, or you weren't officially married."

"And you know this . . . how?"

Myra laughed. "Because Mr. Rutledge told me so. I was married to him, you know. He absolutely insisted we take a honeymoon for the very reason I just stated. And before you can ask, it was about as eventful as my honeymoon was with Charles, except for the water bed."

"Well, damn, Myra!"

The two women went off into peals of laughter as they dived into the box of files Alexis had been working on.

"All I can say is there better be a smoking gun or a rabbit in the hat in this box, or I'm going to be . . ."

"Pissed?" Annie said as she held her sides to keep from laughing.

"Yes, pissed."

Chapter 13

Myra divided Alexis's box into two piles, handing the top stack of files to Annie and keeping the bottom half for herself.

"I think if we knew there was a prize for finding something, we'd both be a little more gung ho, do you agree, Myra?"

"I do. But since there is no prize in this box, let's just wade through it and hope we find something that screams, 'Here I am!' "

The two women sifted, stacked, mumbled, and muttered as they pawed through the neatly stapled papers inside each manila folder, ripping some apart, tossing others. The kitchen looked like a blizzard had descended upon it.

Myra was down to her last two files, and said so. Annie said she had three more to go when Myra suddenly said, "Annie, did you ever hear of a reporter named Virgil Anders?"

Annie stopped what she was doing, and said, "No, why?"

"He's in this file. He worked as a reporter for the *Balti-*

more Sun years ago. I guess you wouldn't have heard of him since you were living in Spain. I never heard of him myself. This file says he was an investigative reporter like Ted Robinson."

"Why is he in that file?" Annie asked, inching closer to Myra to look at the file in her hands. "Oooh, maybe he was investigating Hank. Do you see anything like that?"

"No. But these papers say he was writing a book."

"On Hank Jellicoe? Did it get published?"

"I don't know. The end of this report," Myra said holding up a sheet of paper, "says Virgil Anders dropped off the face of the earth. We can try Googling him or call the *Baltimore Sun* and ask how to get in touch with him. Oh, Annie, this might be the smoking gun we're looking for. If he was important enough to include in these files, he must be someone we need to talk to. Oh, here comes Charles, let's ask him."

Charles Martin stood in the open doorway, dismay written all over his face. "Ladies, how am I supposed to prepare breakfast with this mess all around me?"

"Never mind breakfast, dear, Nellie and Elias are bringing it in a little while. Listen to me, Charles, and think back to Hank when he was in his midthirties. We think we found something. To your knowledge, did anyone ever write a book about Hank?"

"Several, Myra. I thought you knew that. Hank had his own biographer, a scholar from somewhere that I can't remember, but he was notable. Hank wouldn't settle for anything less than notable. But it wasn't until much later, when he was in his late fifties. I actually read one of them, and it was boring. Let me see if I can remember his name. Ah, it was Franklin Fodor. There might have been an *e* on the end of his last name. Does that help? What will Nellie and Elias be bringing in the way of breakfast?"

"Homemade coffee cake and fruit. I'm thinking we could use some soft butter. Kathryn likes jam on everything, so some of that, too. We have to supply the coffee. If the terrace is dry, breakfast outdoors would be lovely.

"That's not the name in this folder. The name here is Virgil Anders, and he was a reporter for the *Baltimore Sun* when Hank was in his midthirties. That's the box we were working on. Since Nellie is bringing breakfast, do you think you can check Mr. Anders out while Annie and I shower and get ready for whatever the day is going to bring us?"

"I'll do it right now. Ted might be able to come up with something. I'll give him or Maggie a call. First things first, though, I'm going to run the dogs."

Within seconds, the kitchen was silent and empty.

Forty minutes later, as Annie and Myra descended the back-kitchen stairs, the dogs rushed to greet them. Both women stared in amazement at the tidy kitchen. The boxes of files were packed, their covers intact. "Whatever would we do without him?" Myra smiled.

"We'd either survive, which we did once before, or flounder. I'll make the coffee. Myra, when do you see us actually leaving for Vegas? I need to make new reservations."

"Annie! You own a Gulfstream. All you have to do is call and tell them when you want to leave. You don't have to make a reservation. You said yourself it only takes ninety minutes for them to ready the plane and file a flight plan."

"Myra, I have to reserve the plane. My people use it, too, you know. I'll call and tell them I have first dibs. Did I say that right? I'll just put them on standby. So, when do you see us leaving? We're going to have so much to do to plan for Kathryn's party. Then if we close for that one night, I have to have the staff go through the cancellation process and make refunds, that kind of thing."

"Let's shoot for this weekend. By then we should be through with all of this," Myra said, waving her hands at the boxes on the floor. "I hear Charles; maybe he found out something. I think it's going to be a glorious day, Annie. Look at that sun!"

While Myra rummaged for plastic plates and utensils and Annie fixed the coffeepot, Charles reported what he'd found—nothing. "Virgil Anders was a young reporter, in his midtwenties when that file was compiled. He started to work for the *Baltimore Sun* when he graduated from college. From the short bio I read, it appeared he was a rising star. He had what his editors called journalistic gut instincts that never seemed to fail him. When he was on a story or a report, he worked around the clock and never gave up. There is no mention of a book other than one of his bosses saying he wouldn't be surprised to hear someday that Virgil was writing the great American novel. There was a picture of him that I printed out. Handsome lad.

"That was all I was able to find out. There isn't anything else. It's like this report says, the lad dropped off the face of the earth. In this day of Facebook, YouTube, Twitter, and the like, there is no mention of him anywhere. As he's older now, that didn't surprise me, so I called Ted, and he's on it. I'm sorry, ladies."

"I think we should call Maggie," Annie said. Charles bristled, which was Annie's intent.

"Maggie has sources that go far beyond Ted's sources. And she gets her results quicker than Ted does. Yes, I think we should call Maggie. What do you think, Myra?"

"Definitely call Maggie. I'm sorry, Charles, she is just so much quicker and faster at things like this. Did you ask

any of *your people* to see if they can come up with anything?"

"Of course I did. They're on it, too."

"Well, there you go! The more people we have working
on this, the quicker we'll get results," Annie said. "You
don't look to me like you think this is important, Charles.
I do for some reason. Whoever compiled those reports
must have thought it was important, or they wouldn't
have put it in the file. It might turn out to be nothing, but
it's all we've come up with so far. You always told us that
small, insignificant details can sometimes turn out to be a
rabbit in the hat or that smoking gun everyone just waits
for."

"Oh, by the way, Charles, I'm going to go to Las Vegas
this weekend with Annie if we get all this cleared away.
I'm not sure how long I'll be there. You can man the fort
with the dogs while I'm gone, can't you?" Myra asked.

"Of course. It will do you good to get away for a few
days. If you think of anything else you need me to do, just
call down to the war room. Either way, call me when Nellie and Elias arrive. The girls are stirring," he said over his
shoulder.

Annie made a *tsk* sound with her tongue. "Your husband is ticked off, Myra."

"I know, dear, but it's not because I'm going away. He
truly resents outside help, and Maggie has one-upped him
a few too many times. Manly pride and all of that." She
giggled to show what she thought of that.

"I'm calling Maggie right now," Annie said.

Myra gathered up a tray to carry out to the terrace. She
stopped for a second to appreciate the promise of a beautiful day, to listen to the birds chirp, and to gaze up at a
truly cloudless sky.

She was followed by Annie a moment later, carrying the

coffeepot, which she plugged into an outlet on the minibar.

"Maggie has her teeth into it. She promised us something by noon at the latest. I explained about Charles's calling Ted and Charles's general attitude. She just laughed. You a betting woman, Myra?"

"Good Lord, no. There is no doubt in my mind that Maggie will cross the finish line first. Do you agree?"

"I do. Especially when she's pitted against Charles *and* Ted. We should do something nice for that Abner person."

"You did do something nice, Annie. That Abner person now owns beachfront property thanks to you."

"But, Myra, he's worth every penny of the bonuses Maggie is forced to pay him for his invaluable information. Can you imagine if that boy were to get caught? Whatever would we do?"

"What's with that *we* stuff, Annie?" At Annie's frantic look, Myra hastily added, "I was just teasing, Annie. The young man has truly proved invaluable to us, and we *would* figure out something if he were to get caught. We would, wouldn't we, Annie?" There was such anxiety in Myra's voice, Annie felt her insides start to crumble.

"Of course," was the best she could mumble in a normal-sounding voice. At least she hoped it sounded normal to Myra, who looked so relieved Annie knew she'd pulled it off.

"Let's just sit here and enjoy the early morning until the girls and Nellie arrive. There must be something pleasant we can talk about. I do love a bright, sunny summer morning, don't you, Annie?"

Bright, sunny summer mornings did nothing for Annie. She muttered something to appease her friend and went back to worrying about Maggie and her special hacker friend.

*   *   *

As Annie and Myra sat in silence, struggling to find pleasant things to talk about, Maggie was on her way to a meeting with Abner Tookus at a small café in Georgetown. She arrived first, asked for a table in the very back of the room, and waited for her friend. She'd deliberately chosen this particular café, a favorite of Abner's, knowing he wouldn't kick up too much of a fuss in public as opposed to over the phone when she told him what she wanted him to do.

Maggie looked around the rapidly filling café. Obviously no one ate breakfast at home anymore. A truly sad state of affairs, in her opinion. To while away the time until Abner arrived, Maggie spooned eight packets of real sugar into her cup of coffee as she watched most of the patrons flip open their copies of the *Post* to pore over it while they waited for their food.

When she felt the air stir around her, Maggie looked up and gasped. "Abner! Oh, my God! What happened to you? Are you going to a funeral? You look just like Brad Pitt! You got a haircut. How much did that suit cost?"

Instead of answering her final question, Abner said, "Nothing happened to me. No, I am not going to a funeral. Thank you for the compliment, but I'm much more attractive, and he's *old*. Of course I got a haircut, because I had the time to do it since you've been leaving me alone. It's none of your business how much this suit cost, but I will say this, you paid for it. Moving right along here, the answer is no. Absolutely no to whatever this little breakfast meeting is all about. By the way, this shirt is pure Italian silk, and this stunning Hermès tie is one of a kind, as was the price. I'll have the two-egg pancake special."

Maggie decided to take a different approach with Abner this morning, remembering how she'd been accused of being so abrasive. "You hate me, don't you? After all I've done for you."

Abner appeared to be unmoved as he brought his coffee cup to his lips. "That's not true. I love you. I have always loved you. But you kicked me to the curb and chose that freckled lout with the red hair. I'm almost over you. If you burst into tears, I will be unmoved. You wanna go there, be my guest. Furthermore, I can get any girl I want just by snapping my fingers. I do not think you can say the same thing about men. Whatever, this is pointless, I'm taking the ten o'clock shuttle to New York. The only reason I agreed to meet you is that I was coming here anyway for breakfast. Your turn, Miss EIC."

"You are so cruel. I do love you. I will always love you, too. When I hear Whitney Houston sing that song, I always cry because I think of you and how it can never be," Maggie whimpered.

"Cut the bullshit, Maggie; what do you want?"

"Why do you care if you aren't going to help me?"

"So I can get my jollies off when I say no once again."

"I want you to find someone. Actually, our mutual benefactor wants you to find someone. The benefactor with the deep pockets, who paid for all that lovely beachfront property she is going to rip right out from under you when I tell her how uncooperative you are being."

"You're tearing my heart right out of my chest. You win some, you lose some."

"I'll be sure to express your sentiments verbatim, and you can damn well pay for your own breakfast. Did you see how much Canadian bacon is these days, and you ordered a double order? You are a user, Abner Tookus. All she wants is for you to locate someone for her. How hard can that be, you crud?"

"Oh, so one minute I'm Brad Pitt, and now I'm a crud. You are not endearing yourself to me. How much?"

"You are so shameless I am ashamed to admit I know you. Whatever it takes. That's for the first part. The second part is a little more . . . ah . . . delicate."

"And that would be . . . what?"

"A little hack job. I'm sure you can handle it. It will pay very well."

Abner chewed on his Canadian bacon, a thoughtful expression on his face. "Details."

"Our boss wants you to find out everything you can on a man named Virgil Anders. A long time ago he was a reporter for the *Baltimore Sun*. His name came up in an FBI file. The man disappeared and was never seen or heard from again, is what we're being told. The only other thing I know and was told to tell you was, he was writing a book. When he disappeared, he was in his midtwenties."

"And the second part?" Abner asked as he calculated the payout versus how much time he would have to spend tracking down Virgil Anders.

"Well, like I said, it's a little more . . . I think the right word is 'delicate.' "

"I don't do delicate," Abner sniffed as he watched the waitress add more crushed ice to his glass and then fill it with pulpy orange juice.

"I know, but this is . . . special. We want you to hack into the Witness Protection Program."

Abner started to choke. Orange juice and pulp flew in all directions as he reached for napkins to sop up the mess, his eyes so wild Maggie grew alarmed. Diners turned to look at what was going on in the back of the café.

"Now look at me! I have to go back home to change my clothes. Were you born crazy, or did you study up on how to be a nutjob?"

Maggie ignored him as she slapped down some bills on the table, and hissed, "We need to take this outside. I can't take you anywhere without you making a scene. What's wrong with you, Abner?"

His eyes still glazed, Abner followed Maggie out of the café.

"All you had to do was tell me you weren't capable of doing it. That I would have understood. Instead, you spewed orange juice all over the table, and now you look bedraggled. I told *them* you weren't the man for that job, but *they* thought so highly of the work you've done in the past, they insisted I ask. I told them, Abby, that it wouldn't matter even if they said you could name your price.

"Look, I'm sorry I upset you. I don't want you to give this another thought. If you don't want to work on the Virgil Anders case, either, tell me now. I'll find someone who needs the money more than you do. Listen, thanks for coming. I'll see you around."

Still in a daze, Abner Tookus watched Maggie walk away. He knew in his gut her step would falter and she'd turn around for one last go at him. But she didn't falter, and she didn't turn around. In fact, she sprinted across the road the moment the light turned green. He watched as she swiped at her eyes.

Maggie Spritzer was crying.

Abner looked down at his Hugo Boss suit and knew he had to get it to the dry cleaners stat. Then he'd head over to the *Post* building and try to make peace with his unrequited love. Brad Pitt, eh?

Chapter 14

Muttering to himself, Abner Tookus stepped into his private elevator, private because he was the owner of the renovated warehouse, which would take him to the spacious loft that he himself had restored. He had nine hundred square feet of actual living space, a bedroom, a luxurious sitting room, an outrageous bathroom, and a state-of-the-art kitchen that he never used. The remaining three thousand square feet of the loft were used for his business, which had no name. Other than "hacking."

At a glance, any first-time visitor would have likened the huge room to that of NASA's mission control. There were computers everywhere. Lights flashed, and muted pinging noises could be heard from all directions. A bank of televisions was mounted on one of the middle walls, each tuned to a different channel. The temperature was a controlled sixty-one degrees and never ever fluctuated.

Abner stomped his way into his bedroom, which resembled a harem gone wild. He did love veils and beads and bright colors. The art that hung on the walls had to do with voodoo, because when all his high-tech equipment failed him, which was hardly ever, he stuck pins in a wide range of voodoo dolls and laughed while he was doing so.

He was aggravated now as he stripped off his Hugo Boss suit and fired off a text to the person he was supposed to meet in New York. "Sorry, Trump, old boy, another time, another place."

Five minutes later, Abner was in a pair of cutoff khaki shorts, grungy sneakers, and a muscle shirt. He ran his hands through what was left of his hair and spiked it up with some gel. Now he felt like Abner Tookus, hacker extraordinaire.

Abner stumbled when the words *Witness Protection* rumbled through his brain as he made his way to his workstation. He sat down on his swivel stool, hit buttons, scooted the stool across the room to punch more buttons. He repeated the process so many times in the following fifteen minutes his stool left scorch marks on the shiny wood floors he'd installed himself, all the while the two ominous words kept ricocheting around and up and down inside his head.

While he waited for results to flow through his computers, he started to text three of his closest friends, hackers almost on his own level. Within seconds, all three colleagues agreed to meet up with him within the hour.

That was good; he'd have Virgil Anders locked up tight, sealed in an envelope by the time they arrived. All he had to do was decide if he was going to hand-deliver the envelope or messenger it to the *Post*. Well, damn, he hadn't even agreed to do the job on Virgil Anders, and here it was all wrapped up. Well, damn again.

Abner had always prided himself on being nerveless, never allowing himself to get rattled. But he was rattled now, and he admitted it to himself. As soon as his friends got here, he would bounce everything off them and see what they thought. *Witness Protection*. No one but no one had ever penetrated their program. They'd never lost a witness, either, thanks to their security.

Abner sniffed and stuck his nose high in the air. The only reason the WPP had never been penetrated was because he had never tried. He *never* failed. Ever. Then why was his big toe itching? He wiggled his toes inside his smelly sneakers, but the itch wouldn't go away.

Frustrated, he kicked off his sneaker. He watched as it sailed across the room. He really had to get some of those Odor-Eaters and put them in his sneakers. Or, horror of horrors, wash the damn things. He did, after all, have a fancy-dancy washing machine, complete with a rack specially for washing and drying sneakers. Worst-case scenario. Christ he was edgy.

Abner almost jumped out of his skin when the buzzer sounded to indicate his friends had arrived. He walked over to the elevator and sent it downward. He waited while it lumbered back up. He found himself grinning from ear to ear at his friends' appearance. They all looked and dressed just the way he did. Tim, Bart, and Stella, the seniors of the group, were in their very early thirties, all computer geniuses, all with PhD's. The three younger men trailing Tim, Bart, and Stella were their trainees. All three trainees were in doctoral programs. They were here to observe, to listen, and to keep quiet.

They knuckled one another as they made their way into the climate-controlled work area. Abner fished out stools from under various counters. Everyone took a seat. Refreshments were never served in this area. Six sets of eyes looked at Abner like he was the Messiah ready to lead them . . . *somewhere*.

"I have been offered a job, guys. Then a second later the job was withdrawn because the person who offered it said they thought I couldn't do it." A gasp went up from the little crowd that clearly stated that was the next thing to blasphemy.

No one asked a question, because Abner was their leader, and disciples never questioned their leader. "We all know there is nothing out there we can't crack. That's such a given it doesn't even bear thinking about, much less discussing. However, this assignment is a little outside the norm. What would you say if I told you my client wanted me to hack into the Witness Protection Program?"

One of the big three said, "I think the question here is, do you *want* to do it? That then brings a second question, which is how much is it worth? Then the granddaddy of all questions is, if you or we, as the case may be, get caught, and I am not saying that will happen, who takes care of you or us if we all work on this?"

Abner dropped his head to stare at his one bare foot. Did he want to do it? Hell, yes, he did. Cracking the WPP would be like an Olympian's winning the gold medal. "Yes, I do want to do it. And I'm smart enough to know I need your expertise. This particular job I think I can say with confidence is a 'name your own price' deal. As to who would come to our aid . . . the name I was given on past jobs was Miss Lizzie Fox. I would assume that still holds. I will confirm all of this once we all agree that we want to do it. A show of hands will do. Not the trainees, but if they have any input I'd like to hear it. As always, their fee comes out of your share. We still on the same page here?" Six hands shot into the air.

It was never about the money with these guys, Abner knew. The money wasn't important to him, either. He pretended it was with Maggie because he loved to haggle and walk away the winner. The thrill, the high, came from doing something no one else was capable of doing, then walking away free as the breeze. The cherry on top was laughing all the way to the bank.

"We're in," Stella said. Five heads nodded in confirmation. "Is this just a meeting to feel us out or do you want us to start to work? Just tell us what to do."

"Yeah, yeah, I want you to start on this. I have to go crosstown to deliver a package and talk to our client. I will broker the best deal I can, you all know that. I also have to garner a little more information. This is what I know so far. . . ."

Abner was almost to the door when one of the trainees tossed him his sneaker. Abner caught it, made another mental note to buy some Odor-Eaters, and was in the elevator, his heart pumping like a racehorse.

Abner arrived at the *Post* on the stroke of noon. The security guard frowned at his attire as he handed over a visitor's pass on a lanyard. His face grim, Abner stalked to the elevator and rode it to Maggie's floor. When he exited the elevator, he could see her getting up from her chair the moment she spotted him. She had the strangest look on her face, one that he'd never seen. He stomped his way to her office, slapped the envelope down on her desk, and said, "It's three million dollars. Take it or leave it."

Maggie almost broke her hand signing a chit for him to take to the accounting office. She tried to swallow past the lump in her throat. She waited.

Abner leaned over her desk. Maggie rolled her chair backward so she could see him better. "I'll take the job. Give it to me in five sentences." Maggie did in such a shaky, so-unlike-her voice that Abner felt pleased. He was doubly pleased to see that her hands were shaking.

"Three million bucks, and Lizzie Fox defends me and whoever else I might involve in this. I want it in writing right now, and I want half the money up front, like in *now*. Before you agree"—he leaned even farther across the desk—"I want you to know I hate your guts!"

Maggie knew she was going to choke any second. Her eyes burned with tears. A dozen witty comebacks flitted through her mind. Wisely, she kept them to herself. "I have to get authorization, you know that," she managed to squeak out.

Abner backed away from the desk and stood in the doorway. He watched as a single sheet of paper worked its way out of the fax machine. Lizzie's agreement. Maggie motioned for Abner to pick it up. Abner didn't move. He wiggled his fingers to indicate Maggie was to get up and hand it to him. She did, her hands trembling even more. Abner pretended not to notice.

Maggie looked down at her BlackBerry. She read the brief message and nodded. "Your new employer has authorized payment. You are to go to the Sovereign Bank, and they will issue a bank check. All you have to do is show your ID. Thank you, Abner," she said, her eyes shiny with tears.

"This finishes us, Maggie."

Maggie gulped and nodded. Somehow or other, she managed to say, "I know."

The moment the elevator door closed, Maggie rushed to her desk and burst into tears. Her thoughts were all over the map. Even before she realized what she was doing, she removed her engagement ring and dropped it into her desk drawer on top of a pile of candy wrappers. She cried harder and didn't know why. She didn't know why she took off her ring, either.

On his way to the Sovereign Bank, Abner kept swiping at his own burning eyes. The worst feeling in the world had to be loving someone with all your heart and soul and that person not returning or acknowledging that love.

His banking done, the money deposited to his money market fund, Abner left the bank. When he returned to his loft, he'd write checks to his three colleagues, then transfer the rest to one of his secret offshore accounts.

Life was going to go on no matter what happened. Abner picked up his feet, his smelly sneakers slapping at the pavement as he jogged to his loft instead of taking a taxi. He concentrated on the monumental task that was ahead of him as his feet continued to slap at the hot pavement.

While Abner was jogging his way home, Maggie, tears rolling down her cheeks, perused the papers that Abner had slapped on her desk. She rifled through them and nodded miserably. A perfect job. As always. Abby had come through for her once again. But at what cost? She stacked them neatly into the fax tray, pressed in the number, and within seconds they were on the way to Pinewood, where Charles would pluck them out of the machine, make copies, and give them to the Sisters.

"Yeah, Maggie," she whimpered tearfully.

"Oooh, here comes Charles. He looks like he's been sucking on a lemon," Yoko whispered.

"Ladies! I come bearing information, compliments of Maggie. It seems her source for gathering information has some magical sources of his or her own. Her source was able to locate Virgil Anders. Even with all his records being erased or expunged. As I said, magical." The sour lemon was in his voice as he handed out stapled files to each of the women. "Once you read through this as I have, tell me what your next plan of action is. In the meantime, I will make us fresh lemonade and some sandwiches."

The Sisters finished reading Maggie's report at the same

time. Nikki whistled appreciatively. "This is amazing. How in the world does her source do this?"

"I don't think we want to know that, dear," Annie said. "We have it all, that's what's important." There was no way she was going to tell the Sisters the papers in their hands had cost three million.

"So, Virgil Anders lives in Cresfield, Maryland. The town is a Mecca for seafood lovers with the best blue crab and oysters, bar none. Small town with a hometown feel to it. Anders lives in a gated community on the water. He's lived there in the same house for the past thirty-five years. He's right on the Chesapeake Bay, off Tangier Sound. We can get there easily from here in a few hours. Just this past spring, I heard a commercial on the radio calling Cresfield the Crab Capital of the World," Nikki said.

"Virgil Anders is handicapped. He lives in a wheelchair. He has a specially equipped van with a hydraulic lift to get him in and out. His house, which is a Tudor according to Google Earth, is valued at $1.5 million. He has no visible means of income, but monies are deposited into his bank account on the fifth day of every month. The sum is always the same, $10 thousand. Out of that he pays for his food, a housekeeper, a male nurse, his car expenses, and his taxes at the end of the year. The money comes from an annuity. There is no mortgage on the house. He owns the specially equipped van outright. He has one credit card with a limit of $25 thousand. He appears to use it a few times a year, mostly for online shopping, some clothes, books, videos, that type of thing. His bank balance, or maybe his money market account, shows a balance of more than $600 thousand. I guess that's money he saves from his monthly checks that come out of the annuity," Kathryn said. "What kind of annuity pays that kind of money for all these years? This isn't making any sense."

"The annuity is Hank Jellicoe, would be my guess," Myra said. "Mr. Anders was simply too young back when this started to have any kind of annuity that is so robust. My guess would be blackmail. Oh, girls, we really need to go and talk to this man, and the sooner the better."

"He's not married," Yoko said. "This picture of him standing in front of the *Baltimore Sun*'s building shows he was a handsome man in his youth. Did he become crippled when he dropped off the face of the earth, or did that come later?"

"Look at page four on the bottom. He was in Angel Mercy Hospital for eighteen months. When he was released, that's when he disappeared," Isabelle said. "I wonder if he was in a car accident. There's nothing in here anywhere that says what happened to him."

"On page five, middle of the page, it says he never gets company, never makes phone calls, and doesn't receive any calls. His housekeeper is the one who said that, and she's been with him from the outset. The only people who come to the house are the meter readers, the pool people in the summer, and people to clear away the snow in the winter. He's had three different male nurses since he moved where he is currently living. Nothing suspicious about any of the three. The first two relocated down South and the third one, the current one, has been with him for twelve years. In short, the man is a recluse," Alexis said.

"Well, if he's a recluse, why does he need a van that he is capable of driving?" Annie asked. "And where does he go when he does drive the van?" The Sisters shrugged.

"What do you think, Charles?" Myra asked.

"I don't know what to think," Charles said. "I'm beyond amazed at the thoroughness of this report in such a short period of time. I wish there was some information as to how the man became incapacitated. I realize hospitals thirty-five years ago must have kept records, but I'm sure they were destroyed by now. I'd like to see if we can find out anything from there, possibly one of the old record-keeping people might still be alive. I'll work on that if you all agree." The Sisters nodded.

"Girls, how will we get in to see Mr. Anders?"

As one, the Sisters burst out laughing. "We just show up. We simply say Hank Jellicoe sent us, and I think those gates will open like magic. We know good old Hank had to cut his losses and is on the run, so I don't think we have to worry too much about Mr. Anders being able to reach him. I do wonder, though, what will happen to the man's annuity," Nikki said. "If we decide, down the road, that the man deserves it, then I say we help ourselves to some of Hank's money we have stashed away." The others agreed.

"Let's plan our strategy," Annie said, clapping her hands gleefully. "I think we are onto something, girls."

Chapter 15

Nellie's breakfast and Charles's luncheon were long gone, as were Nellie and Elias, when the Sisters trooped back to the kitchen and resumed their task of going through the files on Hank Jellicoe. "We're doing this just to make sure there isn't something else in here that can help us find that skunk," Annie said, diving into her box of files.

As the Sisters worked, they chatted among themselves as to who was to go to Cresfield to seek out Virgil Anders. They batted it back and forth for over an hour when it was finally decided that it should be Annie and Myra since they were of an age with Virgil Anders and he might be more receptive to talking with them.

"This reminds me of when we trapped Hank, Stu, and Fish in Florida," Isabelle said. "Do you suppose or even think that if he is the one who set up Virgil Anders in Cresfield, and we don't know that for a fact, possibly he has other houses in that gated community the way he had in Florida? Just another safe haven right out there in the open and a way to keep his eyes or someone's eyes on Virgil Anders."

"For thirty-five years!" Nikki exploded.

"It's called long-range planning," Myra said. "Charles explained that to me once. Covert agents always look to the future, when the day might come when they have to go to ground. We just talked about this all yesterday. If Hank established a house or even several houses in that gated community years and years ago, no one is even going to think of going there to look for him, assuming they even know about it. Back then, that particular community wouldn't have been a gated community. Those things didn't spring up until recently, when privacy became the name of the game," Myra said.

"You're probably right. No one but us is looking for Virgil Anders, and the only reason we're looking for him is that we have the FBI files. I think it's definitely a feather in our cap that we're the only ones who know about Mr. Anders," Kathryn said. "This way, we won't be tripping over anyone."

"Are you and Myra okay with going to Cresfield?" Nikki asked Annie.

"Of course, dear. I think the question that is more important is are you girls comfortable with Myra and me going? I don't have a problem with all of you coming along as backup if you want to do that. If we are successful in getting Mr. Anders to talk to us, we can wire up and, whatever he divulges, you all can act on it right then and there. I think that's a plan if you all agree. Charles can arrange for a van that will hold us all. When we reach our destination, Myra and I can switch to a car and you all can go to ground somewhere. I always wanted to wear a wire. Myra does, too, don't you, Myra?" Annie's tone clearly said Myra damn well better want to wear a wire.

"Absolutely, dear. I just can't wait to say, over and out, this is vigilante number one calling vigilante number five."

"You're such a poop sometimes, Myra. Where is your sense of adventure?"

"It *went to ground* along with the girls when we left the van for the car." At the expression on Annie's face, Myra burst out laughing.

The rest of the day and into the evening found the Sisters sitting in the middle of the floor shaking their heads. "Nothing here to help us other than the Virgil Anders stuff," Yoko said as she strapped tape around the boxes she'd been working on.

"At least we got something. And we now have a plan. I suggest we trundle these boxes to the living room so Charles can take them back to the war room and secure them," Myra said as she finished her last box of files.

"I'm for bed myself, girls. I know it's only nine o'clock, but Myra and I were up all night, unlike you girls, who managed to snatch a few hours' sleep. If we plan to be on the road by seven-thirty, I want to be well rested."

Once the boxes of files were stacked neatly near the entrance to the underground tunnels, the girls filed up the stairs behind Myra and Annie. At the top of the steps they all splintered off as they trailed to their rooms.

Tomorrow was another day.

Promptly at ten o'clock, Annie pulled up to the security gate at Cresfield Villas. Both she and Myra were wearing wires under their linen jackets. They could have posed for anyone's mother, grandmother, aunt, or sister, with their coiffed silver hair, subdued makeup, subtle perfume, and not-quite-haughty manner. They were driving a rented shiny black Mercedes. The Sisters were less than half a mile away and tuned into the listening devices.

A guard stepped out of the gatehouse, a toothy smile on his face that his parents had to be proud of. "Can I help you?"

"I certainly hope so. We're here to see Virgil Anders. Before you can ask, no, he is not expecting us. His old employer asked us to stop by and give him some documents. I wonder if you could ring him and explain to him that it will only take a few minutes. Mr. Jellicoe needs his signature on several documents."

When the guard went back inside his little gatehouse, Annie and Myra both had a clear view of him speaking on the phone. The guard was frowning as he tried to relay all that Annie had told him. He came back out of the gatehouse, the frown still on his face, and said, "Mr. Anders isn't seeing any visitors today. He said to tell you he's sorry for the inconvenience."

Annie smiled. "Not as sorry as Mr. Anders is going to be if he doesn't sign these papers. He will have to vacate the premises by noon tomorrow if he doesn't sign on the dotted line. Try explaining that to Mr. Anders, please."

The guard returned to the gatehouse. He was clearly distressed at what he was saying and hearing on the other end of the phone. Annie, trying to play it cool, shifted into reverse and was about to back up the Mercedes when the guard held up his hand. "Mr. Anders said it was all right to let you in. You will have to leave your car over there in the parking lot. One of my people will drive you in a golf cart to the house. It's standard procedure. The association doesn't like cars parked on the roads. It will just be a minute. I called up to the clubhouse to send down a cart. Beautiful day, isn't it?"

"It appears to be," Annie said. "How are we to get back here to our car?"

"Mr. Anders will call the clubhouse for you. Have a

pleasant day, ladies." The bar lifted, and Annie drove to the visitors' parking area, which held no less than a dozen cars.

The golf cart was driven by a chubby little blonde who looked to be about ten years of age. She prattled on and on about what a wonderful place Cresfield Villas was during the summer months, when all the tourists arrived to savor the pleasures of Cresfield. When she stomped on the brake five minutes later, Annie and Myra were jolted forward. "Ooops, sorry about that, this is only the second time I've driven the cart." She hopped out and offered her hand, first to Annie, then Myra. And then she was gone.

"Nice," Myra said, indicating the exquisitely manicured grounds that led up to what looked like a solid mahogany door. Before they could even ring the bell, the door was opened by a pleasant-looking white-haired woman wearing an apron. Her voice was as pleasant as she looked when she invited Myra and Annie indoors.

"Follow me; Mr. Anders is on the lanai. He likes to take the morning sun with his coffee." The woman, who said her name was Marion, opened the French doors, announced the visitors, then withdrew, closing the doors behind her.

The lanai was awash in colorful flowers and flowering vines, trailing from the overhead cedar beams that deflected the sun. Virgil Anders literally sat in the middle of the flowering space. "Ladies," he said by way of greeting. "Obviously, I can't get up." He extended his hand to be shaken, the grip powerful. Both women gave back as good as they got. He nodded approvingly. "I had no idea you were coming. Who are you?" he asked quietly.

"I'm Myra Rutledge, and this is Anna de Silva. We lied to the guard, Mr. Anders, and I do apologize for that. Mr. Jellicoe did not send us. But he is the reason we're here."

"We need your help, Mr. Anders." Annie carefully related the details on how they came to find him.

"I really believed Jellicoe when he said no one would ever find me. I really did. All these years later, and suddenly, here you are. I never thought it would happen. What do you want from me? If that man finds out you're here, it won't be good for you. It will be worse for me. You do know that, right?"

"Are you saying you don't know Hank Jellicoe is on the run? Haven't you followed his demise this past year?"

"Yes and no. People like Hank Jellicoe make their own rules. You might think he's on the run, but he isn't. He's holed up somewhere waiting for just the right moment to strike. He's one hell of a strategist, I will give him that. As to following the man . . . I've done nothing but do that for the past thirty-five years. I am sitting in this wheelchair because of him. You really have to leave. I can't talk to you. If I do, I could lose all this," Anders said, waving his arm about. "I shouldn't have agreed to allow you in here, but with him, you never know, I couldn't take the chance that you were legitimate. Like I said, who the hell are you? Oh, Christ, I know who you are! I thought you looked familiar. You really have to get out of here. Please."

"Nothing is going to happen to you, Mr. Anders. I personally guarantee it. All I have to do is make one phone call and you will have twenty-four seven security beyond your wildest imagination. No one will be able to get to you, not even the infamous Hank Jellicoe. I want you to believe me," Myra said.

"Guaranteed?"

"Guaranteed," Annie and Myra said as one.

"Make the call."

Myra hit the speed dial on her phone. She quickly explained the situation, then went quiet as Charles told her what to do. She powered down, and said, "Your *new* security will be in place by the time we leave here. Do you want to wait for it to be put into place, or should we begin our discussion?"

"Where's the rest of your posse?"

"A half mile away. We took a vote, and we all agreed you might be more apt to talk to Annie and me since we're of an age. We know most of your story," Myra lied, "so just talk, and we'll fill in the blanks."

Anders leaned back in his wheelchair and closed his eyes. "Journalism is in my blood. I knew that when I was ten years old and started my own school newspaper and sold it for two cents a copy. When I graduated from college, I went to work for the *Baltimore Sun,* doing all the crap you have to do at entry level. I finally worked myself up to reporter status and from there to investigative reporter. I did okay for myself, too. Today I would be called a rising star. I was also full of myself, another today term. My ultimate goal, as it is with all reporters, was a Pulitzer. The big one, the one that makes or breaks you.

"I thought I had it in Hank Jellicoe. I worked night and day researching that guy. I had tons, bricks and bricks of stuff on him. Some of it good, most of it bad, I have to say that. It was my intention to write a story on him for the paper while I was working on a book about him. Hell, I'd even sent out a query to a publisher, and they were hot to see it. I even had a title for it. *Man, Myth, Monster.*

"At that point, all I had was my research. I hadn't interviewed a soul. How the hell he found out about it is something that, to this day, I don't know."

"What did you find out that resulted in your sitting in that chair, Mr. Anders?"

"That he was in bed with just about everyone, the CIA, the FBI, terrorist groups—but they weren't called terrorists back in my day. I almost had it nailed down, too, but then my snitch or my source took off on me. He'd told me that Jellicoe arranged security for high-profile contractors and the like. He was just getting his toes wet on the military stuff at that point in time. He actually arranged for kidnappings, then rode in on his white horse to rescue them. He got not two bites of the apple, he got three great big bites when they paid high dollars for his protection, then he had their companies pay the ransom, and after that, they were so grateful when he rescued them, they gave the son of a bitch a bonus.

"Headlines around the world. Three or four deals like that, and he was untouchable. Then he crawled into bed with all the different agencies and named his price. By the time the guy was forty, he was a billionaire."

Annie laughed. "Not anymore. We have his money."

"I'll be damned. But he got away. I'm sure you know he has safe houses all over the world, don't you?"

Myra shrugged. "For all the good they're going to do him. We think he's here, and by 'here,' I mean the Washington area. We're waiting for him to come to us."

"What happened to your book, Mr. Anders?" Annie asked.

"His people came to my apartment and took it. He didn't dirty his hands. He had some of his goons work me over, and this is the result. I was in the hospital for eighteen long months. The day I was discharged, two men showed up and brought me here to this house. They parked me and this wheelchair right here where I'm sitting and left. Hank Jellicoe arrived about ten minutes later. It was the weirdest encounter I ever had in my life. He was actually chatty, inquired about my health. He explained that he had brought along a housekeeper who at that precise moment was making us coffee. And he told me he'd hired a nurse for me. He explained about the house, how it was now mine.

"It has everything. Every year a brand-new van with a hydraulic lift is delivered. He told me I would be paid a stipend . . . that was the word he used, 'stipend,' of ten thousand dollars. And all of this would continue," Anders said, waving his arms about, "as long as I kept my mouth shut and lived out my days here in the splendor he had created for me. At the age of twenty-seven, as I was then, that was not what I wanted to hear, but I kept my mouth shut. I knew I was never going to be able to walk again, and back in those days handicapped people had no rights or benefits, so I had no alternative but to take the deal. Which brings me to my next question. What are you going to do with this information?"

"Is this place bugged?" Annie blurted.

"I don't think so. I've looked but have never found anything. Doesn't mean it isn't, though. Maybe your people, the ones who are going to protect me, can sweep the joint." Annie simply nodded.

"Let's assume for the sake of argument that this lovely lanai is not bugged. Do you seriously want us to believe . . . and remember who you are talking to here . . . that you never worked on that book from that day on, a book that could have earned you a Pulitzer?"

"No, I'm not saying that at all. In fact, I'm still working on it. Actually, it's finished up to the point where he escaped. I'm waiting to write the final chapter."

"Where is it?"

"I can't tell you that. At least not now."

"But if Jellicoe knew you wrote it, and that you had given it to us, we could flush him out that much quicker. If you were so afraid of him, why did you write it?"

Anders looked down at his legs. "Because I had to. After twenty years, I thought he'd forget about me, the book, and all this crap. That's when I started on it again. I remembered just about everything I'd written because I'd done it with a pencil. You know, notes, the way a reporter works. That's how I could remember it. It's taken me these past fifteen years to get to this point. I'm sure you know I can get out and about. I go to the gym twice a week for upper-body exercise. Then I go to the library, where I work on the book. No more than an hour and a half at a time. Usually I go to the library first, then to the gym. I keep the flash drive in a locker. I rented three lockers aside from the one I normally use. I paid cash for them so there's no record that I rented them. I'm friendly enough with the owner that I think if anyone had come around asking questions, he would have alerted me."

"Do you have any objections to letting us copy the flash drive and returning the original to its hiding place? Is it a key or a combination? What's the locker number?"

Anders sighed. "Gold's Gym. It's right in town. The locker is seventeen, and the combination is four right, nine left, and six right. When are you going to do it?"

Myra smiled. "Right this very second. It will be back in place inside of an hour. Do not fret about it. I'm not understanding any of this. The man cripples you, then he comes here, acts like your new best friend, and sets you up like a king. Why?"

"Because the son of a bitch is crazy. Do you know what bothered him the most? Not the fact that I had ferreted out what he'd done and was still doing. No, that didn't faze him at all. What got to him was the monster part. *Man, Myth, Monster.* I did the book in three parts, the Man part, the middle part was the Myth, and the ending, which I hadn't written, was the Monster part. He did all this, set me up, gives me money, to prove to me he isn't a monster. He liked the Man part because I depicted him as the tough bastard he is. The Myth part, he liked that, too, because he said everyone is a bit of a myth, and it keeps people guessing. It was the Monster part that ripped his guts, and my useless legs are the result. He's crazy."

"I think we all agree on that. I have one other question. Do you know if Jellicoe was married? We know he was, but we can't pin down the time frame. And we don't know what happened to his wife, and we understand they had a daughter," Annie said.

"I can't help you there. I never heard or saw anything to indicate a wife or child. Now what?" Anders asked uneasily.

Now what indeed, both women thought.

Chapter 16

Less than a mile away, the remaining Sisters entered Virgil Anders's gym. A buff, ripped trainer walked up to them, a dentist's delight, as he smiled and asked how he could be of help.

"We'd like to look around and see if this is the right gym for us," Isabelle said.

"Well, we have everything. And we have personal trainers if you're looking for one-on-one training. As you can see by the chart on the wall, we're competitively priced. This is a state-of-the-art facility. Our membership is quite large." The trainer waved his arm in all directions to show members working out in various sections of the gym. "We have Pilates, aerobics. The classes are full for this session, however. A new session is scheduled to start in two weeks."

"Do you mind if we walk around, check out the equipment, and maybe talk to a few of your members?" Kathryn asked.

"Sure, take all the time you need."

"Where are the locker rooms? Are the men separated from the women?"

"Yes, but there is a connecting door. In case of overflow. Right now we're jamming, and some of the members have had to double up. By the way, we really don't advertise this, but we have a small Internet café down the hall from the locker rooms. Sometimes we have people wandering in here who want to use it or to get a quick bite to eat. We try to discourage that because it's really intended just for members."

"How convenient," Alexis murmured as she moved off.

"Watch my back," Nikki hissed to Kathryn as she headed toward the locker room.

"Got it," Kathryn said, trailing behind Nikki.

"Isabelle, play up to the muscle boy, and I'll watch the door," Yoko hissed as she danced her way back the way she'd come. "I'll sign the guest book for all of us." She smiled to herself as she heard Isabelle asking how long it had taken the trainer, who said his name was Adrian, to acquire his *perfect* body.

Yoko was studying the snapshots of before-and-after members tacked to a large bulletin board near the front door. When it opened, she looked up and into the startled eyes of a tall, well-built man. Without batting an eye, she turned and fished out her phone. She sent a text to Nikki that simply said, *Feds are here.*

She looked toward Alexis, who nodded. She moved off toward Kathryn, who was offering encouragement to a balding man with a potbelly dripping sweat down his designer workout shirt. Her back to the newcomer, Alexis mouthed the word *Feds.*

Kathryn looked down at her watch as she opened the louvered door leading to the locker room. There was no sign of Nikki. She opened another door and was in a hall-way. This had to be the way to the Internet café. Nikki was just coming through the door from the café and slip-ping the flash drive into her pocket, when Kathryn said, "The Feds are here. No time to put that back. Grab a ba-nana or something so it looks like you came in here for food."

Both women sauntered down the hall and out to the main part of the gym. Isabelle was still cooing with Adrian, while another trainer was talking to the new-comer. Yoko was still by the door.

"We've been here sixteen minutes," Kathryn muttered. "Time to get out of here."

"He's going to follow us. Are we sure he's a Fed?" Nikki asked, looking across the room at the newcomer. Not bothering to wait for a response to her question, she said, "Yep, he's a Fed all right. What do you think, Kathryn, should we take him out here or wait till he gets outside?"

"Either/or. Don't they travel in pairs?"

"There is that. Okay, we take him out here and get the other one outside." She nodded to Yoko, who was watch-ing her intently.

Yoko walked over to Isabelle, who was inching her way toward the second trainer and the newcomer. "Hold still, hold still," Yoko suddenly squealed. "You have a spider on your neck. Don't move. Oooh, it looks like a black widow. I bet it has that little red dot on its stomach. If you don't move, I can get it."

The newcomer froze, as did the second trainer and Adrian, who managed to gasp, "We do not have spiders in this gym."

"Well, you do now." Yoko reached up, her fingers poised. She touched the newcomer's neck, and he immediately slid to the floor, unconscious. "Oh, well, I tried. You better call nine-one-one right away. Black widows are deadly. I don't think I want to join your gym. Come on, girls."

The Sisters all gaped at the man sleeping peacefully on the floor. The members that saw what had happened crowded around, jabbering and gesturing at the sleeping man. "Someone really needs to call nine-one-one," Kathryn shouted as she bolted through the door Nikki was holding open for her.

"Where's the other one?" Isabelle shouted as the Sisters hit the parking lot at a dead run, all of them saying the same thing. "They now know about Virgil Anders."

"I thought we were off-limits and untouchable," Kathryn snarled as she raced to a black sedan that screamed FBI, the girls behind her. Kathryn ripped open the door as Nikki reached for the man's arm and pulled him outside and onto the ground. Alexis stomped on his chest while Kathryn took his gun, his cell phone, his wallet, and his keys.

"That's federal property. You can go to prison for this," the agent said as he struggled to get up and speak.

"Obviously, you have me mixed up with someone who cares. I don't. If anyone is going to prison, it's going to be you. We're off-limits and untouchable, and you damn well know it. In other words, your boss broke the rules, and now you're going to pay for it."

"Why are you taking his junk?" Isabelle asked curiously.

"Because I can." Kathryn laughed.

"Well, that works for me." Isabelle giggled. "Let's handcuff him to the door just for fun."

"Okay," Kathryn trilled as she reached into the car for a set of cuffs in the console.

"Where's my goddamn partner? What did you bitches do to him?"

"I don't much care for your tone, Mr. Super Shit Agent. Alexis, do something."

Alexis raised her foot and stomped down on the man's nose. She winced as blood spurted in all directions. "Is that okay?"

"Just perfect. But we didn't answer his question. Your partner is inside the gym. He got bitten by a black widow spider. Oh, I hear the ambulance now." After handcuffing the Fed to the door, Kathryn dusted her hands dramatically, and observed, "Girls, I think our work here is done."

"This was hard work. Let's go get a nice cool drink," Alexis said, as she removed her foot from the agent's chest. The man's arm snaked out, but Kathryn kicked him so hard in the side she heard a rib snap. She shrugged as she followed the girls to the van.

"Burn rubber, Nikki," she shouted as she literally fell into the van, strong arms reaching to pull her to safety.

"How the hell did they find us?" Kathryn said, still in her snarling mood. "I didn't spot a tail on our way here. There's no way the FBI could know about Virgil. We have the files from Mitch Riley. Yantzy can't have seen them, so like it or not, we screwed up, and those guys followed us. We're slipping, girls!"

"Unless there's a GPS bug on this van," Nikki said. "We did not have a tail on the way up here. We need to get out of here. Kathryn, turn on the GPS and find an alternate route back home, just in case they have tails ready to pick us up on the route we took here."

Annie stared at the wheelchair-bound man, a thoughtful expression on her face.

Virgil Anders finger-combed his hair as he stared up at the two women towering over him. "What? Why are you looking at me like that? What are you thinking?"

Annie sat down on one of the cushioned chairs at the table. "I was wondering how it is that you never tried to leave here. I understand your comfort level and zone, and I even understand your fear. You're a prisoner, but then you already know that. Did you ever even try?"

Virgil Anders looked down at his legs and then up at Annie. "No. I never tried. The thought was always there in the back of mind, but I never acted on it. What that meant was that I had to work extra hard not to get carried away with a possible escape. When it did happen, all I had to do was remember those two goons and the eighteen months I spent in the hospital. I knew if I tried, they'd kill me. It's just that simple, and if you can't understand it or *won't* understand it, then it's your problem. I'm alive. For all intents and purposes I have a good life. There is nothing I need or want except to be able to walk again, and that's not going to happen. In case you haven't noticed, I'm an old man.

"Maybe you can understand this. A day doesn't go by that I don't try to plan an escape, a day doesn't go by that I don't plan Hank Jellicoe's death. It's what has kept me going. I was engaged to be married when this all happened, did you know that?"

Annie and Myra shook their heads.

"Well, I was. I guess there's no harm in telling you this. Her name was Margie Evans, and she came to see me every day in the hospital. Then when they brought me here, they told me I had to cut all ties. I knew they were watching me so I . . . buckled. I told myself I did it for Margie's safety, but I was a coward. That's the bottom line."

Myra felt so sorry for the man sitting in front of her, she dropped to her knees and reached for his hands. "Do you want us to find her for you?"

"And have her see me like this? No! Not while Hank Jellicoe is still out there. No!"

"Mr. Anders, you said she stuck by you while you were in the hospital and came to see you every day. That has to mean she knew what your condition was, and she was okay with it. When you were at the library on the computer, didn't you ever *try?*"

Anders shook his head. "I opted to let sleeping dogs lie. I would like to know that she's okay. I think about her as much as I think about Hank Jellicoe and what might have been."

If Anders was going to say anything else, he was interrupted by the sound of the doorbell.

The alarm on Anders's face was so palpable that Myra and Annie were on their feet in a second. "No one called. How did they get past the guard? That guard carries a gun. You must have been followed!" This last sentence was almost a shriek of panic.

The French doors opened, and Avery Snowden stepped onto the lanai. He introduced himself and the men standing behind him.

Anders sagged in his wheelchair.

"Charles said an hour, and the hour is up right now, this minute," Annie said happily.

Myra held out her hand. "You're in good hands, Mr. Anders. Thank you for talking with us. We can see ourselves out."

Annie held out her hand. Both women had turned to leave, when Anders called out, "What about my book? What are you going to do with it?"

Annie laughed, a sound so strange even Avery Snowden looked startled. "Why, publish it, of course!"

Outside, Myra looked at Annie. "Oh, dear, we forgot we have to call for the golf cart to take us back to our car."

"Not so, Miz Rutledge," a deep voice said from the side of the house. "I'll be more than happy to drive you to the gate."

"I do love security, don't you, Myra?" Annie said as she tripped along behind a burly man who was roughly the size of a tree.

True gentleman that he was, the guard drove like a race-car driver. When they reached the gatehouse, he got out first and helped Myra and Annie step down from the SUV. "Where's the guard?"

"Sleeping." The security man, who'd said his name was Sam, looked at his watch. "He'll be napping for another two hours. If you notice, we put a temporary sign on the gate saying because of electric problems, the gate will be closed for several hours. Have a safe trip back home, ladies." Sam tipped an imaginary hat and careened back the way they'd come.

"Well, that was productive!" Annie said, climbing behind the wheel of the rental car.

"We're going to publish Mr. Anders's book! Annie, I don't think you should have made such a rash promise to Mr. Anders. What if we can't find a publisher for it, and what if it isn't any good? It just might be the ravings of a cranky, justifiably used-to-be reporter bent on vengeance."

"We can worry about that when the time comes. One way or the other, we will publish it even if it's in excerpts in the *Post*. People love stuff that is serialized. That's when a publisher snaps it up, then the author becomes published. Most of the time it happens like that. Let's cross our fingers that Mr. Anders is not the exception to that rule," Annie said.

"You have an answer for everything, don't you, Annie?"

"Since I can't depend on you, I have to come up with my own answers. Look, there's the van." Annie pulled the rental car into a parking space at a strip mall. Doors opened and doors closed. The Sisters piled out, all of them jabbering ten miles to the minute.

When Annie suggested that they stop at a little Greek place in the mall to grab something to eat before heading back to their home base, Nikki said that was not a very good idea and that they needed to get out of the area ASAP.

When Myra protested, Kathryn told her that Nikki was right and that all would become clear when they found a place to eat. "Please, let's just get back into the van and make tracks. And by the way, we're taking a different route back to Pinewood. All will become clear in a few minutes."

After twenty minutes of deafening silence, Alexis said, "There's a little Italian place over there. We should be far enough away now, so let's grab something to eat." The women ran across the lot to get out of the blistering heat. The delicious smells along with the arctic coolness inside the little restaurant was a balm to their sweaty faces and thumping hearts. The heady aroma of baking pizza, garlic, basil, and aged cheese was overpowering.

"I could stay here forever. I just love Italian restaurants. If I had to choose between smelling something like this or the finest French perfume, I'd choose this." Nikki sighed.

"The AC in the van wasn't working, and before you can ask, five women descending on a gym translated to five new memberships, so it was a piece of cake getting in and out of the locker room. And miracle of miracles, down the hall from the main gym was a small, for want of a better word, Internet café for members. They serve sandwiches and soft drinks along with juice and coffee, and they have five computers for members. I copied the files on the flash drives, sent copies to Charles, Jack, and Bert, one to Maggie, and one to Lizzie. I also made a copy just for us. I was in and out in sixteen minutes. Yoko timed me," Nikki said proudly.

"Well done, girls," Myra said, as Kathryn placed an order for three large pizzas with the works. "Two pitchers of root beer," Alexis added.

"Okay, girls. What did Nikki just leave out? Clearly something happened, or we would be eating in that Greek place in the strip mall and not riding around on back roads to get home. Out with it. NOW!"

"As Nikki said," Yoko began, "she had no problem getting the flash drive and copying it. But while she was doing it, a Fed walked into the gym, and—"

"Are you absolutely sure it was a Fed?" Annie exclaimed. "What happened to our immunity? It wouldn't be CIA since they'd be risking a major problem if they were caught operating on U.S. soil. So it had to be FBI."

"It was," Yoko assured her. "I took him out by pretending to try to save him from a black widow spider. How dumb is that. He obviously knew just who I was and still let me get close enough to send him to the floor, unconscious, with no obvious violence.

"Then we left the gym, shouting for them to call nine-one-one, and pulled his partner from a black FBI sedan. When we left, he had a bloody nose, a cracked rib, and was handcuffed to the door of the car. Oh, and Kathryn has his gun and badge. She thought we might want to send it to President Connor as a present. Or failing that, maybe Director Yantzy would like them."

"We don't know where we screwed up, Annie," Isabelle said, "but they got on to us somehow. And they must know that we are interested in Virgil Anders. What are we going to do now?"

Annie gave Myra a signal, and Myra got up, went to the restroom, and called Charles to tell him what had happened and to arrange for Virgil Anders to be moved to a safe location somewhere unknown to either Henry, call me Hank, Jellicoe or possibly soon-to-be-ex-director John Yantzy and his FBI hooligans.

When Myra returned and gave Annie a thumbs-up, Annie said, "Let's talk, girls. Myra and I will go first. We think it's safe to say that, for the moment, at least, we can cross Mr. Anders off our worry list. Mr. Snowden and his men arrived as we were leaving. He's in good hands and at this very moment is being moved to a safe location. The FBI is not going to be able to take him. And even if he had been left in place, I don't think there's any way Jellicoe can get to Mr. Anders even if he managed to secure some kind of help by way of perhaps a few old cohorts.

"Now that we have *the book,* I think we should let it be known that we have it. Knowing *the book* is out there swinging in the breeze might force his hand. By the time we put the book into play, Mr. Anders will be buried so deep that no one without authorization from us will be able to get to him. Having said that, I'm open to any and all thoughts."

"I read the opening lines of Mr. Anders's book," Nikki said. "Would you all like to hear it?"

"What a foolish question, dear. Of course we want to hear it," Myra said, speaking for the others.

"This is how it goes. *I heard about the man. I was not impressed. I read the myth attributed to the man. I was not impressed. I met the monster man in person. I was impressed.*"

"Oh, my goodness," Myra gasped.

"Sounds like a runaway best-seller to me," Annie quipped. The others agreed.

While they waited for their pizzas to arrive, the Sisters slipped into their friendship mode and playfully poked and jabbed one another as they laughed and kibitzed about their outing at the gym. Then, one by one, they all got up to hit the restrooms to wash their hands.

Left alone, Myra looked at Annie. "What's wrong? What's bothering you?"

"The girls. You just witnessed all of them together like I did. Old times, all of them working in unison. Again. Think back to the separation. Now they're all back in the fold, and all of them have issues with the men in their lives. Even Maggie, although she won't admit it. I'm worried about all of the girls. I knew they had a strong connection to one another. I'm just now realizing how strong that bond is. What if they can't go back to having normal lives again? What then, Myra?"

"Oh, Annie, I don't know. I have to admit, Charles and I did discuss this very thing a few days ago, and he is as worried as you are. That's not to say I'm not worried, because I am. I think this is something the girls are going to have to work through on their own. I don't think we should interfere. A nudge here or there, a few well-chosen words of advice, but that's it."

Annie whipped out a small bottle of hand sanitizer and motioned for Myra to hold out her hands. She squirted liberally. "Here come the girls. Shhhh."

"Like you have to tell me that," Myra murmured under

her breath. She managed to work up a bright smile just as the waitress set down three glorious-looking pizzas.

The Sisters went back to their easy, comfortable banter as they devoured the pizza and swigged down the frosty root beer.

An hour later, Kathryn leaned back in her chair, and said, "Either I was starved or that was the best pizza I've ever eaten." Alexis took issue with that statement and said the best pizza was from a place in Arlington named Tony's. The girls were off and running again as each one offered her opinion.

Annie nudged Myra's leg to drive her worried point home. Myra nudged back.

Myra reached for the check, whipped out some bills, and left a more-than-generous tip as the girls gathered up their bags to leave the restaurant.

The conversation during the ride back to Washington was mostly speculation on what was going to go down once they decided how to handle Virgil Anders's book.

"Anders nailed the title," Isabelle said. My gut is telling me that Hank Jellicoe is going to go nuclear when he hears that book is out there. We need to figure out how we're going to safeguard ourselves. The man knows where we all live. He's been to Pinewood, and Myra's electronic gate is not going to keep someone like him out."

"We need to stay together. One on one, none of us is a match for him. And what about the guys and Maggie?" Alexis asked anxiously.

"I say we all stay out at the farm until we resolve this," Nikki said. She turned to call out to Annie. "What is this going to do to your and Myra's trip to Las Vegas?"

"A trip is easy to postpone. When we get home, we'll fall back and regroup. Call everyone to meet us this evening at the farm. We need to come up with a plan," Myra said.

"Then we should recruit Jack," Yoko said. To Annie's and Myra's dismay, the girls went off into peals of laughter.

"They don't look too worried to me," Annie said. "Unlike you and me."

"Oh, Annie, that's because they are together. They are so tuned to one another, they are convinced that as a unit they can do anything, and that means capturing Hank Jellicoe. And, before you can ask me, no, I don't think that's going to work this time around."

"I just love it when you are so cheerful and confident, Myra. Has it escaped your mind that you and I are the brains of this group?"

Myra laughed. "Don't ever change, Annie. If you change, I won't know what to do."

"You'll figure out something. Stop with the pearls, or the girls are going to think you're worried."

"Point taken, dear."

Chapter 17

Director John Yantzy slammed the door of his office, his face purple with rage, the veins in his neck thick as straws. "I don't believe this! You're supposed to be two of my best agents. That's why I assigned you to this case. A rookie agent wouldn't have screwed up like you two just did!

"You, Carpenter! You let a goddamn woman wrestle you out of a Bureau car and handcuff you to the goddamn door! And if that wasn't bad enough you allowed a second woman to stomp on your nose and break it! You're a goddamn senior federal agent, for crissakes, and you let this happen. And . . . they took your gun and your damn badge!

"As for you, Finn, you let some midget sell you a bill of goods about a black widow spider on your fucking neck! Son of a bitch, how stupid can you be? That Oriental vigilante is every bit as lethal as that bastard Wong. They're married to each other, for crissakes.

"I'm putting both of you on unpaid leave for what you allowed to happen. Well, say something!" Yantzy bellowed. "Oh, and the local police filed a report. That's going to be in the papers in the morning. The only god-damn good thing you did was not use the word *vigilante*. I'm waiting."

Both agents stood at attention, but neither said a word.

"Okay, let's pretend that you're in the fifth grade, and I'm going to ask you questions. Who the fuck is Virgil Anders? Why did the vigilantes go to see a man in a wheel-chair?"

"I don't know, sir. The guard at the gate told us Mr. Anders was wheelchair bound and has lived there for over thirty years. It was the two older women who went to visit him, Rutledge and de Silva. They told the guard to tell Anders they had papers for him to sign. When he was first called, Anders said that he didn't want to meet them. That's when they told him if he didn't meet with them, he would have to move out tomorrow, so Anders agreed to the meeting. The guard called for the golf cart to transport the two ladies.

"Visitors have to park their cars outside the security gate and be driven to wherever they're going. It's a rule of Cresfield Villas. That was all the guard could remember. The other five women stayed in town and went to the gym. Finn stayed in town when they separated, and I followed Rutledge and de Silva."

Yantzy's face was still a mottled purple. "Get out of here, both of you. I want a report in triplicate on my desk within the hour. I will call you when I want you back here."

If they'd had tails, those tails would have been between their respective hind legs as they slunk from the director's office.

Yantzy made a fist and socked it into the palm of his left hand, again and again, until the pain in his hand shot all the way up to his elbow. He cursed long and loud as he looked at the calendar on his desk. The minute he'd heard what had gone down, he'd sent out a BOLO (be-on-look-out) far and wide. But the damn vigilantes were, as usual, one step ahead of him, and by the time he sent in a second team to clean up the first team's mess, Virgil Anders was gone, and the housekeeper, who professed to know nothing, was packing her belongings to move in with her sister in Bowie. And here he was holding a bag of shit with nowhere to dump it.

Yantzy's gaze went back to the calendar. "Span is going to have a field day with this tomorrow. Unless . . ."

The night was soft and dark, with a balmy breeze. The trees whispered among themselves, a lullaby to the chirping birds who had gone silent for the night. Overhead, a full moon lit up the lush garden, the stars twinkling overhead.

"This is the perfect ending to a . . . very interesting day," Nikki said, sipping from a frosty glass of lemonade.

"What I find interesting is that no one has showed up to arrest us," Kathryn said. "We did render two FBI agents helpless. All right, all right, we assaulted them."

"Tomorrow is another day," Alexis quipped.

"Darling, Director Yantzy stepped over the line. He's not going to come out here, nor is he going to arrest any of us," Myra said. "Do you agree, Charles?"

"I do. For several reasons. One, as you said, he stepped over the line. Two, you girls took them on, made fools of his two agents, and walked away. Three, is or isn't Director Yantzy going to tell Director Span about that little episode? I think not. His agents certainly did not cooperate with the locals when it came to identifying you, since if they had, you would have already had Virginia police out here. But, girls, we do have a large area of concern. The FBI now knows about Virgil Anders.

"We were lucky in that we relocated Mr. Anders to safer quarters, thanks to your quick thinking and actions. Mr. Anders is *not* off-limits to the FBI. I can guarantee the Bureau is on top of that with every available agent at its disposal. Eventually, they will find Margie Evans, Mr. Anders's former fiancée. We don't know how much Mr. Anders confided in Miss Evans. I would think he shared everything as young people do who are in love. My people are searching the entire Baltimore area for her as we speak.

"We do have an edge in that respect. It might take the Bureau a while to find her, whereas we were on it immediately. And, don't forget, it's been over thirty-five years. All trails go cold after so much time. He's going to have to work fast."

"Do you think Hank Jellicoe knows about Margie Evans?" Isabelle asked.

"Absolutely he knows," Charles said. "That's why time is of the essence in locating Miss Evans. I'm certain my people will prevail. The only problem I foresee is the lady balking and not caring about Mr. Anders after so many years. From her point of view, he dumped her and disappeared from her life. She could be married with children and grandchildren and not want to get involved in Mr. Anders's problems at this point in time." Charles smiled at Myra. "However, there are some loves that endure for all time."

"Do you think there is even the remotest possibility that Hank Jellicoe would somehow use Mr. Anders? I guess what I'm asking is, would he do something like that not knowing that we know about the book Anders was writing?" Myra asked.

"Of course. Mr. Anders is the equivalent of a safe house in Hank's mind. If he wanted to, he could hide out at Cresfield Villas for years, and no one would be the wiser. Remember, he's the one who set all that up. He'd make it work for him in some way. Just in case. Hedging his bets, so to speak. But once he finds out the book is out, he'll scratch that location and not go near it," Charles said.

"But, Charles, might not he think that what you just said is how we would all think? He wouldn't go near the place when that's exactly where he would go?" Annie asked. "Did that make sense?"

"Yes, I know what you mean. Of course there is always that possibility. It's the same principle as keep your friends close, your enemies closer. He'd lie low in the beginning, stake out the place for a while, watch and wait for the authorities to back off, then he'd make his move.

"Having said that, I don't think he'll go that route. The reason I say that is Cresfield is not around the corner. All the action will be here and in the District, which he knows like the back of his hand.

"If there's nothing else, girls, I'm going to get back to work."

The girls waved him off.

"All of this is not computing for me," Isabelle grumbled. "Maggie hasn't called. I almost expected her to come out here to the farm this evening. She's always full of ideas. I wonder if something is wrong."

"I can top that. I haven't heard from Jack since I sent him the manuscript," Nikki said. "Someone should have called us by now to comment on the book."

Kathryn started to laugh and couldn't stop. Gasping, she said, "This is just my opinion, but I think the guys are trying to give us what they think is a dose of our own medicine." The others went off into peals of laughter as they gathered up the glasses and snack plates to carry them into the kitchen.

"Time for bed," Annie said. "Good night, Gracie." She snickered under her breath, knowing that none of them would understand the reference except Myra, who'd been a great fan of George Burns.

When the Sisters convened for breakfast the next morning, the pleasant aroma of soap, hair spray, and subtle perfume fought with the tantalizing aromas from what Charles was concocting. With all the chatter going on, it was obvious the Sisters were leaving Pinewood.

"Time for me to check in. Today, the last of Lizzie's files has to be incorporated into our system. Alexis has her work cut out for her, so the sooner we get that out of the way, the sooner we can take over Lizzie's ongoing cases," Nikki said. Alexis agreed.

"I'm going to my office and work on the blueprints. I want to have something to show you, Annie, by the weekend," Isabelle said.

"I'll be in Vegas, so don't rush on my account. I'm sure I will approve whatever you come up with. I think I'm going to leave tonight now that we've taken care of Mr. Anders. Charles can handle anything that comes up in regard to Miss Evans and whatever else is going on. You haven't changed your mind about going, have you, Myra?"

"No, I can be packed in twenty minutes. I'm looking forward to the bells, whistles, and bright lights. We can be back here in four hours if you need us."

"Well, since we're splitting up, I think I'll call the depot and hire on for a run," Kathryn said as she fished a strip of bacon from the platter that Charles was holding out.

"Don't forget to give me enough notice when you want me to take your slot machines in for repair."

"I will, dear," Annie said. "What do you have planned, Yoko?"

"A solid day's work at the nursery. I have to put my order in for the autumn chrysanthemums. I'm actually late doing so. We need to stay in touch."

Ever the worrier, Annie asked again if anyone had heard from Maggie. The Sisters shook their heads. "As long as you're all going back into the District, someone should stop and check on her."

"I can do that," Nikki said.

"And no one has heard from the boys, is that right?" Myra said. Again the Sisters shook their heads. Her face puckering with worry, she looked over at Charles and asked him if anyone had checked in after receiving Virgil Anders's manuscript.

"No one has checked in, Myra. I thought it a little strange myself." He expertly flipped pancakes, his expression so neutral that Myra felt compelled to say, "Do you know something you haven't shared with us by any chance?"

"No, dear." He held out a plate that Myra reached for.

Eating in the kitchen meant the Sisters didn't have to obey Charles's rule of not discussing business while dining. "What do you think that means?" Isabelle asked.

Kathryn grinned. "Boys being boys would be my guess. I'm not worried about them, but I am concerned about Maggie." She looked down at her plate and handed it over to Charles to refill with his airy buttermilk pancakes.

"What are the boys going to do once they're finished with Lizzie's office?" Annie asked.

"I think that's part of the problem. Speaking for Jack, he doesn't know what he wants to do. He could go back to

his old office, they want him, but he's dragging his feet,"
Nikki said.

"Bert has been talking about opening his own office,
but I think it's just talk. He's like Jack; he doesn't quite
know where he fits these days," Kathryn said.

"Harry's fine," Yoko said. "He's acting normal. Well,
normal for Harry. He hasn't said anything to me at all
about the boys. Normally, he tells me everything. Maybe
they all need an assignment from us, something for them
to sink their teeth into."

"I can't worry about that now, I want to get on the road
and back to the office. It's going to be a busy day. Alexis,
are you ready?" Nikki asked.

"I'll be right behind you. The only thing left for me to
do is oversee the cleaning crew I hired to come in this
morning to shampoo the carpets and clean the windows,
that kind of thing. I want the offices to smell nice and fresh
when the new lawyers take over. After that's done, I'll take
my things to the office and set up shop."

"Bye, everyone. Sorry to leave you with the cleanup,"
Isabelle said as she reached for her bag, which had several
rolls of blueprints sticking out of it.

Yoko hugged Myra and Annie, then Charles. "I'm sorry
about not helping with the cleanup. I'll call when I get to
the nursery.

Kathryn was the last to gather up her things. She whistled for Murphy, who was lost without Grady. He barked
at the door and pawed it to get out. Kathryn whistled
again, and he settled down.

Lady and her four rambunctious pups yipped and
yelped as they realized all their friends were leaving them.
"They'll be back," Myra said soothingly. She handed out
bits of bacon to appease the dogs.

"We'll clean up. Charles, go along to your lair," Annie said, opening the dishwasher in preparation to loading it.

When Charles was out of sight, and the dogs were romping in the yard, Myra looked at Annie, and said, "Is there a reason why you volunteered to have us clean up this mess?"

"Shame on you, Myra. The girls were in a hurry to get back to town; they do have lives, you know. Charles cooked. Who does that leave but us? I wish you would stop thinking everything I do is devious."

"You are devious, Annie. Admit it!"

"And you aren't?" Annie sniped.

Myra knew she could never win an argument with Annie. She threw her hands into the air. "Now, why are we cleaning up the kitchen? What do you want to talk about?"

"Maggie. I'm worried about Maggie. She has *never* ever not returned my phone calls. The moment I got up this morning, I went online to read the *Post*. There wasn't a word in the paper about any of this. She had the information at noon yesterday. That was more than enough time to put some kind of teaser in the paper, but I didn't see anything. That's why I'm worried. Maggie never sloughs anything off if the order comes from me."

"What do you think it is?" Myra asked as she dropped two tablets into the dishwasher.

"That's just it, Myra, I don't know. Maggie has always been like an open book. I would like to know what it is if we're going through with our plans to leave for Las Vegas this evening."

Myra opened the door for Lady and her pups to come back indoors. "I think, Annie, we should go ahead with our plans. Nikki will ferret out whatever is wrong. I'm sure of it."

"I hope you're right. What time do you want to leave? I have to call the pilot to get the plane ready."

"How does eight o'clock sound? We'll get there for the shank of the evening with the time change. Who knows, tonight might be our lucky night, and we'll take Babylon for a pokeful of money."

"Keep dreaming, Myra. Keep dreaming."

Chapter 18

Nikki breezed into Maggie's office and flopped down on the chair facing the EIC of the *Post*. "Hey, how's it going, Maggie? We missed you out at the farm. I volunteered to stop by and see if anything was wrong when you didn't respond to any of our texts and phone calls. Is something wrong, Maggie? You look terrible, so I guess I just answered my own question. You want to talk about it?" It was all said in one long, breathless outburst.

Maggie leaned forward and pointed to her desk drawer, which she opened. Nikki stared down at Maggie's emerald-cut engagement ring nestled among a slew of candy wrappers. Her eyebrows shot upward. "Ah, man trouble. Join the club, girlfriend. What happened?"

"I haven't been sleeping, hence the dark circles under my eyes. Worse yet, I've lost my appetite. I feel like I'm going to wither away to the bone. I don't know if I want to be engaged, and I don't know if I want to get married. To Ted."

After a moment of utter silence, Maggie shook her head

once, and said, "Anyway, I'm too young to be Mrs. Robinson."

"Ahhh."

"There's a little more to it than that, of course. Can you love two people, Nikki?"

"Sure. But that's when it gets tricky. I've seen all the movies, so have you. You have to ask yourself which one of those loves you can't live without. Did you ask yourself that question?"

"I did. I didn't come up with an answer. I'm thinking of kicking both of them to the curb, resigning, and taking a road trip out West to get my head on straight."

"Do you think that will work?"

"No," Maggie blurted. "My problem is I'm a know-it-all. But in all fairness to myself, I usually am ahead of the curve and two jumps ahead of both guys. It's not that I am impressed with myself. Well, I am, a little bit, but they let me get away with it. Take Ted. He lets me walk all over him. If I say jump, he says, how high? I have to constantly keep testing him to make sure he lives up to his potential, or he slacks off. He really is the best of the best, and we've been together a long, long time. Plus, I love his cats, and they love me. The sex is spectacular, but there is more to life than sex. I can't even remember how or why we got engaged. I guess it seemed like the thing to do at the time. And I hate these damn acrylic fingernails that I have to keep up with to show off the ring."

"Aaaahhh."

"Then there's Abner, who has never, ever failed me. Ted hasn't failed me, either, but with Abner it's different. In case you don't know, Abner is my snitch and my hacker. He has bailed us out so many times, I've lost count. He charges outrageous sums of money for what he does, but it isn't the money with him. It's kind of how he courts me. He looks for the most part like the bad end of a well-used mop, but then so does Ted. They're both into grunge for some reason. Maybe it's a guy thing. I don't know. Right now, as we speak, Abner and his crew are trying to hack into the Witness Protection Program. If he gets caught, he'll go away for like forever. I had to browbeat him, challenge his expertise before he would agree to do it. Never mind how much Annie is paying him and his crew for the job. We already made a payment.

"He was all dressed up that day, Nikki. Nice summer suit, fresh haircut; he smelled all citrusy, and his shoes were polished. He looked like Brad Pitt only better. I thought my heart was going to bang right out of my chest. We got into it, and he said he loved me, had always loved me, and I knew . . . know that, Nikki, and still I kept baiting him. He pretty much told me to kiss off, this finished us, never to call him again. He's said that before but he didn't mean it. He meant it this time. And before you can ask, we have never had sex, but I have sure dreamed about what it would be like.

"When he walked out of here, I knew he meant every word he said. He just looked like I killed him, and he had yet to lie down. When he left, I sat here and cried for hours. That's when I took off my ring, and I haven't put it back on since."

"Aaaahhh."

"What if he gets caught, Nikki? You don't mess around with those Federal marshals. No one has ever penetrated the WPP. Nor have they ever lost a person they put into the program. God, I didn't have all that much to give him to begin with. Just a woman and her daughter whose last name was originally Jellicoe. What if I was wrong and I have him doing all this for nothing and he gets caught. I'll

just die, Nikki, I'll simply die." Maggie continued to boo-
hoo.

"But you say you're never wrong, Maggie. Either you
believe in yourself or you don't. Why are you second-
guessing yourself now? Don't do that, don't go there.
You're upset because you can't decide whom you love
right now. Look it square in the face and own up to it.
Work from that point on."

"What if he gets caught, Nikki?"

"It's a little late for what-ifs. As you said, it's happening
right now. If something goes awry, we call in Lizzie. Lizzie,
my firm, and anyone else we can call on will be on board.
Do you think he'll succeed in finding Jellicoe's long-lost
wife and daughter?"

Maggie swiped at her eyes. "If they're in the program,
Abner will find them. That's a guarantee." Fresh tears ran
down her cheeks. "I'll never see him again. I'll never know
if he's the one or Ted is the one."

Nikki got up off her chair and walked around to hug
Maggie. "True love always finds a way, believe it or not.
Same principle as that old ditty that the truth will set you
free. There is every possibility that when you walk out of
this building, you might bump into some stranger who
turns out to be that one true love. You have to be open to
everything. And, Maggie, you have to be honest with Ted
and Abner, but most of all you have to be honest with
yourself. If you can do that, whatever happens, you will be
able to handle it."

Maggie nodded tearfully. "How's things with you and
Jack?"

"A bit rocky, but we're working on it. Now tell me,
what did you think of the book we got from Virgil Anders?"

Maggie swiped at her eyes again as she rummaged on

her desk for what she wanted. She finally came up with a piece of paper with what looked like a hundred scrawled notes on it. "Since I couldn't sleep, I worked on this last night. I'm running it in tomorrow's paper on our book page. Big headline. 'Best-Seller to Rock Alphabet City. Writer is Anonymous.' For now.

"If Hank Jellicoe is within our distribution area, he's going to see it and make his move. Hey, if nothing else, all those damn agencies are going to go nuts."

"Now you sound like the old Maggie I know and love. Good going. You really should call out to the farm. Everyone is worried about you. By the way, Annie and Myra are planning to leave for Las Vegas this evening. You might want to check in and tell them to fly safe. Annie's big on that, as you well know."

"I will. Come on, I'll walk you to the elevator. Thanks, Nikki."

Nikki grinned. "For what? All we did was have a little girl talk."

"Easy for you to say. I owe you for this one."

"Okay, I'll collect one of these days."

Back in her office, Maggie managed to while away her time until she saw Ted settle down at his desk and turn on his computer. When she looked up again, Espinosa was doing the same thing. She waited until Ted looked in her direction. She took a long deep breath and motioned him to come to her office. Espinosa pointed to himself, and Maggie shook her head.

"Close the door, Ted," Maggie said quietly.

"What did I do now?" Ted asked as he hopped from one foot to the other.

"You didn't do anything, Ted. Why do you always ask me that when I want to talk to you?"

"Well, duh. Because at these little meetings you always

rag my ass. So, what is it this time? What didn't I do to your satisfaction?" Maggie's stomach turned sour at the expression on Ted's face.

Maggie took another deep breath. "I don't want you to say anything until I finish what I have to say. I'm sorry, Ted. It's not you, it's me. I mean that. I want to apologize to you for . . . for so many things. I don't want to be engaged. I don't want to get married. I'm . . . I'm just not ready for that kind of commitment. I don't know if I ever will be. I do love you. At least I think I do. Don't look at me like that. I'm trying to be honest here. I just feel . . . all twisted and frazzled and I can't eat or sleep.

"What . . . what I'm trying to do right now until I can get a fix on things is to simplify my life. To pick out the areas that appear to be giving me the most angst and deal with them until I know which direction I want to go in. Just so we're clear on this. From this point on, we're friends. I don't know right this minute if that means friends with benefits or not."

Ted closed his mouth and stared at Maggie. He didn't say a word when she held up her hand to show it was minus the ring. She reached into the drawer and took it out and handed it to Ted. "What you do with it is up to you, Ted. I can't give you any guarantees that I will ever ask for it back. Okay, you can say something now."

Ted fought a head rush. Now that he was officially off the marriage hook he didn't know what he felt. "So we are officially unengaged but will maybe or maybe not be friends with benefits, which means maybe or maybe not there will be sex? Do I have that right?" he said, rubbing the ring between his fingers.

He was momentarily stunned at how cold the diamond felt in his hand. For some reason he thought the beautiful stone should feel warm and full of fire since diamonds were supposed to be a girl's best friend and a guy's route to the poorhouse.

"Yes, that's what it means," Maggie managed to say.

Ted opted for the high road. When in crisis, never let them see you sweat. He tried for a light tone and was surprised when he pulled it off. "Okay." He suddenly felt so relieved he had another head rush. "You got my assignment sheet?"

"Right here," Maggie said, handing the assignment sheet over. "Espinosa is with you for the day."

Still tripping on the high road, Ted grinned and realized he wasn't forcing it. "See ya."

Maggie blinked, then blinked again. "Well, he took the wind out of your sails, now, didn't he, Maggie? I should feel like a huge weight has been lifted off my shoulders," she continued to mutter to herself. "Crap!" she said succinctly.

Maggie slid her feet out of her sneakers, fumbled under her desk for her heels, and put them on as she dialed Pinewood, spoke hesitantly at first, then more forcefully with Annie. Her sigh was so loud when she powered down after the call that she thought it could be heard all the way out to the street. *The truth will set you free.* Yeah, right. Then why wasn't she feeling free?

Backpack in place, Maggie marched toward the door. She offered up a sloppy salute to her office as she made her way to the elevator, Ted's and Espinosa's eyes glued to her back. She pretended not to notice.

"Abner Tookus, here I come, like it or not."

Forty minutes later, Maggie rang the doorbell to Abner's loft. This was the first time she'd ever been here. She wondered why Abner had never invited her before. Maybe it was because she always suggested they meet at some out-of-the-way place or at her office at the *Post*.

She looked upward when a thick cloud blotted out the sun. An omen?

"Who is it?" a female voice queried from the speaker. Maggie jerked backward. Taken by surprise, she mumbled, "Maggie Spritzer. I need to speak to Abner. It's an emergency."

"Hold on."

Hold on for what, Maggie wanted to ask but wisely kept silent. When she heard the female voice again it was definitely frosty cold. "Abner said he has no interest in speaking with you. He said to tell you to go away."

Maggie bristled but kept her cool. "Tell him I wouldn't be here if it wasn't an emergency, and I will go away after I talk to him. Tell him if he doesn't speak with me, I will turn him in myself and suffer the consequences."

"Hold on."

This time there was no dialogue, but the buzzer on the door sounded. Maggie opened the door to a dark foyer. Then a light came on, and she could hear the elevator on its way down to the ground level. She had to use all her strength to slide the thick iron gate open. Inside, she pressed a button. The elevator started to rise. She could see blinding white sunlight at the top. The cloud cover must have moved on. When she rose to the top, she again had to use all her strength to slide open the gate.

Maggie saw it all in one quick flash, the deep comfortable furniture, the shiny hardwood floors, the sparkling clean windows, the colorful art on the walls, the beautiful throw rugs, and one of the most unusual fireplaces that she'd ever seen in her life. The kitchen, what she could see of it, looked like it belonged in a magazine layout. But what stunned her the most was the snowy white cat sitting on the back of one of the chairs and a Yorkshire terrier playing with a soft red ball on one of the rugs. Abner had animals?

He came out of nowhere, his hands jammed into his jeans pockets. He offered no greeting, just stared at her.

In the whole of her life, Maggie had never been this nervous. "Just hear me out, Abner, then I'm out of here." Her voice was so shaky she could hardly believe it was her own. Abner made no comment, he just kept staring at her.

"This is . . . lovely . . . I had no idea . . . and you have a dog and a cat. That's so nice, Abner. Listen, we're calling off the job. My boss said you can keep the money we paid you. I don't have the words to tell you how sorry I am that I involved you. I . . . I have such a bad feeling you might get caught. I don't want that to happen to you. I wouldn't be able to live with myself if you got caught. I . . . ah . . . want to apologize for all the times I . . . I took you for granted.

"Obviously something is wrong with me, I just don't know what that something is. I'm working on it, so I'm at square one." She wiggled her finger to show the absence of her engagement ring. *The truth will set you free.* "I didn't give back the ring because of you. I gave it back because of me. I need to find myself again. And to tell you . . . to tell you . . . I do have feelings for you. I don't know if it's love or not. I'm starting to think I don't even know what love is. Well, that's all I came to say. I won't come back, I won't call you again, either. Don't . . . ah . . . think too badly of me, Abner. I'm just glad I got to talk to you before . . . in case something happened. Bye, Abner."

Maggie wondered if her high heels would support the short walk to the elevator. Did she really think Abner was going to wrap her in his arms and say . . . what? He hadn't said a word, had stood still as a statue. His expression had been totally blank. There was no forgiveness there. Probably never would be. Her eyes burned unbearably as she used her shoulder to open the gate to the elevator. Just as it started to close, Abner's arm snaked through the opening between the bar. He shoved a manila folder into her hand. The last thing Maggie saw was the dog and the cat and Abner and his crew staring at her. A moment later the elevator was on the way to the ground floor.

And Abner hadn't said a word.

And the truth will set you free. Screw you, Nikki. I don't feel free. I feel like I was just buried under a ton of rock.

In the cab on the way back to the *Post*, Maggie opened the envelope Abner had jammed into her hand. She pulled out several sheets of paper and in doing so she noticed bits and pieces of the checks she'd given to him. He'd torn up the checks. The papers . . . he'd successfully hacked into the Witness Protection main database and found Hank Jellicoe's wife and daughter.

The sound that erupted from Maggie's throat was so bloodcurdling, the cab driver swore and jammed on the brakes.

"You no throw up my cab. You get out here, Missy."

Chapter 19

"They know I'm here!" Annie hissed to Myra, as they walked through the doors of Annie's casino. "See how everyone is scurrying about. It's good to be feared, don't you think, Myra?"

Myra laughed as she walked over to a slot machine and dropped in four quarters. "You just made a dollar, Annie."

"Stop wasting your money. Let's go into the Harem Bar. It was redecorated while I was gone. I want to see the finished product. My exact words to the decorator were to use good taste. People in this town have different versions of what good taste means. People spend a lot of money in bars, did you know that, Myra? They do, especially the high rollers. Money just flows for some reason. I find it decadent myself," Annie said virtuously.

At the entrance to the bar, Myra stopped in her tracks. Her jaw dropped as did Annie's. "Well, it is named the Harem Bar," Myra said.

"Oh, my God!" Annie said. "*This* was *not* what I mean by good taste. This is . . . it's an abomination! There are actually people in here. Do you believe this? Well," she huffed, "first thing tomorrow, we are going to have to redo this. We meaning you and me, Myra.

"These veils and beads have got to go. I don't think I ever saw a real grapevine with real grapes hanging from an indoor ceiling. I've never seen gold goblets in a bar, either. And would you look at those . . . those sheer pantaloons the waitresses are wearing. That's a string bikini underneath all that . . . that gauze."

"But, Annie, look at the crowd! Look at the bar, it's six deep. All the tables are full, and people are flashing money. I bet you make a fortune here at night."

"Do ya think?"

"I do." Myra had a horrible vision of showing up in the morning, dressed in farmer's overalls, ripping out the grapevines and veils. "Maybe you shouldn't be so hasty. Do you have a personal table here?"

"I do, but I can't see it with all the people. Annie snapped her fingers, but no one paid any attention. She did it again. When she still didn't get any attention, she put her fingers to her lips and let loose with a whistle so shrill Myra thought her eardrums were going to burst. The sudden silence was louder than the previous babble.

With a haughty look on her face that Myra had never seen before, Annie pushed through the gaggle of people till she was eyeball-to-eyeball with the bartender. "*My* table please. *Now!*"

Among whispers of, *she's the owner*, the crowds parted, and Annie led Myra toward the back of the Harem Bar to a table so secluded with veils, beads, and grapevines, they couldn't see a thing once they were seated. "Four beers, two on ice, two frosted glasses, and a bowl of peanuts," Annie said.

"I so love instant gratification," Annie snarled, as the beer appeared like magic. "I didn't want to waste time with mixed drinks. Bottoms up, Myra!"

"I do like your style, Annie," Myra said as she took a long, draining gulp of the beer. "Okay, now what?"

"Two choices. We can tie one on. Or we can observe. Or we can go up to the penthouse and do whatever we want, which is probably go to bed. You call it, Myra."

"Oh, dear, I just thought of something, Annie. Did you turn your phone on after we got off the plane? I forgot," Myra said, as she fished in her bag for her phone. "Maybe there's news at home. Ah, I have five missed calls."

"Me too," Annie said as she clicked buttons.

"Ooooh, this is so interesting," Myra murmured under her breath as she watched Annie power down. "I think we should head upstairs to discuss . . . this latest news."

Annie slapped two twenty-dollar bills down on the table. Myra noticed that her hands were trembling. Rightly so, because her own hands were just as shaky.

"This is just so amazing. I don't think I could ever get used to the noise, the bells, the whistles, and all this. . . ." Myra said, waving her hands about as they fought their way to the exit. "But you're making money, so I guess you trade one for the other."

"The city that never sleeps. No clocks. Time has no meaning to most of these people. It gets old real quick. Fish loved it. I like it for about a week. I'm thinking it's going to take a lot of work, not to mention money, to renovate the Harem Bar.

"Maybe I should just let it ride for a while. It might grow on me. And like you said, it seems to be thriving. Who knew people were into veils and grapevines? We need to keep up with what's *in*."

"Forget that *we* stuff. This is your bailiwick. Mine is a

farm with dogs and horses and acreage. How long are we staying?"

Annie jabbed her finger on the button of her private elevator. "Let's go home tomorrow. Stuff is happening back there, and we need to be in the thick of it."

"Then why are we here? I thought we were going to plan Kathryn's party. You said you needed my help."

"I might have stretched the truth a bit." At Myra's stormy expression, she said, "All right, I lied, okay? We are here to plan the party, but we can do that in an hour. I can do all the picayune details from the farm. I thought we needed a little break. We're getting stale. Our imaginations are starting to atrophy. Haven't you noticed? We need some *action*! Vegas is chock-full of action. We were just part of it.

"Oh, I can't win with you, you're such an old poop. Thank God, here we are," Annie said, stepping out of the elevator that led them straight into the penthouse. She locked down the elevator and proceeded to turn on every light in her personal quarters. "Take note, Myra, there are no reminders anywhere of Fish. I dumped everything, even had the place painted, fumigated, installed new carpet, the whole nine yards. It was like he was never here. I hope I get over the mistake called Fish soon. Okay, okay, let's call Charles and see what's up. I'll get us some drinks while you do that."

"I wish you'd shut up, Annie. You're like one of those windup dolls with extralong-life batteries."

"And you're like a slug, Myra, with all those last names. No one has as many last names as you do," Annie sniped.

Myra held up both hands. "Truce!"

"Okay. Put him on speaker and follow me into the kitchen."

Myra looked around at the gleaming modern kitchen

that had to have cost a fortune. "Do you ever cook when you're here, Annie?"

"Are you out of your mind? If I cooked, all these nice shiny appliances would look used. I just dial seven for room service. Bourbon? I have Madagascar and Elijah Craig. Either will knock us on our asses inside of fifteen minutes. In other words, it's premium, not that swill you have back at the farm."

"Whatever. On the rocks. Okay, I'm calling Charles now, so be quiet."

Charles picked up on the first ring. The amenities over, he got right down to it. There was such awe in his voice that Annie and Myra were both stunned when he said, "Maggie's source cracked the Witness Protection database. We now know where Hank Jellicoe's wife and daughter are.

"We need to make a decision on who is to visit them. It has to be understood that we will not interfere in their lives, Myra. There has to be a reason why the WPP put them there in the first place."

"I think we're all in agreement on that, Charles. Where are they?"

"Not on the phone, Myra. Even though they're secure, we can't afford a glitch of any kind right now."

"Understood, dear. We're coming home tomorrow."

"I rather thought you would. Are you having a nice time?"

Myra looked at Annie. "No."

"I see."

"No, you don't see, Charles, so stop saying that. Anything else we should know before we leave here?"

"One other thing. Check the *Post* online in the morning. The book section. Maggie will run her teaser as a banner headline. Newest Washington tell-all. The District will run with it, and I guarantee every TV and radio station will be on it like leaves on a tree. You'll get home just in time for the fireworks. Did you win anything yet?"

"I lost a dollar but got some free drinks, dear."

Charles laughed as he broke the connection.

"You heard it all, Annie. What do you think?"

"I'm thinking it's going to flush out Jellicoe. I am concerned about the wife and daughter. I can't believe . . . well, I do believe that Maggie's source was able to . . . you know, do what he did. And he returned the money. Actually, he tore up the checks in little pieces and told Maggie he never wants to see her again. She was crying when she left the message. Oh, and she broke off her engagement to Ted. These young people today are a pure mystery to me. Do you understand them, Myra?" Annie asked fretfully.

"No. The girls are all having trouble with their relationships. It's obvious to me, and it should be to you, too, Annie, that they are trying to keep it from us. Why, I don't have a clue. Those damn pardons just ruined everything, Annie."

"I know, I know." Annie poured generously.

A very long time later, as both women teetered toward their bedrooms, Myra said, "That was some very fine bourbon. I think it's the finest I've ever had. It was so fine we drank it all."

"Shut up, Myra."

The sun was creeping over the yardarm when Myra opened her eyes. It only took a second to realize she had a pounding headache. She sniffed to see if any tantalizing aromas might waft her way the way they did back at the farm when she woke. Then she remembered Annie's aversion to messing up her new appliances.

In the bathroom, Myra swallowed some aspirin, took a

shower, and dressed. When she made her way to the kitchen, Annie was just uncovering a room service order. "When I'm in residence, I have my own personal chef. I think you will find this breakfast as good as any Charles might make. Do you have a hangover?"

"Not really. I had a headache when I woke up, but after my shower it went away."

"See, it pays to drink good bourbon. Do you want me to ship some home to you, or I could have Kathryn take it back when she does the slot-machine run."

"God forbid. No. What time do you want to leave, Annie?" Myra said as she helped herself to some fluffy scrambled eggs.

"I already called the airport. I was up a full hour before you, and look at this . . . I printed out the book page from the *Post*. As always, Maggie did a good job, and I'm sure that Washington is in turmoil as we speak. Every damn politician will think the book is about him. Actually, when you think about it, it is kind of funny that any of them would consider himself the man, the myth, the monster."

"Vanity is a terrible thing," Myra said. "Who cares about the other politicians; we only care that Hank Jellicoe reads it or finds out some way. He's going to go over the edge, Annie. I feel it."

"I know. I feel it, too."

The women ate in silence. Annie poured from a second pot of coffee and got down to business. "We came here to set up a party. So, let's do it."

Ninety minutes later, Annie dusted her hands dramatically. "See how easy that was? It's so nice to threaten and delegate and know the job is going to get done. We cleared all the decks, the notices will be posted on all the doors, security is taken care of, the menu is done, the cake is ordered.

"I ordered a special birthday candle in the shape of a rocket. Notices will go out to all our customers who have reservations for that particular weekend. We're done, Myra. Do you want to go downstairs and do a little gambling until it's time to leave for the airport?"

"Sure, why not? My limit is a hundred dollars. Does this mean you're going to leave the Harem Bar as is?"

"Guess what, Myra, they wire fresh bunches of grapes on those vines every single day. Customers just reach up and pluck off a bunch and chomp down. I read that on the in-house report in my mail. I find that absolutely amazing. But to answer your question, yes, for now I am going to leave it as is."

"Good girl, Annie. It's always wise to retreat when things are working."

"No one likes a smart-ass, Myra. Not even me. Get out your hundred bucks and let's hit the casino floor. I'm feeling lucky myself."

"What about this mess?" Myra said, pointing to the table and all the dishes.

"Didn't you hear me about delegating duties? Someone will come up from the kitchen and take it away. I am, after all, the boss."

"And a damn fine one you are," Myra said, linking arms with her old friend. "You do know I will kill you if I lose my hundred dollars, right?"

"Oh, boo-hoo, Myra!"

Chapter 20

The neighbors, all six of them, all in their late eighties and slightly dotty, along with a mind-your-own-business group that lived over a thirty-acre spread, said the house owned by retired professor Simon Jordan at 911 Sherman Way in Manassas was the prettiest house on the street, with its flowering beds and landscaped shrubbery, not to mention the rolling-golf-course lawn. But that had been all said years and years ago. These days most of the residents of Sherman Way didn't even know what their own names were, much less their neighbors'.

The assessment of the six neighbors was wrong about everything concerning the property except for one thing. It really was the prettiest street, but Sherman Way wasn't really a street, it was a road that surrounded thirty acres. Retired professor Simon Jordan no longer lived at 911 Sherman Way. Retired professor Simon Jordan was dead. Five years earlier, the professor had gone to France to a symposium as a guest speaker. He died on a lonely country road in a fiery car crash with no credentials remaining to identify him. Even his dentures had melted. He had been buried in a small local cemetery by a caring vicar and a group of Good Samaritans. His simple marker said, *One of God's Children.*

The six dotty neighbors never knew this, because at one point, retired professor Simon Jordan did return to take up residence. Those same dotty neighbors considered Simon Jordan a whippersnapper, saying he was only sixty-six years old. He had a passport that said he was Simon Jordan and a valid Virginia driver's license if anyone cared to look at them. If asked, several of the oldsters would have claimed to have seen their neighbor time and again, but no one asked. Why would they?

The "new" retired professor Simon Jordan, the one with teeth, returned from France and took up residence without a blip of any kind.

The contents of the house at 911 Sherman Way didn't change at all on the first floor. The second floor was another story entirely. Except for one bedroom and bath, the other five bedrooms had had their walls knocked out and computer equipment installed bit by bit, all purchased from the Virginia, Maryland, and Delaware area. The basement, which was totally dry, held three humongous, deep freezers, all jammed to the top with the finest food money could buy. It could last years, even if the power went out. In that case, emergency generators kicked in within three minutes. Win-win for the present-day Simon Jordan.

The library held enough reading material to last into the next millennium. After all, professor Simon Jordan, old or new, was a lover of the written word.

With all his family gone, Simon Jordan was left alone. Even his nearest and dearest friends were gone, too. Put even more simply, no one gave a good rat's ass what he did or where he went, which had worked just perfectly for Henry, call me Hank, Jellicoe, from the moment he had assumed retired professor Simon Jordan's identity.

Chapter 21

The Five Musketeers, as Ted referred to the little group, settled up their bill and waited for Espinosa, who said he had to make a pit stop.

"Beautiful day," Bert said.

"Stunning," Jack said.

"I hate it," Ted said.

"The only reason you hate it is because Maggie dumped you. Right now you hate everything and everyone. Look at that beautiful sun! Feel the warm breezes. Life is good, you're just too stupid to know it," Jack said. "Give her time, she'll come around. Where else is she going to find a dumb cluck like you?"

Espinosa pushed through the door, looked at his friends, eyebrows raised. "What?"

As if on cue, five cell phones vibrated, buzzed, chirped, beeped, and chimed. Faster than the wind, all five men held the phones to their ears. Again, as if on cue, all five powered down and were left staring at each other on the sidewalk.

"I don't want to talk about this right now. Shall we adjourn to my *dojo* and finish up our business? I say *our* business before we tackle what just happened," Harry said.

"You know, Harry, a ninety-minute lunch is one thing, but anything over that we're off the clock. Maggie will have our hides if we don't check in."

"What part of 'she dumped you,' aren't you getting? Even though this is the modern age of technology, unless she has a tracking system keyed to your DNA, she has no way of knowing where you are at any given moment," Harry said. "It was an order, in case you failed to notice."

"Oh, okay," Ted said agreeably. "We'll meet you there. Joe here is driving today. At some point we have to cover some diplomat who is arriving at Dulles around four. Too much information, huh? Okay, okay. C'mon, Espinosa, let's hit the road."

Harry hopped on his Ducati, which was parked at the curb, and roared off, leaving Jack and Bert puffing on cigarettes near the curb.

"Harry doesn't have any patience, Jack, you know that. I'm ready to commit, so you better make up your mind. What's the problem here?"

"I haven't talked it over with Nikki yet. Yeah, I've been meaning to but . . . the time just never seemed right for some reason. Things have been strained as you well know. Did you talk it over with Kathryn?"

"No. But I'm not married, Jack, you are. That means I don't have to talk something to death. I can make my own decisions."

"Are you saying I'm a wuss or, worse yet, pussy whipped?"

"Well, yeah. Hey, Harry has offered us a golden opportunity. Both of us are more than qualified to do what he wants. In this economy, you can't sneeze at 150K a year.

It's a win-win for us and for Harry. He gets to go to the trials, and he might even ace it and be the number one martial-arts expert of all time. We owe Harry, Jack."

"Yeah, we do owe him. Damn, it's a big undertaking for Harry. I never thought he'd step out of his comfort zone and go for something like this."

This was the expansion of Harry's business. Shortly after his stint with Hank Jellicoe, Harry and Yoko bought up the derelict buildings on the block where his *dojo* stood. With all the alphabet agencies in Washington and Virginia clamoring to have their agents trained by one Harry Wong, Harry forged ahead.

When he first approached Bert and Jack, Harry explained how he wanted to train and go to the martial-arts trials in Bangkok the following year. "I'm tired of being number two," was his bottom line. "If I win, and we all know that's a given, we will have agents coming here from all over the world to be trained by the three of us. You two are good. I won't deny it. You can run this business while I train. I have contracts through the next five years, so that guarantees your salaries. Expenses, too. Lizzie has all the incorporation papers in place. Maggie has all the advertising we talked about ready to go once you guys sign on. The contractors tell me three more weeks and we'll be up and running. Four new classes are on hold. Seven are up and running. The waiting list is around the corner."

"I'm in," Jack said. Bert clapped Jack on the back. A moment later, both men were on the run as they sprinted down the street, picked up speed, and ran full bore toward Harry's *dojo*. They arrived sweaty and flushed, but there was a light in their eyes that made Harry laugh out loud.

"We have ten minutes before my next class starts. Talk fast, boys."

"The girls found Hank Jellicoe's wife and daughter. I sure as hell would like to know how they did that."

Ted cleared his throat. "Don't be stupid, guys. Maggie did it. She has this guy on a leash who, I swear to God, can ferret out anything. I know it sounds corny, but he's like magic. But you pay for it. Big-time. It blows my mind that someone . . . anyone . . . actually cracked the Witness Protection Program. It's never been done, and they've never lost a person under their protection. And this damn guy did it!"

"Yoko said Annie and Myra are on their way back and should be here late this afternoon," Harry volunteered. "Listen, as long as we're all on the same page, call Lizzie, have her overnight or fax the contracts, get your kick-in monies in place, and let's get this show up and running."

Espinosa looked at everyone, and said, "Alexis just sent me a text saying Charles would like us all to go out to Pinewood for dinner. Can you guys make it?"

"Yeah, sure," they all agreed.

Harry waved as he walked to the back of the *dojo*, where his students were trickling in.

"So now what?" Ted asked.

"What indeed?" Jack said.

"Guess we'll head on home then since we're unemployed. I need to get out of this suit and tie anyway. We'll meet up with you at the farm, okay, or do you want to ride out with me and Jack?"

"Don't know how long we'll be with the diplomat. No sense hanging around waiting on us. We'll head on out as soon as we're finished," Ted said.

The foursome splintered off, with Jack yelling to Bert to stop by the house after he changed.

Jack parked on the street, then entered the house he shared with Nikki. All manner of thoughts and emotions ripped through him as he walked through the house and upstairs to get out of his suit. He dressed in khakis and a bright yellow shirt, one that Nikki had bought him. She had a passion for the little green alligator sewn on the shirts. He smiled when she'd presented him with a shirt in every color of the rainbow.

These days she was barely talking to him. But she was talking, so that was better than nothing. It was when she froze him out that he became a basket case. God, if he could only unring the bell.

Jack sat down on the edge of the bed and let his mind race. What should he have done differently? Where had he gotten off the path? Why wasn't he working double time to fix things between himself and Nikki. Was this *all* his fault? Shouldn't she share some of the blame for their current situation?

Jack flopped back on the sweet-smelling bed and stared up at the ceiling. *Goddammit, I want yesterday back.* For the first time, he admitted to himself that he wished the Sisters' pardons had never come through. How sick was that? Pretty damn sick, he answered himself.

Not liking where his thoughts were taking him, Jack bounded off the bed and walked down the hall to one of the spare bedrooms both he and Nikki used as a home office. He turned on the fax machine, powered up, and called Lizzie. He could hear little Jack laughing in the background. He found himself laughing when Lizzie explained that little Jack was trying to walk in Cosmo's shoes. She promised to fax the contract papers, congratulated him on the good sense to incorporate with Harry, then signed off. Jack felt better when he broke the connection. Talking to Lizzie always made him feel better for some reason.

Eyes on the fax machine, one ear tuned toward the

doorbell, Jack yanked out his cell phone and, before he could think twice, he hit his speed dial for Nikki. "Hey, babe, how's it going?"

They made small talk until Jack had enough and said, "Listen, Nikki, I have something I want to talk to you about. I should have discussed this with you sooner, but as you know, of late we . . . haven't been talking much. How do you feel about me going into business with Harry? Bert is going to join, too. As you know, Harry bought up the entire block where the *dojo* is, and he's going to expand.

"He wants to train for the trials in Bangkok, and he wants Bert and me to run things. Pay is 150K guaranteed for each of the next five years. I want to do this. I need to put some distance between me and the law for a while. It's a hell of a commitment, but I owe Harry. I have to put in 100K as my share, but I'll own a third of the business. Lizzie is handling the details. I guess I just want to know if you're okay with this. Are you?"

"I am okay with it, Jack. Why would you think otherwise? Actually, I think it's the perfect solution for the three of you. You're coming out to the farm, aren't you?"

Jack sighed. She actually had a lilt in her voice, and she sounded like she wanted him at the farm. Well, damn. "Yeah, I am. We've been like two ships passing in the night, Nikki. I think it's time we collided. Thanks, Nik, for understanding." Nikki laughed. Jack blinked. It was almost like old times—the easy laughter, the teasing—but there was something still missing. Even a fool could tell that. He struggled to find what it was, but it was too elusive. Still, he felt better for having talked to his wife.

Jack was halfway down the steps when the doorbell rang. He opened it, motioned for Bert to come in. Overhead, he heard the fax machine ring. He motioned for Bert to follow him back up the steps.

"Our contracts! We overnight the originals back to Lizzie, and we're in business. I think it's going to work out, Bert. I just got off the phone with Nikki, and I told her. She's okay with it. I feel like a load of bricks just fell off my shoulders. Did you talk to Kathryn? By the way, where is she?"

"She was in Rhode Island early this morning. She's on her way back. I did talk to her, and she thinks it's a good idea. I think I was surprised, but I also had the feeling if I had told her I was going to dig ditches for the gas company, she would have been okay with that, too. That's another way of saying she doesn't give a shit what I do."

"C'mon, Bert, cut her some slack. So she isn't ready to get married, so what? It's not like the old days when women wanted men to take care of them. Women today are career oriented, they know how to juggle and make it work for *them*. *Them* being the operative word here. Your mistake, and I'm saying this as a friend, was when you let her know you didn't approve of her doing overland trucking. Saying that was a man's job was like the kiss of death. I do have a suggestion, however.

"Ask her if you can go along on her next job. Ride shotgun. Get the feel of the road, see why she doesn't want to give it up. Understanding is half the battle. I'm not saying it's going to work, but what the hell do you have to lose at this point? Play your cards right, and she might even let you take the wheel. Hell, she might even let you blast that air horn a time or two." Jack guffawed at his own wit.

"Some days I really can't stand you, Jack. I would hate every minute of it. But if you think it'll work, I'll take a shot at it."

"Some days I can't stand you, either, Mr. Ex–FBI Director. It won't work if you have an attitude about it. You have to dive in like taking the trip is the most important thing in the world to you. Women love it when men buckle. They feel superior then. C'mon, Bert, let's face it, women are smarter than men. You just gotta be grateful that they let us win once in a while."

"Harry's right, you do suck, Jack. I was never good at pretending."

"Well, you better start practicing, or you're going to lose Kathryn, that's my gut feeling. Just be open to it, Bert. If it's meant to be, it will be. If not, you move on."

"Easy for you to say. Did you read these contracts?"

"I'm reading them right now. Do you really think Lizzie would screw up?"

"She's a woman, isn't she?" Bert growled.

Jack looked up at Bert as though he'd sprouted a second head. "There are women, then there are women. Lizzie is in her own category. That means she does *not* make mistakes."

Both men scrawled their signatures on the last page of the contracts. Jack scooped them up, shoved them into an overnight envelope, filled out the air bill, then closed the envelope while Bert called the overnight courier, who would pick up the envelope from the front stoop before six that evening.

As Jack was bounding down the steps, Bert's cell rang. His heartbeat kicked up several notches when he saw that the call was coming in from the Hoover Building. "Shit!" He put his finger to his lips when he saw Jack standing in the doorway. "Navarro." He listened, then said, "What can I do for you, Director Yantzy?" Jack rolled his eyes.

Bert continued to listen. Finally, he managed to say, "I'm a private citizen these days, Director Yantzy. I'm also gainfully employed." He listened again, and said, "Try hauling me in and sweating me for seventy-two hours! Just try it. I don't have to tell you anything, and why do you think I know where the *Post* got some book they're tout-ing. I still have a few friends at 1600 whom I can call if you try pulling a fast one." Bert went into listening mode again. "I'm a private citizen, I can say whatever the hell I feel like saying. Right now, I'm done saying anything. Have a good day, Director."

"Sounds like he's got his panties in a wad," Jack said, laughing.

"Guess the countdown is on. Let's call Maggie and see what she's running in tomorrow's paper. Maybe instead of calling her, we should pop in on her like old times. You know, before the *breakup*."

"Dude, you really do not know anything about women. Maggie would see through that in a nanosecond. She is al-most as sharp as Lizzie. Call her," Jack said. "Tell her we're going to have dinner out one night to celebrate our new venture. Maggie loves going out to dinner. Especially a celebratory one. What are you waiting for? Call her, al-ready."

Bert reared back when he heard Maggie bark a greeting. He went into his spiel the minute she said, "Speak."

"Ah, listen, Maggie, I called for a couple of things. First off, Director Yantzy just called and wanted info on the book story you're writing. Do you want either Jack or me to pick you up for dinner at the farm tonight? Annie and Myra are on the way back.

"And then there is the really good news. Jack and I signed on with Harry. We're going to be running the *dojo* while he trains for the martial-arts trials in Bangkok. Would you like to come to dinner with us one night to cel-ebrate? Also, Jack said to ask you what you're going to run with in tomorrow's papers."

Bert listened, then realized he had dead air on his cell. He powered down, looked at Jack, and shrugged. "She doesn't need a ride, thank you very much. She can get there on her own. Said Yantzy is an asshole, but we already know that. She said congratulations and let her know when and where the dinner is.

"She's happy for Harry. Delighted that Myra and Annie will be at the farm. Tomorrow's article is going to have an added word: terrorist. Man. Myth. Monster. *TERRORIST!* She said she has it all blocked out already, whatever that means. Then she broke the connection. She sounded strange, like maybe she's getting a cold."

"You stupid ass. She sounded like that because she's been crying. Women sound like that after a good cry," Jack said knowledgeably.

Bert thought about it a moment, and said, "Smart-ass!"

"Terrorist, huh? Well, that is the buzzword these days. Nothing like that word to rile up the populace. Hope Jellicoe sees it. If he objected to being referred to as a monster, imagine what he'll do when he sees himself referred to as a terrorist. Ooooh, we all need to start shaking in our boots."

"Seriously, Jack, where do you think that bastard is?"

"Right under our noses. For all we know, he could be parked right outside this house. You know it as well as I do. Keep your friends close, your enemies closer. He thinks like that."

"You got anything to drink?" Bert asked.

"Coffee, soft drinks. I think there's some ice tea in the fridge. Name it."

"Make some coffee, Jack. I think better with a cup of coffee."

Both men walked down the steps and into the immaculate kitchen. "Guess we're out of coffee. Shit. It was my turn to do the grocery shopping. See this list, coffee is right at the top. Sorry, Bert."

Bert shrugged. "I like this house, Jack. I like the color scheme, like that it isn't cluttered and like how it feels . . . homey. My apartment looks like some guy from Budweiser lives there. I never got around to . . . you know, doing the finishing touches. I was sort of hoping my cleaning lady would fix it up, but she just cleans."

"This is all Nikki's doing. She has good taste. This is not my house, Bert. I just live here with Nikki. She wanted to put my name on the deed, but I said no. Before the girls' pardons came through, I paid rent to her."

"That's a good thing, Jack. You have your priorities straight."

"Yeah. She could kick my ass out into the street anytime she feels like it. I might be knocking on your door someday with my bags."

Bert laughed as Jack poured tea over glasses filled to the rim with ice cubes made from tea. "Got a spare bedroom. I'll charge you rent, too. How come these ice cubes are brown? Jesus, you didn't make them with rusty water, did you?"

"No, Nikki makes ice-tea ice cubes so the ice doesn't dilute the tea."

"That's clever," Bert said. "Isn't it?"

"Women do shit like that," Jack said. "Nikki puts an apple in her pot roast gravy. Would you ever think of doing that?"

They were off and running then, one thing following the other. The end result much later was that the two of them agreed that neither one of them was even half as smart as his significant other.

"And we came to this conclusion stone-cold sober," Bert cackled. "Just for the record, Kathryn does not cook."

"Maybe you could give her a gift certificate to some

cooking classes for her birthday, which—by the way—is just weeks away. I'm kind of looking forward to going to Vegas for the event. Things around here have been rather dull. It will be nice to see Lizzie and little Jack again. What *are* you getting Kathryn for her birthday?" Jack asked, a devilish glint in his eyes.

Bert's voice was serious when he said, "I was thinking of giving her a gas card for diesel fuel for her rig."

Jack's jaw dropped before he bellowed his outrage, a sound that could be heard all the way to the Capitol. "You *WHAT?* Damn, Bert, that's right up there with buying something with a plug on the end. You don't *ever* give a woman something with a plug on the end. Or mud flaps. Another no-no is peat moss or manure for their flower gardens."

Bert looked like he was going to cry. Jack took no pity. "I refuse to deal with stupid."

"C'mon, Jack, help me out here. Jewelry, flowers, candy?"

"Forget the candy. By the time they finish eating it, they'll be on your case because they gained weight. The only word you'll hear is *fat*. Stick with the jewelry. You can't go wrong with sparklers."

"Kathryn doesn't wear jewelry."

"Maybe she doesn't have any to wear. Did you ever think of that, Mr. Stupid?"

Bert groaned as he refilled his glass with ice tea. He groaned again when Jack went off into a fit of laughter. "Screw it. Something will come to me. Don't help me anymore, Mr. Know-It-All."

Chapter 22

Jack Emery slid out of the car. Immediately, the fine hairs on the back of his neck started to dance. He looked around at Myra's compound to see what had triggered his sudden sense of déjà vu.

Bert stopped in his tracks and stared at Jack, sensing something wrong. His shoulders stiffened as he looked around. *Danger.* He automatically dropped into defensive mode, as did Jack. He found himself reaching to his left side, where he wore his gun and holster when on active duty. Out of the corner of his eye he could see Jack doing the same thing.

No guns. Civilians don't carry guns. "I *feel* it, but I don't *see* it. Someone is watching us," Jack hissed.

"Where?" Bert hissed in return.

Jack moved his head to the right to indicate the dense forest beyond the perimeter of Myra's fenced property.

"We're standing ducks," Bert continued to hiss. "On three, head for the kitchen door. One! Two! Three! You know the drill, run like an alligator is after you—zigzag."

Both men blasted through the kitchen door, breathless,

to the dismay of the dogs, who were barking and snarling while Charles, Nikki, and Isabelle just stared at them.

"Good Lord, what's wrong?" Charles said. He whistled sharply to the barking dogs, who went silent immediately.

"When was the last time you had this place swept for unauthorized surveillance?" Jack bellowed.

Charles looked momentarily blank. He shook his head. "Inside or outside?"

Jack looked exasperated. "Jesus, Charles! Both!"

"Avery checks the house once a week. We're bug-free. As to the outside, I have no idea. We sit here on over a hundred acres."

Jack's exasperation continued. "If you recall back in the day, I perched in those damn trees and watched this place for months, hoping to catch all of you doing whatever you were doing at the time. I sat perched up in those trees until I froze. Then I hired someone to sit in for me until I ran out of money. Ask Nikki, in case you forgot."

"Are you saying what I think you're saying, Jack?" Nikki asked.

Jack shrugged. "Yeah."

Something in Nikki's eyes flickered. "Well, we did say we wanted to draw *him* out and make him come to us."

Isabelle clenched her fists and her jaw as she headed for the door. "Is *he* out there?"

"Whoa! Easy, Isabelle," Jack said, reaching for her arm. Isabelle jerked free, her intention clear; if Hank Jellicoe was out there in the woods somewhere, she was ready to take him on. One on one. Bert blocked the doorway. Isabelle's eyes filled as her shoulders slumped. Defeated, she walked back to the kitchen table and sat down. Nikki patted her shoulder from behind.

Charles was heard murmuring on the phone. When he powered down he said, "Avery will be here with his men in short order, and they'll sweep the woods. They have some special equipment that will jam any feed going to Hank if it's out there, but first they have to find it. Having said that, I think we will be dining indoors this evening instead of on the terrace."

Cell phones chirped and were answered. Myra and Annie's plane had just landed; they'd be here within the hour. Maggie was less than a mile away. Kathryn was just leaving the trucking depot and would arrive, depending on traffic, in less than an hour and a half. Ted and Espinosa were behind Maggie but not by much. The sound of Harry's Ducati could be heard at the entrance to Myra's property. They all knew Yoko would be with Harry. All present and accounted for, with the exception of Alexis.

"So we're hiding out?" Isabelle bellowed.

"For the moment," Charles said. "It's always best to know what your adversary is about, you know that. Once you figure it out, then you attack. Do not let your emotions rule here, my dear."

Charles was right, and Isabelle knew it full well. She mumbled something that sounded like an apology, hanging her head in the process.

Jack thought he'd never seen Nikki look so grim. He toyed with the idea of saying something flip but changed his mind. Bert moved from the doorway but still close enough if Isabelle changed her mind and bolted.

The kitchen monitor over the doorway pinged as it showed Maggie Spritzer at the gate.

She blew into the kitchen like a wary wind, her gaze taking in the tenseness. "I know something," she blurted.

"Well, don't just stand there, spit it out," Jack said.

"Who died and left you in charge, Jack Emery? Never mind. Listen," she said, yanking at a chair and sitting down. "I remembered something. I can't say exactly when this happened, but I can nail it down when I get back to the paper. I always go in early to peruse the paper just as it hits the streets. I've been doing it forever. Anyway, I saw this article, I read it, and didn't think too much about it, but then for some reason I went back and read it again. It still didn't register anything with me, but I've thought about it off and on over these past months. I don't know why it bothered me, I just know it did. I finally figured it out.

"There was a fire in town in this four-office medical building. They never found out who set it, but it was arson. The insides were burned to a crisp, all the doctors' files. The doctors were partners, but they dissolved their partnership and none of them wanted to go to the expense of rebuilding, and the insurance wasn't enough for it anyway. They sold off the property, it was leveled, and a new twenty-four-hour clinic was built. It's actually up and running now. There was a dermatologist, an OB-GYN, a plastic surgeon, and right now I can't remember what the fourth one was, but it doesn't matter. The plastic surgeon is/was Julia Webster's old partner, Dr. Laura Valentine. Julia was one of your Sisters. I think, and this is my gut talking now, that Hank Jellicoe went to that plastic surgeon and had a makeover. Then he got to thinking he had a witness, so he burned all the files. I can't find the doctor. The best I could come up with was one of her nurses, who said Valentine packed it in after the fire and took her losses.

"She said Dr. Valentine couldn't afford the malpractice insurance, so she sold her house in Rockville, and no one knows where she went. She was a single woman with no ties, and as the nurse put it, free to roam the world. So, what do you think?" she asked breathlessly.

Charles, his eyes wide, managed to sound sincere when

he said, "I am impressed." Everyone in the room knew Charles was jealous of Maggie and her sources, which sometimes outperformed his own.

"Well, that certainly bolsters my ego," Maggie said tongue in cheek.

"If you're right, Maggie, and I suspect you are, that certainly would explain how Jellicoe can be out there moving around with no one knowing who he is. I think what you were saying without really saying it was that you think Jellicoe had something to do with the doctor's . . . ah . . . disappearance," Charles said.

"Yep, that's what I'm saying!"

"So, we're saying Hank Jellicoe could look like just about anyone, and we'd never know it. And we also think he's got surveillance out there in the woods," Isabelle said.

"Listen, this morning when I was over at Annie's farm, one of the contractors stopped by, then this man came by and . . . he was meandering around like he knew the property. He didn't do anything wrong, but looky-loos way out here are not the norm, and you can't really see the farmhouse from the road, so the man had to drive in like he knew where it was. All he said was it was nice to know someone was going to refurbish the old house after so many years. Then he left. I didn't think anything about it till just now."

The little group descended on Isabelle like a flotilla of locusts, all of them shouting, "What did he look like?"

"I can do better than tell you, I can show you. I'll sketch his likeness." Isabelle walked over to her leather bag, which she'd tossed in the corner with a dozen long rolls of blueprints still sticking out of it. She pulled out a white artist's pad and a charcoal pen and went to work.

The group was so intent on watching Isabelle's deft

strokes they didn't know that Alexis had entered the kitchen until her dog Grady raced through the house to chase the others.

"Hey, I know that guy. I saw him not two hours ago."

The little group turned and gawked up at Alexis, their mouths hanging open.

"Why are you all looking at me like this? Who is that guy?" Alexis said, pointing to the sketch on Isabelle's pad.

"We think it might be Hank Jellicoe," Nikki said. She went on to explain what Maggie had told them and about Isabelle seeing the man she was drawing at Annie's new farmhouse. "Where did you see him, Alexis?"

"Are you kidding me? No, I guess you aren't. I was backing out of my driveway and there was this car parked at the curb. Just as I was about to cut the wheel, this guy started to roll and I had to slam on my brakes. I rolled down my window and let him have it. He got out of his car, and before you can ask me, it was black, either a Toyota of some kind or a Honda. He apologized profusely, saying he meant to put the gear in reverse. Yada yada yada. He said he was sorry for upsetting me, and he could tell I was upset. And I was. Damn, that's him!"

Then they were all babbling at once as Isabelle added a few more strokes with her charcoal pen. She eyed it for a moment, then ripped the sheet off the pad and stuck it to the refrigerator with two magnets. The group moved backwards to study the sketch from all angles.

"It doesn't look anything like Hank Jellicoe," Nikki said.

"That's the beauty of it. That tells us the plastic surgery was a success," Bert said. "I would know that son of a bitch in a dark room, and this sure as hell doesn't look like him. That's how he's able to move about out in the open with no one having a clue as to who he is. If he had the balls, excuse me, ladies, to step into Isabelle and Alexis's world, he sure as hell must feel pretty confident."

Charles moved over to the kitchen door and opened it. The dogs barreled through, their hearing picking up the men tramping through the woods beyond the fence just as Ted and Espinosa arrived, followed by Annie and Myra ten minutes later.

Another long explanation followed for the benefit of the newcomers. They all stared at the sketch tacked to the refrigerator. All agreed that it did not resemble Hank Jellicoe in any way.

"It's him, I'm telling you, that's Jellicoe," Maggie said adamantly.

"No one hates that bastard more than I do," Ted said. "Maggie's instincts are always spot on, so if she says it's him, then it's him."

"Suck-up," Jack hissed.

"Screw you, Jack. Look at his ears. I always thought that for a guy he had weird ears, they were too small for the size of his head. Did they seem out of proportion to you, Isabelle?"

"Not when I was looking at him face-to-face. It didn't register. But I guess so, because they're smaller on the picture. It registered in my subconscious, and it came out in the drawing. Let's all agree that this is indeed Hank Jellicoe."

Harry slapped at the refrigerator so hard it moved. "Why are we standing here?"

"Because we need to have a plan," Jack said. "The guy looks like he could be anyone's neighbor. He could be living anywhere. How do you suggest we find him, Harry?"

"Let's concentrate on finding Dr. Valentine. Charles, that is your area of expertise. People just do not drop off the face of the earth unless they have unlimited monetary resources like Jellicoe."

"I think I can handle it if you all take care of the dinner preparations."

There was a wild flurry of activity as everyone moved to do Charles's bidding.

Annie poked Myra on the arm. "I think we might be coming into the home stretch, Myra."

"I think you might be right, Annie."

Chapter 23

Even though there was chaos in Myra's kitchen as the Sisters bustled about, and the guys were talking above a comfortable decibel level, they could all hear Murphy's joyous bark as Kathryn roared through the gate and parked. Murphy bolted out of the car and raced to where the other dogs were running up and down along the fence even before she could open the driver's side door to let herself out.

Bert held the door open, looked down at Kathryn's face to judge her mood. She smiled, and his world turned bright. He kissed her lightly and put his arm around her shoulder. "Just in time for dinner," he said.

"Good! I'm starved," Kathryn said, "but right now I'm more thirsty than I am hungry." She headed for the refrigerator for a cold bottle of water. She blinked at Isabelle's sketch, then frowned. "Hey, I just saw this guy not an hour ago at the depot when I signed out. Who is he? How come you have his picture here?"

Bert grabbed Kathryn's shoulders and whirled her about. "You saw that guy! That's Hank Jellicoe."

"No, it wasn't Jellicoe. I'd know that SOB anywhere. The guy I saw was just some guy checking on a load that was an hour late. I heard him telling the manager he was expecting eighteen hundred weed whackers. He was pretty upset when the manager told him there was no paperwork on file. The guy was really upset and threatening to sue, the whole nine yards. I was signing out, and that's how I heard what was going on. No way, that was not Hank Jellicoe, but the guy at the depot sure does look like this sketch. You do this, Isabelle?" Isabelle nodded.

Then they were all talking at once, with Kathryn refusing to believe she'd literally been eyeball-to-eyeball with Hank Jellicoe and didn't even know it. Eventually, when Maggie repeated her story again, she came around to agreeing with the others. "Now, all we have to do is find out where that son of a bitch lives and go after him."

"Easier said than done. He's coming to us. One by one," Nikki said. "He's taunting us like a little kid. You know that game we all used to play when we were kids, catch me if you can. He thinks he's giving us an edge because we'd never catch him otherwise. It's a game to him now."

Charles appeared in the kitchen doorway just as Annie announced that the steaks were done. A bit of confusion ensued as everyone grabbed something and settled it on the dining-room table. Myra poured ice tea while Harry dropped twice-baked potatoes on each plate. Bert handed the huge salad bowl to Ted, who started to pass it around the table.

Yoko looked around the table, and said, "Screw your rule of not talking business at the table, Charles. Either we talk business or Harry and I are leaving." Harry smiled from ear to ear as his little lotus flower showed off her muscle.

"Fine," was all that Charles said by way of agreement or disagreement.

"How's that grilled tofu, Harry," Jack asked.

"Just fine, Jack. How's that bloody meat some poor animal gave up his life for? Not to mention that with my exceptional hearing, I can hear your arteries fluttering."

"Smart-ass." Jack dug into his twice-baked potato.

Charles looked around the table. "I think it's safe to say Mr. Jellicoe has some sort of surveillance at each of your homes. If you'll excuse me, I think I'll head out to speak to Avery and see who we can put on this immediately."

"It's dark out there, dear, be careful," Myra said.

"Always, Myra. Always. Seven dogs watching my back is about as good as it gets, don't you think?"

Myra shrugged.

"I think we should discuss Jellicoe's wife and daughter now," Nikki said. "How are we going to handle that?"

"Very carefully, dear," Myra said. "We can't in any way jeopardize their safety."

"Understood, Myra. I've been thinking about it all afternoon. How about this? We have Kathryn head out to Oklahoma in her rig. We all split up and meet there. Guys, what do you think?"

The guys gawked at her. As one they all thought the same thing—they were actually being asked for their opinion.

Bert was the first to respond. "Sounds perfect to me. I can ride with Kathryn if she'll have me. I've been dying to do a road trip." Kathryn grinned from ear to ear. Bert wanted to puff out his chest and roar. One look at Jack told him he was overdoing the whole deal.

"You're going to love it, Bert. Kathryn took me along once. It is one of my most memorable experiences," Myra said.

"This is just my opinion, but why should everyone make the trip? Won't that throw up all kinds of red flags? Remember now, we don't want this to come back to Maggie or her source in any way," Ted said. Espinosa seconded Ted's assessment.

"My original thought was Jellicoe would somehow follow us, and we could take him out before we reached the ex-wife. But if you guys think that won't work, I'm open to any and all suggestions. We need to plan this out and not go off on any wild tangents. We have time on our side, and we're not kicking the clock," Nikki said. The others agreed.

"I think we need to wait to see what Avery Snowden and his boys come up with before we make any concrete decisions. Bert and I have time before things start popping at the *dojo*. Harry's Master won't be arriving to start his training for three weeks. So, that's our window. Also, remember, the president gave Span and Yantzy thirty days to grab Jellicoe or she would replace them. They're a good week into their deadline," Jack said.

Bert shared his last conversation concerning Yantzy with the others. "The feebs don't have a clue, trust me. When those thirty days are up, those two are history, and you can take that to the bank. This town will go nuts wondering what the hell they did wrong."

"Are we going to try to flush Jellicoe out in some way by using his wife and daughter as bait? If that's the case, I don't like it. It makes me nervous," Annie said. "The safety of the ex-wife and daughter has to be our primary concern."

"But, Annie. Once we catch Jellicoe, the wife and daughter are safe. They won't have to stay in the Witness Protection Program any longer. Unless they want to, and they very well might, because it's a way of life now for them. The other question is, if we do catch Jellicoe, maybe the marshals won't want to use their manpower to watch over them, and they'll cut them loose on their own," Myra said.

"That's why we have to be so careful," Nikki said. "So, let's clear up this mess," she said, waving her hands about, "and reconvene."

They were whirling dervishes, even the guys, as they moved in sync to clear up after dinner.

"Eleven minutes and the dishwasher is on! Best time yet," Ted chortled happily. He winked at Maggie.

Maggie shot Ted a look of pure venom. Didn't she just dump him? Didn't she just return his ring? Why was he so damn happy? She almost asked him but changed her mind. Obviously, he was happy with the way things were going. *He's happy, and I'm miserable. What's wrong with this picture?* she wondered.

Obviously, Ted thought nothing was wrong because he continued to babble nonstop to anyone who was listening to him, which meant the other guys.

Shrill barks and the sound of men and dogs heading for the back door drowned out all the conversation. Charles opened the door, the dogs bounded through and raced through the house as Charles and Avery Snowden and six of his men filled the kitchen. In their hands they held equipment that looked like it belonged on an intergalactic space vessel. "There's no way to tell how long this has been in the woods. Long story short, Jellicoe has a setup where he can monitor our comings and goings. Avery dispatched two teams to check out your homes. For now we think our best course of action is to stay here, especially the girls. What do you want to do, Maggie? If you decide to leave, can you temporarily stay at the paper or a hotel?" Charles asked.

"A hotel, dear, if you feel you can't be away from the paper. Just bill the *Post*," Annie said.

"I'll do that." The other girls agreed to stay at the farm, even Yoko. The guys said they could handle anything that might come their way. And then they all settled down to strategize.

Every light in the house at 911 Sherman Way in Manassas was on, lighting up the dark night. Hank Jellicoe, a.k.a. professor Simon Jordan, prowled the premises like a caged lion. On one hand he was delighted that his three appearances with the vigilantes had gone off with no one the wiser. He galloped up the steps into his computer lair and within a nanosecond saw that the video surveillance monitor that kept track of the comings and goings at Pinewood was nothing but white snow accompanied by the scratchy sound of static. "You're one up, Charlie," Jellicoe said before he picked up a heavy paperweight and threw it right through the monitor. He knew that in the next few hours, all the monitors would look the same way. Thanks to good old Charlie Martin. He started to curse, once again making up new cusswords to add to his already burgeoning cursing vocabulary.

How long before the three women he'd shown himself to would put it together? He couldn't come up with a time. He started to prowl again, but this time he fired up a cigar. He paced up and down the second-floor hallway, his booted feet coming down harder and harder on the plank floor until he was practically whizzing up and down the hall, the fat cigar clenched between his teeth, the smoke billowing upward.

"Think!" he said to the empty hallway. "If this were Afghanistan, and this was happening there, what would you do? What did you do in Iraq when this happened?"

An evil grin split his features, and his eyes darkened. "You go back to your starting point, that's what you do. Get your gear and grab the devil's horns. They think because they found your surveillance equipment, you'll move on. That's exactly what old Charlie would think. Well, think again, Charlie."

Jellicoe walked into the bathroom and doused his cigar under running water. Then he headed down the steps and on to the basement, where he opened box after box until he had what he wanted. Then he walked into the four-car garage and debated which vehicle he should drive. He finally opted for a Hummer that he'd purchased a month ago but had not taken on the road as yet. When he'd first found this property, the garage had held a tractor and a top-of-the-line John Deere riding lawn mower that were now rusting away in the barn to make way for his own vehicles.

Jellicoe spent an hour sorting through everything he would need to spend a night in the woods. He chuckled. All the gear, the canisters, too, were compliments of the Pentagon and the engineers at NASA. He looked down at one of the small canisters before he slipped it into one of his many pockets. One squirt to any part of his body and he could walk within a foot of any dog and it would never pick up his scent.

A second small canister went into another pocket. One spray to a dog's back and the dog, no matter how vicious, would stand still for a full two minutes. Just long enough to slip an audio device under its collar. It had taken beaucoup bucks and some of the best biochemists in the world to achieve that little feat. Too bad he hadn't gotten a patent on it.

No one, not even the top brass, had been able to figure out how he'd managed all those tracking dogs in the third-world countries he'd worked in. Even back in the day, when he was just providing security for the top corporate executives, the brass couldn't comprehend the massive bonus payouts. He chuckled again. Figure out a price, put it on your own head, and sooner or later everyone started to believe you were worth all those zeros.

Time to saddle up. Jellicoe looked down at his watch. Two-ten in the morning. He liked this time of the day, the dark when he could blend in with that darkness and be invisible. Maybe he should check out his surveillance monitors one last time before he left the house.

Jellicoe stomped his way through the house and up the steps and down the hall to his war room. He flinched when he saw all the blank screens and heard the static that was filling the room. So they'd found all his monitoring devices. Well, he'd suspected they would eventually. He hadn't planned on it happening so soon, though. He cut the power, happy to see that his hands were steady as a rock.

"Plan B is now in effect, ladies," he muttered as he stomped his way back down the hall, down the steps, through the house, out to the garage, and into the Hummer. He rolled up the garage door, backed out without turning on his lights, then locked the garage doors with the special digital locks he'd installed, another perk from the Pentagon.

Another way of saying that the house located at 911 Sherman Way in Manassas was a fortress, all compliments of the Pentagon's generosity.

"Get ready, Charlie, I'm on my way. You're out of your league now. Survival of the fittest. You know how that goes, right, Charlie?" Maniacal laughter filled the Hummer.

*   *   *

Charles Martin stopped in the kitchen and poured himself a glass of ice tea, which he gulped down in two swallows. The air stirred around his ankles: Grady and Murphy. Both dogs loved it when Charles took them out in the middle of the night for a run.

Charles opened the screen door, and the dogs raced into the darkness. He reached behind the door, flipped open the cabinet, and took out a cigar. He debated a moment as to whether he should put on one of the terrace lights. No— like the dogs, he loved the cover of darkness. He settled himself on one of the springy padded rockers and fired up his cigar.

He'd always loved the night, the softness of the dark, the blanket of stars overhead. The thin slice of moon that danced its way behind one cloud, only to peek out and dance behind another one. On nights like this, the trees whispered their own gentle song to lull the wildlife into a peaceful sleep. On this night, however, his ears were tuned to the dogs. So far so good.

As Charles puffed away, the two dogs patrolled the fence the way they always did on these middle-of-the-night excursions because they knew when they returned there was a chew bone waiting for them.

Both dogs heard the whistle at the same time and inched their way to the fence. Ears straight up, tails tucked between their legs, they sniffed, then stood on their hind legs to paw the fence. They stayed in that position just long enough for dark hands to slide underneath their collars. Another short whistle, and the dogs bounded off, back in the direction of the terrace, where their treats awaited them.

Charles handed out treats. The dogs flopped down and started to chew contentedly. The fine hairs on his arms moved. Charles doused his cigar, looked across the yard in the darkness, and said, "I know you're out there, Hank." He offered up a sloppy salute before he called it a night.

"I know you know, Charlie." In the darkness, Hank Jellicoe offered up a crisp salute in return.

Chapter 24

Charles bustled about the kitchen, the seven dogs under his feet as they moved about. "You know the drill, boys and girls. Outside for a good early-morning run, then you get breakfast."

The smile on Charles's face was only half-wattage as he remembered the eerie feeling he'd had earlier when he had stepped outside to smoke his middle-of-the-night cigar. There was something niggling at the back of his mind, but he couldn't bring it to the surface. He knew that the more he tried to figure out the elusive whatever-it-was thought, the more elusive it would become. Better to let it surface on its own.

Charles looked over at the kitchen clock and saw that it was a few minutes before seven. The girls would be coming down any second now. It was like he had seven hands as he expertly turned bacon, flipped pancakes, and warmed syrup. He whipped eggs in a bowl to a bright frothy yellow. Kathryn did love scrambled eggs, especially his. He wondered if he'd had another life if he would have been a five-star chef. Probably not.

Yoko was the first one down this morning. She kissed Charles lightly on the cheek and said how good everything smelled. Then she walked to the door and commented on what she thought was going to be a beautiful day. "Summer is coming to a close, Charles. I am not looking forward to winter, but I do love autumn. Which season do you like best?" she asked as she watched all seven dogs frolicking on the lawn.

"Autumn. I do love the smell of burning leaves. I like to see the pumpkin harvest. Myra loves to decorate the front porch with bales of hay, pumpkins, and scarecrows. She did it every year when Nikki and Barbara were youngsters. But then she loved decorating the porch at Christmastime with a monster wreath, huge red-velvet bows, and silver bells. I think she might do it again this year if Lizzie brings little Jack for Christmas. It doesn't get any better than experiencing Christmas through the eyes of a child."

Yoko continued to watch the dogs on the lawn. "How do you tell the four pups apart?"

Charles laughed, a great booming sound. "Myra put nail polish on their tails so she could tell them apart. The colors have silly names like Passionflower Red. I believe that's number Two. Luscious Strawberry is Three. Red Ruby is Four, and Crimson Delight is One." Yoko burst out laughing.

"Well, Red Ruby just yanked off Grady's collar and is heading for the door. Ooooh, she's going to come right through the screen." In a flash, Yoko had the screen door pushed wide and the dogs ran through. Pandemonium ensued as the dogs yipped and yapped as Four, a.k.a. Red Ruby, offered up the collar in her teeth to Charles, fully expecting a treat as her reward. Or at the very least, praise, which Charles gave.

The Sisters all started to talk at once as they did their best to herd the dogs along with treats to another part of the house so they could have breakfast in peace and quiet.

"They certainly are rambunctious this morning," Myra said. She looked up at Charles, who stood frozen at the stove. Alexis stepped up and removed the various fry pans when Charles pointed to the collar he was holding and put his finger to his lips. The Sisters understood immediately as he held out the bright red collar for all to see.

"Breakfast is served, ladies. I want you all to eat hearty as we have a very busy day ahead of us."

The Sisters took Charles's cue and talked about everything and nothing as they picked at the delicious breakfast and watched as Charles pantomimed what he thought the collar in his hands meant. He jerked his head in Kathryn's direction and mouthed the name "Murphy." Kathryn slid off her chair and ran into the family room and removed Murphy's collar. She turned to stone for a moment before she walked back to the kitchen and held out the collar to Charles.

"More coffee anyone?" Annie burbled.

"Absolutely more coffee," Isabelle said. "By the way, did anyone log on to get the news of the day?" She pointed to the refrigerator, where her sketch had hung until Maggie had ripped it off and took it with her the night before with the intention of running it in the morning's paper.

"I was going to do that right after we clean up from breakfast," Nikki said. "Can't start the day without reading the *Post*."

They were off and running, doing their best not to giggle as they rehashed old columns that had run in the paper while Charles dangled both dog collars back and forth. "Today should be a real doozie," Alexis said, pointing to the refrigerator.

Myra walked over to the sink and filled a pot with water. She held up three fingers and mouthed the words, "We're coming to get you, Hank." She motioned to Charles to get ready to drop the collars into the pot of water. "On the count of three, girls."

"We're coming to get you, Hank," the Sisters chorused as one the moment Myra said, "Three!"

"You rock, Myra," Charles said, getting into the spirit of things. He quickly recounted his eerie early-morning experience with the dogs.

"Well, we can take comfort in knowing we didn't say anything he could pick up on in regard to his ex-wife and daughter. That's what I care about right now," Annie said. "Charles, do you think he's still out there in the woods, or has he gone back to the rock he lives under?"

"If he was out there, he's gone now." Charles pointed to the pot of water with the two dog collars. "I think he shot the last arrow in his quiver. I could be wrong, but I don't think so. He'll definitely go to ground now. Wherever he is living is just going to be a memory now.

"On the other hand, I could see him going back to wherever he's been living one last time to erase whatever he thinks he has to get rid of. He's got another place to go, count on it. The man is a mercenary; he thrives on this kind of action. This is all taking him back to the time when he was at the top of his game. He refuses to come to terms with the fact that he's not who or what he used to be, and he's lost his edge.

"Anyone he thought he had in his corner has long since cut him loose. That's the way the game is played. He's acting solo and has been for quite some time."

"So, what's our next move?" Yoko asked. She pointed to the pot of water. "Now he knows we're onto him. How are we going to catch him?"

A shriek from upstairs, then Nikki's footsteps thundering on the kitchen staircase made all the Sisters jerk to attention. "Look at this! Look what Maggie did!"

The Sisters and Charles clustered around the laptop Nikki was holding up for them to see. Isabelle's sketch was on the front page of the *Post* with the headline, DO YOU KNOW THIS MAN?

"Good Lord!" Myra exclaimed. "I don't know if this is good or bad. What do you think, Charles?"

"I'm not sure I can call it either way right this minute. At this point in time, *we* know who he is. The boys at the FBI are going to be wondering who he is about now.

"I see that Maggie has asked all respondents to call into the paper and offered a five-thousand-dollar reward on a positive identification. The CIA might run the likeness, as will the FBI through every database known to man. Depends on who gets to him first." Charles's phone took that moment to chirp to life. He announced himself, and said, "Thanks, Maggie. We're on it."

Charles looked at the Sisters. "According to the first five call-ins, Hank Jellicoe is now masquerading as Simon Jordan, a retired professor. He lives at 911 Sherman Way in Manassas. Ladies, you have the floor."

"By the time we get there, he'll be gone. That's a given," Kathryn said. "I say we send the guys to check it out."

Charles was already punching in Bert's number. He relayed the news and said the boys were on it, and Ted and Espinosa would be taking pictures.

"So for now, we wait. My gut is telling me somehow, some way, Hank has one more rabbit in his hat. I have nothing to base that on except my gut feeling."

Annie's cell phone rang. She looked down at the caller ID. Her eyebrows shot upward. "It's Fergus Duffy! Imagine that!"

The Sisters listened as Annie offered a greeting. Her eyes popped wide, and she could barely get her words out. She thanked Duffy for his call and powered down. "You are not going to believe this. Fergus said the Sûreté called him, whatever that guy's name is, the one on the plane, and said the man pictured in the *Post* is professor Simon Jordan and he died in France and is buried in a small rural cemetery. Seems the vicar, who is addicted to American television and our newspapers, saw the picture in the paper this morning. He was buried as an indigent by the Good Samaritans of his parish because he had no identification on him. The vicar said he took a picture of the body, what was left of it, and forwarded it to the Sûreté."

"Wow!" Isabelle said.

"What? Jellicoe killed Professor Jordan, assumed his identity, is that what we're saying?" Nikki asked.

"Well, dear, if it looks like a duck, walks like a duck, quacks like a duck, then I think it's safe to say it's a duck. The answer is yes," Myra said.

"The boys are on the way to Manassas," Charles said. He smiled indulgently at Myra. "It is indeed a duck."

"What do you think Director Yantzy is going to do?" Alexis asked.

"The short answer is, whatever he has to do. Having said that, Director Span is now in the game if Professor Jordan was killed on French soil. Even though the CIA cannot operate on American soil, it can investigate the death of the real Professor Jordan. But I still think we have the edge here. I'm sure a team of agents is on the way to the *Post* if they aren't there already. Not to worry, Maggie knows what to do should that happen," Charles said.

Hank Jellicoe drove the roads like a bat out of hell, not caring if the police picked him up for speeding. Right now he was so pissed he could chew nails and spit rust.

Goddamn vigilantes. Once again I underestimated them. Stupid fucking dogs. I should have known better.

His eyes on the road, one hand on the wheel, he yanked at the small audio gizmo in his shirt pocket. He fought the urge to bite down into it and crush it into a million pieces.

This was supposedly so goddamned foolproof. They must be laughing their heads off that they found the audio chips under the dogs' collars. And Charlie! He was probably laughing up his sleeve, too.

That hurt, that someone like Charlie could actually outdo him.

A half mile away from 911 Sherman Way, Jellicoe reached up to the visor and clicked it. His garage door would immediately slide up, so when he pulled into the driveway, he could sail right into it and not waste a precious second. Seconds were going to count from here on in.

Minutes later he did just that, slowed slightly, roared up the slight incline, and came to a dead stop just as the doors started to slide down. He cut the engine, got out of the Hummer, and bolted through the house to the second floor and his war room, but not before he opened the electric box and cut the power.

Blank screens stared up at him. He reached behind his chair for the Louisville Slugger he liked to keep handy. First he yanked at the guts of the machines, ripped at some power cords, sliced others. Then he wound up and swung the Slugger time and again. Plastic, Plexiglas, bits and pieces of tubing flew in all directions. Satisfied that the room was a total shambles, Jellicoe tossed the bat across the room.

Did he have hours, minutes, seconds, what? Hours, maybe two. More than likely less. He headed back down to the first floor and the room where he slept from time to time, not that he slept much. No point in calling the room a bedroom if he didn't sleep in it at least four hours a night on a regular basis. It was just a room. As he stripped his clothes off, he was checking out the morning edition of the *Post* on his special satellite phone. If he'd worn dentures, they would have fallen right out of his mouth when he saw, in miniature, a picture of himself under the fold on the front page of the *Post*.

Jellicoe's adrenaline kicked in as he pulled out a set of clothes from the top drawer of the only dresser in the room. Not hours. Minutes. He pulled on slacks and a loose-fitting, long-sleeve green blouse; he clipped on some earrings. A string of pearls went around his neck. He added two garish rings and a few clanking bracelets to his hands and wrists. The last thing he did was pull on a curly gray-white wig. He kicked off his boots and slipped his feet into a pair of serviceable women's footwear. "Welcome to the world of covert espionage, Bertha Tolliver."

Minutes, not hours. Minutes.

Back in the garage, Jellicoe eyed the robin's-egg blue Caddy. He turned the power back on, climbed behind the wheel, pressed the remote to open the garage door, and drove out and down the driveway to the main road.

Little old ladies like Bertha Tolliver would drive like snails and be hindrances on the road. So that was what Hank Jellicoe did. He drove at thirty-five miles an hour and ignored the honking horns and the upraised fingers as he listened to Perry Como and tried to read the text underneath his picture in the morning paper.

Jellicoe's heart beat erratically in his chest as he felt things closing around him. They had put it together, and that bitch at the paper was going to crucify him. The Feds were now on it, too. That meant the CIA had their agents in France already exhuming Professor Jordan's body. For one wild, crazy moment, he felt like he had a noose around his neck. He felt vulnerable for the first time in his life. He did not like the feeling.

"Hey, check out that Caddy," Bert said, craning his neck to get a better view of the ancient car going in the opposite direction. "That's got to be a 1951, maybe a '52. Get a load of those tail fins. Looks like it's in mint condition, and get a load of that old lady driving it. Bet she thinks she's queen of the road."

Jack laughed. "Check out the line of cars behind her. And she doesn't give a hoot. Just tooling along in the sunshine, probably listening to some old guy singing. They called them crooners back in her day. I gotta say, though, that baby looks like it would fetch a bundle from some car collector. Probably more than a Porsche Boxster costs. I was never into cars like most guys. If it gets me there, that's all that counts."

"The old lady must live in that retirement village we just passed," Bert said as he looked in his rearview window. "Bet all the old geezers in there love that car. I know my dad would if he were still alive. He's the one who got me interested in vintage cars. A nice hobby if you're rich, which I'm not."

"Enough with the cars already," Harry said from the backseat.

"Yes, sir, Mr. Wong, sir, we will now cease and desist on any and all conversation pertaining to robin's-egg blue Caddies that only old ladies drive. Old ladies, not old men. How strange is that? Okay, okay, that's my final word. Be patient, Harry, we are almost there."

Chapter 25

Ted Robinson stopped texting and looked up. "Just for the record, 911 Sherman Way used to be called 911 Sherman Lane. Not that it matters. Hell, it's a damn highway, so where do they get off saying it's any kind of street to begin with?"

"I don't think it matters, Ted," Jack said in a soothing tone, taking note of Ted's irritability. "It's a given the son of a bitch will be gone by the time we get there. Who are you texting?"

"Some lady named Annette at the county tax office. She even knows Professor Jordan, says he's a little dotty, whatever the hell that is, but a responsible man of the community."

"You mean the *real* Professor Jordan? She's going to be surprised when she reads the papers and finds out Jellicoe has been impersonating him. Ask her when she last had contact with him," Bert said.

"I already did, and she said three years ago at some equestrian show. That was clearly before Jellicoe assumed the professor's identity."

"Well, here we are," Espinosa said, leaning out the car window. "That mailbox says Jordan on the side. Looks like the driveway is . . . right there." Bert slammed on the brakes, cut the corner short, then straightened out the car. "Stop, Bert, let me pick up Mr. Jordan's mail." Espinosa hopped out of the car and returned with a bundle of papers, catalogs, and assorted flyers. He was back in the car in seconds. "Move on out, buddy."

"What you just did is a federal offense," Jack said virtuously. "You could go to a federal prison for tampering with a person's mail. So? Anything worth reading?"

"If I tell you, then you're as guilty as I am. We'll both be going to the slammer."

"At least we'll be together." Jack guffawed. "So what's in the mail?"

"A magazine called *American Rifle. Field & Stream.* Flyers from Staples, Walgreens, and Walmart with coupons. No bills, nothing personal."

"Nice place," Harry said, when Bert stopped the car alongside a four-car garage. "Any possibility this place is booby-trapped?"

"Nothing is impossible, Harry. I'm kinda, more or less, thinking that bastard left in a bit of a hurry and wouldn't have stopped long enough to tidy up. I say we pick the lock on the back door even though the house can't be seen from the road. Who wants to do the honors? What? No takers. Jack, you're it," Bert said.

"Me!" Jack said in pretended outrage. "Do you think I carry a picklock with me at all times."

"Yeah, I do, I saw it on that knife thing you keep on your keychain; cut the shit and open the goddamn door so we can figure out what's going on."

Five minutes later, with a little goading from his friends,

Jack snapped the lock, and the five of them were standing in a huge kitchen.

"Let's spread out and, for God's sake, don't touch anything. Grab a dish towel or something and wrap it around your hand if you want to pick up something. A paper towel will do," Bert said.

The group split up, Jack and Harry taking the steps to the second floor. Espinosa headed for the basement and Bert toward the garage. Ted covered the first floor.

"The action is up here!" Jack bellowed a few minutes later.

Footsteps thundered up the old pine staircase. "Looks like our buddy Jellicoe got himself in a little snit and busted up this place. Nice setup. We're talking some big bucks here," Jack said as he walked over to the corner to pick up the Louisville Slugger. He hefted it and took a few practice swings. "This baby is what he used to do all this damage. I think I just might keep this as a memento."

"There's nothing salvageable here. He did a damn good job of destroying everything," Bert said. "Maybe the feebs at the Bureau can salvage something, but I doubt it."

"There's nothing here in . . . I guess it's his bedroom. A couple of sets of clothes, extra shoes, and boots. DNA, but that's it. Guess he doesn't care about that," Harry said.

"Okay, let's cover the rest of the house. We might find something he left behind that will give us a clue as to what he's going to do next."

Twenty-five minutes later, all the guys had to show for their efforts was the Louisville Slugger and a wad of paper towels.

"Wonder what the fourth vehicle was that he kept in the garage?" Ted said. He looked over at Bert, "Hey, Mr. Ex–FBI Director, is there any way to tell what kind of vehicle was parked in the fourth bay?"

Bert shook his head, a look of disgust on his face. "Wonder why he didn't take the Hummer. Maybe too noticeable. For all we know, the fourth one might have been a MINI Cooper or some old junk heap that would blend in with all the other cars out there on the road. He travels light, that's for sure. Other than a year's supply of food in those freezers, that's it as far as things being out of the ordinary."

Harry looked down at his watch. "We've been here too long already."

"I hear you," Bert said as he headed for the kitchen door. "Get your pick ready, Jack, and lock this door behind us. Come on, people, Harry's right. We've been here too long already."

"Espinosa, you got it all on film, just in case, right?"

"Got it."

"Ted, you sending all of this to Maggie?"

"Done."

"Then we're outta here," Jack said, snapping the lock back into place. They were back on the highway in less than three minutes.

"What now?" Bert asked.

"We aren't all that far from Pinewood, so head there. Espinosa, upload all your pictures to Charles so he has them by the time we get there," Jack said.

"And what are we going to do once we get there?" Harry asked.

Jack turned around to stare at Harry. "I don't know, Harry. Maybe try to get back into the good graces of the girls? I think that's our top priority, and don't try and tell me Yoko isn't giving you the old silent treatment, either. What do *you* think we should do when we get there? I am open to any and all suggestions." Harry ignored Jack the way he always ignored him.

"Ted," Bert called over his shoulder, "see if you can get online and find out what that old Caddy is worth that we saw on the road before. I'm pretty sure it's a '51 or a '52. I'd give my eyeteeth to have that buggy."

"Wouldn't you be embarrassed to be seen driving something like that on the road?" Espinosa asked. "It's not exactly a chick magnet. Not that you're looking for a chick magnet," he added hastily.

"Are you kidding me? I would be the envy of every guy on the road if I had an old heap like that. Assuming the engine is solid or rebuilt. Looked in mint condition to me. Hey, guys, on the way back, how about we stop at that retirement village and ask around for the owner. She might want to sell. I bet that snappy blue color is the original. Might need some touch-ups here and there. Yeah, I bet it is original in every way except for maybe new tires."

"You are out of your mind, Bert Navarro. You need to save your money for your retirement," Jack said. "Besides, that car probably has sentimental value to that lady. She was alone, so maybe she's a widow, and it was her husband's car. She's never going to part with it because it reminds her of him. In other words, get over it and move on," Jack said, an edge to his voice.

"Very good, sound advice, Mr. Navarro," Harry said, the edge in his voice sharper than in Jack's.

The rest of the trip to Pinewood was made in total silence.

The owner of the robin's-egg blue 1951 Cadillac sat at an antique oak table in the small kitchen of the town house of one Bertha Tolliver. The car was nestled in a carport that had sliding doors across the front. A definite screwup by the builder, whoever he was, back in the day. From his position at the table, Jellicoe could see the roof of the car through the kitchen window but the car was invisible to anyone passing on the street.

Jellicoe was still wearing the curly gray-and-white wig and women's clothing. He was sweating profusely. He got up, went over to the refrigerator, and popped a bottle of Coors Light.

As with all his safe houses, the refrigerator and freezers were fully stocked. The cabinets held staples that wouldn't go bad. With the exception of fresh fruits and vegetables, he could survive here without stepping outside for a year. Right now it was temporary. At least he hoped it was temporary.

Jellicoe noticed that the hand holding the Coors was trembling. He set the bottle down on the table and picked it back up with his left hand. The tremor in his left hand was just as noticeable as in his right. He needed to take a deep breath and get it together. He polished off the beer, then turned on the television set sitting on the counter. First he turned to a local station, but there was nothing on it that pertained to him. He clicked on CNN and sat down. Ten minutes till the top of the hour. He passed the time by popping another Coors and opening a box of saltine crackers and a package of Velveeta cheese. As he had found out over the years, the cheese was like those candy Cheeps or Peeps or whatever they were called. You could keep them forever, and they didn't go bad. He broke off a chunk of the cheese, chewed, then washed it down with the beer. He leaned forward on the table, better to see the seventeen-inch television.

All good things come to those who wait, he thought bitterly when he saw the director of the FBI standing on the veranda of 911 Sherman Way, blathering on and on about how Henry Jellicoe's capture was imminent and that the

Bureau and the Cental Intelligence Agency were working together to make sure it happened.

Jellicoe snorted. Neither one of those clowns could hold a candle to him. Which then brought his thinking around to the vigilantes. They might be one or two up on him, but here he was nonetheless, safe and sound. He made an ugly sound in his throat. He really had to get out of these clothes.

Hank tromped through the town house at 16 Primrose Court. It was twenty-one-hundred square feet, large for a town house. It had everything—modern kitchen, garden bath, good storage, three good-sized bedrooms, a home office, and a nice great room.

There was no computer setup like he'd had at the Sherman Way address. But he did have a computer, fax, and printer. There was even a landline but no voice mail. And he hadn't installed a stand-alone answering machine, either. Old ladies didn't like such contraptions, he told himself. He smiled when he thought about how he'd gone online to read up on the likes and dislikes of seniors. Even though he was a senior himself, what he read in no way applied to him. He remembered the day he'd hung a wreath of bright yellow sunflowers on his front door. Oldsters were partial to door wreaths and decorated porches. Well . . . when in Rome . . .

Old coots, seniors, or whatever the current term was these days, also liked to keep their blinds drawn. They also liked to keep lights on outside set on timers and night-lights in every room. He'd obliged and stayed with the script. They also liked their mail to be slipped through the door and did not want outside mailboxes, where some hoodlum could steal their pension checks. None of the people polled for the article believed in online banking. So he'd put in a mail slot himself and the mail just accumulated on the floor until he paid a visit to retrieve it.

Bertha Tolliver's electric and water bills were paid a year in advance. Receipts were sent along with a single bank statement each month. That was the extent of Bertha Tolliver's personal mail. Bertha had $1,800 in her personal savings account.

Once or twice a year, Jellicoe made an appearance just to check on things and post a notice on the front door, inside the sunflower wreath, which said something stupid like Bertha was going to California and would call when she got back. Bertha, according to the notes the gossipy mailman shared with the other two house owners, was a big traveler since her husband had passed away.

Jellicoe dumped his beer bottles into the trash compactor and headed for the stairs. He turned on the TV as loud as it would go before he stripped down. He'd purposely chosen this particular unit because it was separated from the other town houses and had once been the model to show prospective buyers. He could blast his stereo and TV as loud as he wanted.

Under the cascading shower, he strained to hear the commentator on CNN. He was relieved to hear that they weren't talking about him. He relaxed, soaped up twice and rinsed off, washed his hair again, then soaped up a third time.

The bathroom was steamy when he toweled off and dressed in well-worn khaki shorts and a gray T-shirt that was just as worn. He slipped his feet into worn sandals and made his way downstairs, carrying the laptop he'd brought with him.

Jellicoe had never been a clock watcher, much preferring to go with his own internal clock. Long ago, when out in the field, he learned to tell the time by the sun and the elements. He was sure enough of his capabilities to call the time within a minute or two. Now he was more than aware of time and had reverted to his watch.

It would be time to eat soon. Another one of his internal clocks at work. He walked into the laundry room, opened his deep freeze, and pulled out a package of something. He read the directions, found an oven pan, dumped in the contents, turned on the oven, and slid the pan onto the top rack. Dinner was taken care of.

He booted up the laptop, waited a minute, then settled down to figure out where his life was going and at what speed.

Jellicoe worked steadily for the next two hours, taking only one break to rub at his eyes. He leaned back and closed his eyes. A vision of his wife and daughter appeared behind his closed lids. Crap, he did not want to go there. That was all a lifetime ago. His one big failure. Not that other failures hadn't occurred along the way, but he'd been able to resolve those.

To this day, with all the resources at his disposal, he'd never been able to find his wife, Louise, and his daughter, whose name he could no longer remember. He wondered if his daughter looked like him in any way. Well, the way he used to look, not the way he looked now. Almost his own age, Louise probably had aged well. She'd had good bone structure. He wondered if there was a man in her life, if somehow she'd managed to divorce him in some other country. Did he even care? Of course he cared. She'd bested him just as those damn vigilantes had. Why was it always women who did him in? If he could get his hands on her right now, he'd wring her neck until her eyes popped out of their sockets. And then he'd stomp on her and walk away.

Chapter 26

The boys barreled through the open gates at Pinewood to a robust greeting from the dogs, who yipped and danced for attention. Jack and Bert took time to throw some sticks for the dogs before they all entered the house to choruses of, "Why didn't you call?" and "What happened?" and "What's the situation now?"

Jack took the floor, his eyes on Nikki as he reported their findings in Manassas. He thought he was going to black out when she stepped into his arms and nuzzled his neck. Later, he swore he did black out momentarily when she whispered, "Let's go home, Jack. We need to make our world right again." At that precise moment he knew he would have leapt for the moon if that's what Nikki wanted. He wasn't sure if what he was feeling was his own tremors or those of Nikki. All he knew was he wanted to get the hell out of there as soon as possible.

"All your properties have been checked, scanned, then checked again. You're all good to go. Unless you want a roundtable."

Annie withdrew a huge frosty pitcher of lemonade from

the refrigerator while Myra took glasses from the cupboard. Yoko reached into the ice bin and filled the glasses with Annie's lemonade ice cubes. "I think this calls for a toast," Annie said when she was finished pouring the lemonade. "I think we won this round. Mr. Henry, call me Hank, Jellicoe appears to be on the run."

Glasses clinked. There were smiles all around, then they sobered.

"On the run to *where*?" Ted asked. "We might have driven him so far to ground we'll never find him."

"With his picture plastered all over the *Post,* I doubt that," Charles said. "By the way, Avery Snowden called and said that Virgil Anders is rewriting the end of his book. And Margie Evans, Anders's old fiancée, is on her way to meet up with him. Avery's people found her in the retirement village where she lives. If you can believe this, she never married and stayed true to Mr. Anders. Suffice it to say, both Anders and Margie Evans are ecstatic at the way things are turning out for them."

"That's so wonderful," Alexis said, her eyes on Espinosa, who was suddenly looking like a beaten dog. She winked at him.

"True love is wonderful. Imagine them getting together all these years later," Kathryn said so softly the others had to strain to hear the words. Bert heard them loud and clear, his features lighting up like a Christmas morning when he was a small boy.

"I don't mean to be a wet blanket, but we need to decide what we're going to do about Mr. Jellicoe's wife and daughter. We need to make a decision on something, and we need to make it now," Myra said. "I'd like some input from all of you."

They ran with it. The input ran from "let sleeping dogs lie" to "let's do it, and the sooner the better."

They debated the pros and cons for a good thirty minutes. In the end, it was decided that Myra and Annie were the least threatening and should be the ones to make the visit. Charles frowned the entire time the matter was under discussion. "What if anything do you think the wife and daughter are going to tell you?" was Charles's bottom line.

"That's just it, Charles, we don't know. Maybe something, maybe nothing. If you want, we'll accept you sending several of Avery's men with us just in case. I'm sure Annie and I can blend in as button customers."

"Is that what you think, Myra? Did either of you forget that you are practically household names and the world has seen your pictures?"

"There is that, dear, but I'm sure Alexis can help us out with a temporary disguise to get us through our first meeting. After all these years, I seriously doubt their handlers live on or near the premises. We'll just be two customers."

Another thirty minutes of discussion followed, with the Sisters weighing in on the side of Myra and Annie. The boys tactfully kept their opinions to themselves because, as Harry put it later, "We weren't asked for our opinions."

"Then, arrange it, Charles. Early tomorrow morning will work fine for us. The sooner we do this, the sooner we'll be able to close out that chapter of Hank's life," Myra observed.

"Guess we'll be heading out then," Yoko said as she tugged at Harry's arm.

Another ten minutes went by as everyone had to decide who was riding with whom.

In the end, it was Ted who was odd man out, with no transportation. Myra tossed him the keys to her Mercedes. Ted caught them in midair.

The dogs did their dance, yipping and howling to see their friends being herded into different cars.

Annie was the last one out the door. She listened unashamedly as Bert was extolling the virtues of robin's-egg blue Cadillacs. "Would you mind a short detour on the way home, Kathryn? I can't get that car out of my mind. If I can find the owner, I could call her or write her a letter telling her if she ever decides to sell her car, she should consider me. Look, I know it's stupid, but my dad would have gone nuts over that car. Do you mind, honey?"

Kathryn laughed. "Of course not. I know how you feel. I felt that way when I saw the big rig I wanted to call my own. It's dark, though. Maybe we could go back tomorrow when it's light out. If that car is in good condition, then I'd say the lady garages it, which means you won't see it sitting in a driveway."

"I have to do it tonight. Call me crazy, but I won't be able to sleep. I wanted to follow her when I saw it, but the guys voted me down."

"Then, let's do it," Kathryn said agreeably. "Right, Murphy." The huge shepherd raised his head in the backseat and let loose with a sharp bark before he lowered his massive head to his paws and went back to sleep.

Twenty minutes later, Bert slowed the car as he approached the entrance to the retirement village. "No security, no gate check, just small houses. We can ride up and down the streets and see if anything pops out at us. It's not that late."

It was a nice neighborhood, with shade trees and sidewalks. There was ample street lighting, and lights shone from old-fashioned picture windows. Ten minutes into driving around the meandering streets, Kathryn spied a couple walking two golden retrievers. "Pull over, Bert; let's ask them if they know the lady who owns the car."

Kathryn rolled down the window, poked her head out, and said, "Excuse me, can you tell me if you know an elderly lady who lives here in the village and has a bright blue Cadillac?"

The couple, whose dogs strained at their leashes when they picked up Murphy's scent, looked at one another as they decided if it was safe to talk to Bert and Kathryn. The sight of Murphy pressed up against the back window made their decision. Dog lovers.

"I've seen the car from time to time but not recently," the man said.

"I can't say for sure, but I think the woman lives on Butternut Avenue. I think I saw it a while back when I was walking the dogs one afternoon. John's right, it isn't a car you see all the time. You should come back tomorrow and ask the mailman. He delivers to the village between ten and twelve-thirty. If anyone would know for certain, it would be him," the lady said.

"How many houses are in the village?" Bert asked.

"Seventy-five. This is Phase One. They're going to build Phase Two starting in the spring. Do you have a name?"

A chill ran up Bert's arms when he heard Kathryn say, "No, we don't. My husband is a car buff, and he saw the lady driving it earlier but wasn't able to cross the meridian. He did see her drive in here, however. He just wants to give her his name in case she ever decides to sell her car. My father-in-law, God rest his soul, had a car just like that."

"Understood," the man said. "I still think the mailman is your best bet."

"Well, thanks for your time. Your dogs are beautiful," Kathryn said.

"Yes, they are, and they're our children these days. Our real children don't . . . well, they're busy with their own lives, so we give all of our attention to these little ladies. I hope you're successful in finding the car," the man said, as the retrievers tugged them forward.

"Guess that takes care of that," Kathryn said as she pressed the button to raise the window. "We can come back in the morning, Bert."

"How did it feel when you said your husband is a car buff?" Bert asked in a jittery voice.

"You know what, Bert, it felt kind of nice." Kathryn's tone changed slightly. "Don't push me, Bert."

"Okay. So you're all right with coming back tomorrow morning?"

"Well, yeah, now that you got me all curious about a robin's-egg blue car that knocked you off your feet. What do those babies go for these days, or do you even know?"

"Probably way out of my league. You know what, Kathryn, I can't explain it, but when I saw that car tooling along at thirty miles an hour, it just caught my eye. I can't explain it any better than that."

"You don't have to. Come on, let's go home."

"Do you want to stop at the Squires' Pub for something to eat or drink? Ted asked me, and I said I'd check with you. He's feeling pretty down right now."

"Sure. You want me to text him?"

"If you don't mind." Kathryn obliged.

Back in the District, Ted Robinson was settling himself on a barstool in the Squires' Pub as he looked down at the text message coming in. He sighed happily. Bert and Kathryn would be joining him after all.

The air moved around his stool with a swoosh. "Hey,

aren't you Ted Robinson?" a pretty blonde asked as she took the seat next to him.

"I was when I woke up this morning. Have we met?" *That was certainly clever,* Ted thought.

"No, but I always wanted to meet you. I admire your work. Amy Blandenburg. I work for the *Sentinel,*" she said, holding out her hand. "I tried a couple of times to wrangle an invitation to meet you, but it never worked out. Did I say I really admire your work? I hope I can be half as good a reporter as you are someday."

"You did, but you can always say it again. I don't get all that many compliments. How do you like working at the *Sentinel*?

"It's a job. I'm still paying my dues, I guess. I'm sure it's nothing like working at the *Post.* That's my goal, to move on to a bigger and better paper. What's it like working over there?"

Ted looked into Amy's eyes and saw only genuine interest. She wasn't buttering him up. She was what Maggie used to be. Used to be.

"Want to move over to a booth, or are you here with someone? It's kind of noisy at the bar to talk."

"Sure. No, I'm by myself. I like coming in here before I go home. You know, shoot the breeze for a little while, get rid of the adrenaline rush. I think you have to be a newsperson to understand that. I have other friends, but they have different interests, and those interests aren't something I can listen to them rattle on about for hours on end. Talking to other reporters, even when I know I'm low man on the totem pole, is something I enjoy, and my fellow reporters don't talk down to me, because they were all in my position at one time or another."

Ted nodded as he carried their drinks to a booth in the back. Bert and Kathryn would find him. Settled comfortably, Ted realized he liked the adoration he was seeing in Amy Blandenburg's eyes. And the best part was he didn't feel guilty for being here with her. "You hungry?"

"I am, but let's go Dutch. I don't know you well enough to let you pay for me. Talk to me, tell me what it's like to be a star reporter for a big paper like the *Post*. And then, if you don't mind, tell me about yourself."

Ted couldn't remember the last time anyone wanted to know anything about him. He started to talk and was so intense he didn't see Bert and Kathryn when they walked in. Bert nudged Kathryn, and the couple backed out the door with knowing looks.

Outside, Bert said, "Aha!"

"What does 'aha,' mean, Bert? Maggie gave Ted back his ring. That means he can sit in a booth in a bar with another female companion. I also suspect she's a colleague," she snapped.

"Whoa! I thought you would be on Maggie's side. For whatever it's worth, I agree with you. Does this have anything to do with you and me? Our situation?"

"No. Well, yes, in a way. Couples have to respect each other and their opinions. You tried to muscle me, Bert, and you damn well know it. I don't like being muscled. I told you I wasn't ready to get married, but you pushed and you pushed hard. I might never be ready to marry. I told you all of that up front. You said you were okay with it. Then you weren't all right with it, at which point I suggested we each move on in whatever direction we wanted to take. You backed off, and we're at the position we're in right now.

"In addition to all of that, Ted and Maggie are not your business, nor are they my business. The female in the booth with Ted is not our business, either."

Bert sucked in his breath. "You're right, Kathryn. So, do you want to head home or stop for some Italian?"

"I am hungry, and Italian sounds good. Let's go for it."

Bert felt his body go limp. He'd dodged that one. If he lived to be a hundred, he'd never be able to figure out women, Kathryn in particular.

Back at the Squires' Pub, Ted looked at his cell and the message coming through. Bert and Kathryn had changed their minds and were headed home. Ted felt giddy at the thought that he had Amy Blandenburg to himself.

Chapter 27

Lincolnville, Oklahoma, was any small town in America as Annie drove the rental car through the residential streets. There were sidewalks with giant shade trees and benches underneath. The hardware store on Main Street featured its wares on part of the sidewalk; old-fashioned bamboo rakes sat next to modern-day leaf blowers. It was hard to tell what was in the six or seven bushel baskets with the exception of one that held rosy red apples that people picked up as they walked by. Swanson's drugstore had a sale—Listerine mouthwash was half price if you bought two tubes of Crest toothpaste. Alfredo's Pizza Parlor said a slice and a Coke was your dollar lunch on Fridays.

Annie drove by the courthouse, a redbrick building with white columns and what looked like a shiny, new asphalt parking lot with blinding white lines designating the parking spaces.

"What's the GPS saying, Myra?"

"It says you make a left at the quarter-mile sign, and our

destination is two blocks from there. Are you nervous, Annie?"

"Yes and no. I wish, though, that we had come in disguise. I feel kind of naked for want of a better term. She might recognize us," Annie said fretfully.

"We aren't here on a mission, dear. We're just here to talk. We're going to walk away when we're done talking. The ex–Mrs. Jellicoe is a woman, Annie. She's going to understand when we explain why we're here."

"But what if . . ."

"There are no what-ifs, Annie. It's what it is. If you don't want to do this, and may I remind you that you were the one who suggested this in the first place, you can walk away right now."

"It's not that, Myra. Here is this woman who feels safe and has every right to stay that way, and we're going to invade her life."

"Not in the true sense of . . . invading. Like I said, all we're going to do is talk. I feel strongly that she will not kick us out. I think she'll listen to what we have to say. She is of an age with us, Annie. Surely she has garnered wisdom along the way the same as we have."

"Well, here we are," Annie said as she made a turn into a long, winding road. The house, a redbrick two-story affair, was trimmed in white, with neat black shutters. The lawn was landscaped beautifully; someone loved flowers, because there were colorful blooms everywhere.

"I guess that long, low building at the back end is the place where she does her button thing. I see three cars back there. Customers? Or the help. Here goes nothing, Myra," Annie said, swerving into a space next to a Ford Ranger pickup.

There were flowers here, too, that lined the long line of the building along with low-lying evergreen shrubs. A huge tree in line with the front door cast shade over the front of the building. Tongue in cheek, Annie said, "This looks just like what I imagined a button shop would look like."

Myra smiled. She'd never given much thought to buttons. Buttons were buttons. They were just there, something on clothing to close it up. Who knew?

Both women climbed out of the car and walked to the front door, opened it, and walked into a neat little foyer that screamed cleanliness. Annie rang a bell that was sitting on the counter next to a huge bowl of beautiful lemon yellow marigolds. A set of French doors opened, and a tall, striking woman with a fashionable hairdo entered the foyer. She was wearing a bright red smock over jeans and what looked like a T-shirt. She smiled, and asked, "What can I do for you ladies today?"

Since no one was in the foyer, and it didn't look like anyone was going to invade the foyer, Myra saw no reason to delay matters. She got right to the point. "I'm Myra Rutledge and this is Anna de Silva."

The woman continued to smile as she held her hand out to be shaken. "You look familiar. Have we met?"

"People say that all the time," Annie said. "No, we haven't met, but it hasn't been for lack of trying, Mrs. Jellicoe." There, it was out. The striking woman turned pale under her beautiful tan. She reached for the edge of the counter, her eyes full of panic.

"Please, no one knows we're here. Your secret is safe with us. The reason we seemed familiar to you is because of our own notoriety. We *were* members of the vigilantes."

"Oh, my God, how did you find me?"

"With a great deal of difficulty. Which, by the way, was not legal, just so you know. We tell you this so that you know we mean you no harm. Your secret is safe with us.

For all intents and purposes, we are just two women who want to buy some buttons. If you have any outdated buttons or leftovers, we'll be happy to buy them."

"What is it you want? I just don't understand how you found me. So many years have gone by. For the most part, I no longer think about those early days. I have a wonderful life that is so fulfilling. I have grandchildren, a son-in-law, a man in my life who cares about me, and this business that I built." She threw her hands in the air in despair.

"When we leave here, you will still have that. We would die before we told anyone about you. You have to believe that. We're here about Hank. I'm sure that over the past year you've heard through the marshals or just by reading or listening to the television that the man is wanted. He's been labeled a terrorist. An enemy combatant, if you will. He's after us. But right now, we're one step behind him and closing in fast. At least we hope we are."

"I thought you were pardoned. Are you . . . are you *back in business?* Lord, how stupid that sounded."

"See, now, you're one up on us. When we leave here, you can notify the authorities and tell them whatever you want to tell them, and we'll go to prison. That gives you the edge right now. All we want to do is ask you some questions, then we'll leave."

"Would . . . would you like something to drink?"

"Actually, I would," Myra said, trying to put the woman at ease.

"We have a very nice old-fashioned kitchen in the back. No one will bother us there, and I think I need to sit down. Follow me."

As Myra and Annie followed Louise Jellicoe, a.k.a. Marsha Olivettie, through the factory, Annie said, "Why buttons?"

The woman laughed. "Why not buttons? Right now we are primarily doing children's buttons. Big, bright, and bold colors. I myself was stunned when the orders started flying in. We can't make them fast enough. It was my daughter's idea. Little fingers need big buttons."

"That makes sense," Myra said as she thought about Lizzie's son, little Jack.

Marsha Olivettie opened the stainless-steel refrigerator, and asked, "Is green tea okay?"

"Green tea is fine," Annie said.

Louise handed out the bottles, then took her place across the table from Myra and Annie. "My daughter and I cheered you ladies on and donated to your cause back in the day. We cheered again when we heard you were pardoned. Having said that, it's your turn. Talk to me."

"Tell us why you're in the Witness Protection Program. And how did you get here? I know how the WPP works. What I mean is, what did you know that got you in the program?"

"I·didn't *know* anything, but I suspected a lot of things. I was afraid of Hank. Not in the beginning, but later on he turned into someone I didn't want to know, much less be married to. He was always gone, patriot that he was. He was a zealot, but at the time I just thought he was cruel and inhuman. There came a point in our marriage when I no longer existed to him. I was just there. Almost like a servant. He would talk on the phone and didn't seem to care if I heard him or not. I started keeping a diary. He was doing all kinds of things, deals with the government he shouldn't have made, people covering up, things he covered up. It got to the point where I couldn't tell the good guys from the bad guys.

"Huge sums of money were involved. Huge might be the wrong word; vast sums of money were being sent to the wrong places. Then Hank would ride in like the white knight and save the day. The only problem with that was he set it all up, caused the problem to begin with, then went in and cleaned up his own mess and was rewarded with tons of money. He kept records that I was never able to get to, but my diary was enough to convince the marshals to put me in the program when I told them I was going to expose him if they didn't get me and my daughter to safety. I made a copy of my diary and gave it to a lawyer I knew who didn't have a dog in that fight.

"I guess in the end I convinced them, and they agreed to relocate me and my daughter. They made me swear on a Bible, literally, that my diary was the only copy. Of course I didn't blink an eye when I swore on the Bible, which doesn't say all that much for me. But it was me and my daughter or him. Before you can ask, nothing was ever done with the information that I know of. They swept it all under the rug. I blame the CIA for all of that." Marsha's voice was bitter, her eyes full of tears.

Myra's mind raced. "Does that lawyer still have your diary?"

"I would assume so. I go online every so often and Google him. He is still practicing law. You want the diary, is that it?"

"We do. Could you write us a letter, authorizing him to release it to us?"

"I can do better than that. Not only will I give you a letter, but I will have my local attorney call him and make the arrangements."

"Are you sure you're willing to do that?"

Marsha's shoulders straightened. "I'm sure. Are you finally going to get him?"

"We are. Actually, we had him once, we turned him over, then he got away from some of the most sophisticated operators walking the face of the earth. All *men*, I might add," Annie said.

Marsha laughed, a genuine sign of mirth. "Why doesn't that surprise me?"

"What should we call you?" Myra said.

The smile again. "How about friend?"

"That will work," Annie said. "Is there anything we can do for you before we leave or after we get back to Washington?"

"No. I'm good. Catching that SOB and locking him up for the rest of his life will work for me. Can you promise that?"

Without missing a beat, Myra said, "Absolutely." Annie's eyes almost bugged out of her head. "Are you going to notify your handler that we were here and what we talked about?"

Marsha laughed again. "Tell a man something like that! I-don't-think-so! Your secret is as safe with me as I know mine is with you."

"When will you call your attorney?" Annie asked.

"The moment you're thirty thousand feet in the air. Call me when your plane takes off. I'll wait for twenty minutes and make the call.

"Here's the lawyer's name and phone number. You might want to set down and pick up my diary in person. He's on the way for you. One small change in your flight plan if you came by private jet, which I assume you did." Marsha reached up and tore a piece of paper from a notepad on the refrigerator and scribbled a name and a phone number along with the address.

"Will you stay on here?" Myra asked.

"Probably. My life is here, and, as you can see, it's a good life. I won't kid you, I will sleep a lot easier knowing you've put Hank where he belongs."

"Well, I guess that's it for us. You have nothing to fear from us, just so you know . . . friend," Annie said.

"I want to thank you for coming. It doesn't matter how you got here or what you had to do to find me. I'm just glad that you did. If my diary will help you, then this has all been worth it. Good luck."

"Same to you, Marsha . . . friend. Do you want us to get in touch if . . . when we're successful?"

"I have phones, but they're monitored. If you call this number," Marsha said reaching up for another slip of paper from the refrigerator, "on the first Saturday of the month at two in the afternoon, I'll be there to answer the phone. It's one of the few public phones left in this town, and it's in the drugstore."

Myra pocketed the slip of paper, and the women didn't bother to shake hands. They hugged one another because that was what women who trusted one another did.

Back in the rental car, Myra drove this time. "I thought that went rather well, don't you, Annie? She seems to be a lovely person. Buttons! Who knew buttons could be a way of life."

"What about that guarantee of catching Hank Jellicoe? That might come back to bite you, Myra."

"On which cheek?" Myra laughed. "Call ahead to the pilot and tell him we have to detour to Salt Lake City. I don't think that's exactly on our way, but it should work out anyway. Buttons! Who knew, Annie?"

"Shut up about the buttons already, Myra. I'm going to be dreaming about red, yellow, and blue buttons for the rest of my life."

"Children love bright colors and big buttons. Everyone knows that."

"Myra, erase the word *button* from your vocabulary or I will strangle you."

A devil perched itself on Myra's shoulders. "Button, button, who's got the button?" she squealed, until Annie doubled over laughing.

"Call everyone, Annie, and tell them what we found out and be sure to tell them we're making a short stop on the way. Charles is going to love this, as will Maggie. The CIA covered up for Hank Jellicoe. Now, that is going to blow the lid off Washington, D.C., for sure."

Chapter 28

It was a golden day in Washington, D.C. The sun was shining, the sky was a clear blue, with barely a cloud to be seen. But it was hot and humid, the horrible dog days of summer. It was hard, Bert thought, to try to figure out what kind of day it would be emotionally.

Bert was on his way to pick up Kathryn to travel out to the retirement village to see if he could track down the owner of the car that consumed his dreams all night long. He wished he knew why he was suddenly so obsessed with that stupid car. Kathryn had been tolerant of it all, but the guys . . . the guys didn't really understand it, either.

"Shit!" Bert said succinctly as he made his way to the underground garage where he rented space for his car. Maybe it wasn't the actual car itself but more about the time period when it was manufactured. The fifties. *Happy Days* and all that. Before his time, and he wasn't into the fifties, so then what the hell was it? The color? He looked up at the blue sky and decided it was the exact color of the car he'd seen yesterday. He couldn't remember ever, during the whole of his lifetime, seeing a car that particular shade of eye-popping blue.

The driver? He hadn't gotten that good of a look. Did she remind him of his grandmother? His mother? Or was it the whole package and some long-submerged memory that the car triggered? That had to be it. Some kind of old memory.

Before he could change his mind, Bert sent off a short text message to Kathryn saying something had come up and he'd call her later in the day. He jammed his phone into his pocket, climbed into the car, and headed to Harry Wong's *dojo*, where he knew Jack was working out. His gut churning every which way, Bert pulled up to a red light, stopped, then whipped out his cell and sent a text to Ted Robinson that was short and sweet. "Meet me and Jack at the *dojo*."

When Bert arrived at Harry's *dojo*, he found Jack wandering through the renovation site and talking to the crew about what they were doing.

"Harry's finishing up a class. What brings you here? I thought you were spending the day with Kathryn."

"Change of plans. Listen, Jack, all shit aside, I need to talk to you. Let's go out back, where no one can hear us."

"Does this have something to do with that ridiculous car?" Jack grumbled.

"Actually, it does. I'm trying to figure something out, and I can't get a handle on it. I don't want that goddamn car. I don't know what the hell got into me. It was like I was possessed or something. I need you to help me figure it out."

Jack threw his hands in the air. "Well, let's figure it out quick since it's hot as hell out here. Not that the *dojo* is any cooler, but this sun is brutal. You saw the car tooling down the road. It was going around thirty miles an hour. We talked about that, saying old people drive slow. We all commented on the color, the fins on the Caddy, and wondered if it was in mint condition. We talked about car collectors and what a car like that would be worth."

"Right! Right! There's something else. I'm missing it. Something maybe that my subconscious registered, and it's right there tickling me. Help me out here, Jack; this is driving me insane. You have to know it's making me nuts to give up spending the day with Kathryn."

"Was it the driver? The old lady? Do you think it had anything to do with where we were going and what we knew we were going to find when we got there?"

Bert literally did a twirl around as he pounded Jack on the back. "Damn, Jack, you are good! That's it! Jesus, how could I have been so damn stupid to miss that? You are amazing, I will give you that."

Jack preened, wondering what the hell he had said to make Bert so euphoric.

"We were going. The blue car was coming from the direction we were going to. You know that old saying, when you want to hide something, do it right under someone's nose, right out there in the open. Same principle as keep your friends close, your enemies closer."

"What?"

"Yeah, what?" Harry said as he waved to the last of his departing students.

Jack explained.

"You're still harping on that car, Bert. Give it up already. It would cost you a fortune to store it somewhere. Where are you going to get parts when it breaks down? My advice is to get over it."

"Yeah, well, I wasn't the director of the FBI for nothing. I'm telling you there is something logged into my subconscious about that car, and I can't get it out of my mind. Jack just enlightened me, Harry. We were heading to Professor Jordan's house. When we got there, it looked to all of us like old Jellicoe had just left. You saw that four-car garage. The fourth bay was empty. You following me here?"

Ted and Espinosa suddenly appeared out of nowhere. "Thanks for standing me up last night," Ted growled at Bert.

"Yeah, well, I didn't actually stand you up. Kathryn and I did go to the pub, but when we got there we saw you with that sweet, young blond thing, and since we didn't want to interrupt, we left."

"She's not that young. She's thirty-three, and she works for the *Sentinel*. Her name is Amy Blandenburg, and she is enamored of me. She told me I am her inspiration. A guy needs to hear stuff like that once in a while. We hit it off big-time. And she has a cat, so that makes us both cat lovers. We have a date this weekend."

"Does Maggie know?" the guys chorused as one, shock written all over their faces at this brazen news.

Ted huffed and puffed. "In case you forgot, Maggie returned my ring. She does not want to be engaged to me, and she does not want to marry me. That means I am a free agent, just the way she is a free agent. So, get off my case. Aren't you supposed to be on my side? What's wrong with this picture?"

"Maggie scares me sometimes," Jack said. "I think you should be scared. Scorned women are vicious."

Harry spoke. "I will protect you, Ted."

Ted's legs turned to jelly. He plopped down on the picnic bench, his eyes glassy. "Thanks, Harry."

"Can we please get back to my problem here?" Bert admonished. "The fourth bay in the garage was empty."

"And this means . . . what?" Jack said.

"It means . . . it could mean . . . I think it means there was maybe a robin's-egg blue Cadillac sitting in that fourth bay. It was going in the opposite direction. Like maybe Jellicoe was the driver, and he'd just left Professor Jordan's house. Try that on for size."

"Jellicoe dressed up as an old lady. Is that what you're saying?" Jack said.

"Why not? He assumed the professor's identity. What's to say he can't pretend to be a woman. Something triggered my reaction. Espinosa, you took pictures from the car, right?"

"I did, but in passing. Hell, I didn't even see the driver. I just clicked when you yelled for us to look at the car. Hold on, let me see what I got."

"When something is nothing like what it seems, you need to look into it," Ted said.

"Very astute, Mr. Robinson. I totally agree. I think we should find a vehicle that Mr. Jellicoe won't recognize and drive out to that retirement village and ask some questions."

Bert shared his and Kathryn's experience with the dog walkers from the night before. "We even have a street the couple thought might be where the woman lives. Butternut something or other. They said to talk to the mailman."

"Okay, here is the picture. All you can tell about the driver from this angle is the gray hair. Sorry, guys," Espinosa said.

"Let's head out to Manassas," Bert said. "We need a nondescript car that will not draw any attention to us as we cruise through the village. You know, a sedan of some kind. Old people like Chryslers for some reason. I read that somewhere," Bert said as an afterthought.

"What about the girls? Should we tell them what we're doing?"

The boys stopped, looked at one another, then laughed out loud. The sound was devilish, which meant they were in high spirits.

Forty minutes later, Jack was driving a Chrysler Sebring, and they were tooling down the highway.

"And our plan is . . . ?" Harry said from the backseat. His tone clearly said there better be a plan in motion.

"We drive up and down the streets until we find the mailman. We stop the car. We ask him questions. Then we drive off. We stop. We confer."

"And then we call out to Pinewood with our findings?" Bert said. "Shit! Kathryn is *not* going to like this when she finds out I blew off our day together to come out here with you guys."

"I will protect you, Bert," Harry said in a singsong voice from the backseat.

"What's with all that shit about protecting everyone, Harry? Are you up to something you haven't told us about?" Jack all but bellowed. Harry ignored the question.

"The couple Kathryn and I met last night said there are seventy-five homes where we're going. They said it is Phase One. They're going to start Phase Two after the first of the year."

"That was information we don't need, Bert," Harry said.

"Information is powerful. The more you have, the more successful you will be at dealing with the problem," Bert huffed.

"It's stupid," Harry said.

"My mother had an expression she was rather fond of,

which was, stupid is as stupid does," Jack said. "Okay, according to the GPS, we are a tenth of a mile from the entrance to the village."

"Do you think four guys asking questions of a mailman about an old lady with a robin's-egg blue Cadillac isn't going to come under suspicion?" Espinosa asked. "To me, that's an immediate red flag. Seniors are vulnerable to scam artists who prey on them."

"He has a point," Bert said. "I never thought of that."

"That's because you're stupid," Harry said. "Someone should have thought of it. No, not me, I'm your protection. Now, come up with something or I'm outta here."

"Espinosa and I have press credentials we can flash," Ted said.

"I have my old FBI credentials if the mailman doesn't look too close."

"I have my old D.A.'s Office card," Jack said. "We can swear him to secrecy. That leaves you, Harry. Who do you want to be?"

"I'm the guy who is going to kick your ass all the way to New Jersey. I'm me. I don't have to be anyone but myself."

"That was well said, Harry, and I respect every single word you just uttered. Just for the record, what do you think I would be doing when you kick my ass to New Jersey?"

"Flying," Harry said.

"I think we should discontinue this discussion," Ted said. "Look, there's the mailman, and this street is . . ." He craned his neck to see the concrete posts set at the end of the street, "Acorn. It crosses Butternut. It looks like he's headed to Yellow Squash Drive. I'd never want to live on a street called Yellow Squash Drive. Let's hit on him there. We don't want to be too close to Butternut in case that's really where he is. Is that okay with you, Harry?"

"It is, Ted."

Ted slowed the Sebring and slid to the curb. He got out as did the others. Credentials in hand, the boys approached the mailman, a tall muscular guy with a long blond ponytail and an earring. He was rolling a mail cart in front of him. He stopped and waited.

"Special Agent Navarro, this is District Attorney Jack Emery. Ted Robinson and Joe Espinosa from the *Post*. Harry Wong." The boys held out their IDs and Harry bowed.

"What do you want?"

"First things first. Your driver's license will do nicely. Mr. Espinosa will photograph it. A few questions. Your word that you will not discuss this little meeting. As in ever. Are we clear on that?"

"Yes, sir. I've been assigned this route from the day it was built, that would be four years, two months, and three days."

"Do you know any of the residents personally?"

"No, not personally. I go by addresses and names. Who are you looking for?"

"An elderly lady who drives an old baby blue Cadillac."

"That would be Bertha Tolliver. She lives on Butternut, number 17. She travels all the time, leaves notes on her door. Saw a note yesterday. It said . . ." The mailman squeezed his eyes shut as he tried to remember what the note said. "It said, 'Erma, I tried calling you to cancel lunch but your cell phone wasn't working. I'm going to Seattle and will be back after Labor Day.' There was duct tape at the top of the note and duct tape at the bottom to hold it in place. She put it smack-dab in the middle of a door wreath. Some kind of yellow flowers."

"So she's gone away?" Bert said.

The mailman shrugged. "When she goes away, she takes

her car. How I know this is when I drive around Yellow Squash Road, I can see her car in her carport. I haven't finished my route yet today so I don't know if she's there or not. Try knocking on the door."

"Do you know anyone who knows Ms. Tolliver?"

"No, sir, I don't. What did she do? Never mind, I don't want to know. Can I go now? These people get cranky when their mail is late."

"Remember what I told you. Not a word of this to anyone. One peep, and you'll be a guest of the Feds for an indefinite period of time."

"Not a problem," the mailman said as he moved off. He took one last look at Harry Wong, smiled, and then waved.

"It's my aura," Harry said.

"You know, Harry, you are so full of shit, your eyes are turning brown," Jack said.

Jack climbed behind the wheel and roared down the street. He looked in his rearview mirror to see the mailman offer up a single-digit salute. "Same to you," he muttered under his breath.

"Slow down, Jack. Go around the circle so Espinosa can take some pictures. We can only go around once; any more than that will make a senior suspicious. Okay, Espinosa, get ready."

"Did you get it?" Jack yelled.

"Hell, yes, I got it. I'm a photographer. However, just a bit of the hood can be seen, and you have to be at the right angle, which I wasn't. Ah, yeah, you can see a little blue. The car is there, boys! The mailman must be wrong, or she took a cab and a flight. He sounded pretty sure about how she traveled."

"Jack, turn right here, you made the circle, go slow, house 17, an uneven number, is on the left. We get one shot at this, too. Hit it, Espinosa. Zoom in on the door."

"Got it. Burn rubber, Jack," Espinosa said.

Jack ignored the order and continued to drive twenty-five miles an hour until they reached the highway. He drove for fifteen minutes, the occupants of the car silent until he pulled off onto a secondary road, which in turn led him to the parking lot of a roadside steakhouse. The lot was filling rapidly with the lunch crowd. He shifted into PARK and turned around. "What's it look like?"

"Just the way the mailman said, the note, the duct tape. The wreath is sunflowers, and the note is smack-dab in the middle. I don't get it, what's with the garage doors on a carport when the sides are open?"

Harry offered up his buzzword for the day. "Because whoever built this paradise is stupid, that's why."

"Well, I for one am glad I waited for your explanation, Harry. I can now get on with the business of living," Jack said.

"Eat shit, Jack."

"Okay, we need to take a vote here. Who believes Bertha Tolliver is Hank Jellicoe?"

Every hand in the car went up.

"So, what do we do with this information? Do we go back, circle the house, invade it, or do we go to lunch? If you don't like those two choices, we can go to Pinewood and dump it all in Charles's lap. Bear in mind that if we go back to Pinewood, we're giving Jellicoe hours to split again. That's if he saw us driving by."

"You think he stands by the window watching cars?" Bert asked.

"No. I think he has a camera by the front door, up under the eaves, that looks out onto the street. He wouldn't be there without some kind of warning system or surveillance. He must feel safe here to be so out in the open," Ted said. "I say we head back to Pinewood." The others agreed.

Halfway to their destination, Ted finally asked the question that had been plaguing him. "Do you really think Maggie is going to be pissed?"

"Oh, yeah," Jack drawled. "The thing with women is this. Even when they dump you and push you under the bus, they don't want anyone else to have you. I was never able to figure that out, but there you have it. Since you two apparently have an agreement, you don't owe Maggie any explanations. You are on your own, Ted," Jack said. "But I would advise this: Do not, I repeat, do not sneak around. That makes things worse. Women can come up with a hundred reasons why you did or didn't do something, and you don't have a fighting chance. So, if you go with the truth and don't sneak around, you won't be scrambling to come up with what you think Maggie might want to hear."

"I concur," Harry said.

"Oh, Harry, I so feel the wisdom emanating from the backseat." Jack cackled. Harry reached up and tweaked Jack's ear.

"Guess you're driving, Bert," Ted said, as he got out of the car to help drag Jack's body onto the passenger seat. Bert climbed behind the wheel.

"Harry, you have to stop doing that." Bert grinned.

"Why?"

Bert laughed as Jack slept peacefully.

Chapter 29

The war room in the underground tunnels at Pinewood bustled. Everyone was talking at once. Questions ripped off the walls and ricocheted to the point where Charles whistled sharply for silence. "Enough!"

"But Charles . . ." Isabelle blustered.

His hands still in midair, Charles descended the few steps to the table where the Sisters were sitting, the boys clustered in a tight group behind them. Noticeably absent was Maggie Spritzer. Charles explained her absence by saying she was only a phone call away, ready to change the front page of the *Post* if need be.

"We aren't even sure it is Hank at that house," Charles said.

The room went silent when Harry said, *"We're sure!"* And that was all the confirmation the Sisters needed.

Charles did a harrumph deep in his throat and moved on to what he was going to say next. "Then let me say this. We cannot spook Hank. That means no drive-bys. I have here a map of the retirement village. For starters, there are not seventy-five houses in Phase One. There are

275 houses. You were given erroneous information. For any of you interested, there will be a like number in Phase Two. And there are two mail carriers who deliver mail to Phase One.

"Having said that, there is a recreation center where special events are held—luncheons, birthdays, holiday gatherings, the like. A newsletter is published once a week to alert the residents of coupons at certain supermarkets, the lowest prices at local gas stations, which pharmacies give the best bang for your buck. It's all geared to senior living and making things as good and as comfortable for its residents as possible. It appears everyone is involved in everything. They have over two dozen committees. It's hard to keep track of, but I think I have a handle on it.

"Having said that, your plan, when you come up with one, does not have to be immediate. I think, and this is just a guess on my part, that Hank is going to stay right there in that house for a while. He's got to fall back and re-group, and what better place than where he is? I don't like giving you a deadline, but I feel comfortable saying I think you might have a week to develop a plan and act on it. Do you have a plan?"

"Well, of course we have a plan, Charles," Myra said huffily. "We just have to fine-tune it, and I think we can do that in the next several hours. Don't look so surprised, dear."

"I'd like to hear the plan, *dear.*"

"Well, of course you would." Myra pushed back her chair and stood up. "Because Annie and I are of an age with the women of the Red Hat Society I'm going to tell you about, we think it will work marvelously if we work in sync. It's the Red Hat Society. You boys probably don't know what that is, but I'm sure the girls do. There are chapters all over the country, globally, also. Ladies of a certain age, fifty and up, wear decorative red hats and purple clothing. Very fashionable. They have fun. Let me tell you about the society just to bring you up to speed.

"As I said, there are chapters everywhere, and there just happens to be one in the retirement village, with a very healthy membership. Annie and I signed up earlier online under assumed names, of course. These ladies basically answer to no one but themselves. More or less like us." She twinkled. "They celebrate life at every age and stage. They solidify and support the expansion of the bonds of sisterhood. As we do, girls. Now, are you all following me?"

Not waiting for a response, Myra continued, "The ladies discover and explore new interests and renew abandoned ones. They realize their personal potential and embrace a healthy, life-lengthening lifestyle. That's what it says on their Web site. In other words, they are working to get the most out of life, which I think is commendable, and at the same time they wear gorgeous hats and colorful clothing. Color is in this year, girls. And boys.

"A membership is thirty-nine dollars a year. That means each member who signs on is entitled to have an RHS chapter and be the Queen, complete with charter, inclusion on the Queen to Queens' Newsletter e-mail list, access to online chapter management tools, and it includes her own Supporting Membership. Each Hatter becomes a Supporting Member for twenty dollars."

"Wow!" Jack said. The Sisters glared at him. Jack had the good grace to look ashamed.

"And each member gets a unique, custom RHS keepsake, but as yet we don't know what that keepsake is."

"And your plan has something to do with the ladies in Red Hats?" Charles queried.

"Well, of course it does, Charles. We infiltrate the local

chapter the residents of the retirement village belong to. We arrange a party at their clubhouse. Or on their pavilion. We send out invitations to all the residents to attend. Hank, of course, will get an invitation. It will all be legitimate to cover all the activity that will be going on so as not to spook him. So in summary, ladies and gentlemen, the Red Hat Society is a global society that connects, supports, and encourages women in their pursuit of fun, friendship, freedom, fulfillment, and fitness, kind of like our little group."

"And . . ."

"And, what?" Myra huffed.

"Do you know any of the people on the board at the retirement village, any members of the various committees? How do you plan to organize this in a week's time?" Charles asked, his face registering total dismay.

Myra drew herself up to her full height and glared at her husband. "You said you wanted a plan. I just gave you the plan. You did not say I had to execute the plan. You're the one with the street maps and the locations. That is your forte, Charles."

And then everyone was talking at once.

"Do we get a red hat?" Alexis asked. "If I had the time, I could design us some eye-popping hats. Even so, I bet I can whip us up something that will blow everyone's socks off."

"Where do we come in?" Espinosa asked, his gaze on Alexis. "Is there a top hat or a black hat society for men? How are we going to get into the village?"

"Ask Charles," Myra snapped. "He's in charge of the details. Annie and I just came up with the plan."

"What's the purpose of this special get-together?" Nikki asked. "It has to be something important enough that Jellicoe will buy into it. Something *BIG*."

Suggestions and ideas flowed at the speed of light. Free memberships donated by some civic-minded person. Proceeds going to something that needed to be done or built at the retirement village. Luncheon or dinner catered by another civic-minded person. And on and on it went until the girls threw up their hands and called a halt.

"Don't look at us," Bert said. "We don't know anything about red hats and purple dresses. My mother always wore gray and black. Just tell us what you need us to do, and we'll do it."

"What about the paper? You said Maggie was standing by to possibly change the front page of the paper. You better get something to her quick, or she won't be able to change the front page."

The Sisters huddled. "Even if it's just a tease of some kind," Kathryn said. "I'm sure she can come up with something from the archives or from the Red Hat Web site. But don't we have to call someone at the retirement village to alert them that a party is being planned? By outsiders. Something could go awry if they see it in the paper before we alert them."

"Kathryn's right. Maybe Maggie could call from the *Post*. That would certainly give it all legitimacy and hopefully get everyone on board. We could even hire a party coordinator to set it all up. That's what they do. We pay for it, and it's win-win for everyone. The bottom line here is we want Jellicoe to see the article in the *Post* so he knows it's legitimate when all those red hats invade the village."

Fifteen minutes later, everyone had a task. Charles went back to his workstation, the boys right behind him as he explained the layout of the retirement village.

"You look worried, Charles. Care to share your concerns?" Ted asked.

"Women. Too many women. I'm not sure Hank won't see through it. He's got to be teetering on the edge. I told the girls I thought he was good for a week. I'm not sure about that, either."

"But the girls said that the Red Hat Society is legitimate. He can't fault that. It's a damn retirement village. That's what people do who live in those communities. They're dedicated to keeping everyone busy, so they don't atrophy. They have something going on twenty-four seven. We did a whole section one Sunday on retirement villages all up the Eastern seaboard.

"One old guy told me living in one of those communities was like getting a big group hug every day. He loved it, said it was the best thing he ever did by moving there. People cut your lawn, rake the leaves, shovel the snow, and you just watch them do it. Like he said, what's not to like? It's all included in some kind of fee," Ted said.

"Think of something, Ted, and call it in to Maggie," Charles said.

Ted and Espinosa walked off with a legal pad and pens.

"How are we going to invade his house?" Bert asked.

"I just got started, Bert. I have to think this through. For starters, I would really like it if that vehicle of his could be disabled somehow."

"That is not going to happen, Charles. Think of something else. If we get within sniffing distance of him, he's going to bolt. And I bet he has some serious horsepower under the hood of that Caddy. How about we drop down his chimney? Come in by air. The last time we came in by water," Jack said.

"We have to have a plan to cut off any and all escape routes before we do anything," Charles said. "Whenever there is any kind of gathering with seniors and there are crowds, they usually have ambulances standing by. We could hire a few of those and block the entrances and exits. If you look carefully at this map, there are only two entrances and exits. You can enter by either the south entrance or the north entrance. There is no other way to get in or out of that village."

"Then let's make that work for us. I didn't pay all that much attention to the yards. Could he drive through someone's yard to get to an exit?" Jack asked.

"Not with all those brick walls surrounding the place," Charles said.

"We're going to need a diversion that will seem legitimate. How about a parade?" Bert asked.

"A parade of what?" Harry growled.

"The ladies in their hats, what else? You need to get with the program here. They can parade up and down all the streets, starting with Butternut, where Jellicoe is holed up. Yeah, yeah, I'm liking this. Or that cross street, Acorn. The best hat in the parade gets a prize. Women love prizes. Tell Ted so he can have Maggie put it in the paper. What's the prize, though? Should be something substantial. How about one of those bright red Miatas. For sure that will bring every lady who owns a red hat to the scene. Oh, yeah, this is so perfect I can't stand it. Ted!" Jack bellowed.

"Articulate, my friend," Ted said, his pen poised over his legal pad. Jack laid it all out.

"Now, that's a plan. Where do we get the car?"

"Annie?" Jack bellowed a second time. In short order, Annie gave the okay and said she herself would call the car dealership and order the car. Five minutes after she gave her okay, Ted had Maggie on the phone. She promised to send one of her reporters to the car dealership to photograph a lady in a red hat standing next to the red sports car. The donor, after ten minutes of discussion, was Bess

Gold, who worked in the classified department at the *Post* and a Red Hatter herself. Translation: Bess Gold owned a red hat.

"It's coming together. Do you approve, Harry?" Jack asked nervously.

"I do, Jack."

"Harry, old buddy, you have no idea how good that makes me feel. Just knowing you . . . Okayyy, Harry, I see that . . . that look in your eye that bodes ill for me if I continue along this vein."

"Shut up, Jack. How do we get in the house?"

"Now, that I do not know. Charles, explain how we're going to get in the house, so Harry doesn't get upset."

Charles looked at Harry with his steely gaze. Harry returned the look. Charles was the one who looked away first. Harry smiled. "I haven't worked that out yet, gentlemen. Does anyone know what kind of turnout we can expect? I am the first to admit I know nothing about ladies in red hats and purple dresses. Do any of you know *anything?* Are we talking hundreds, thousands, a few, what? And do these ladies have partners when they participate in events such as this? Crowd control could be an issue."

Ted was back. "Maggie has it going on. She's excited, believe it or not. She said she'll make the deadline and to watch the paper in the morning."

"That's when you should have told her about that chick you met in the bar," Bert said.

"Ha-ha, Mr. Smart-Ass. I did tell her, and she said, 'Have fun.' "

Bert and Jack started to laugh. "Yeah, she said that now. Wait till you have that fun she wished on you." When Harry started to giggle, Ted turned white.

"Stop trying to ruin my day," Ted blustered.

"You ruined it yourself, don't go blaming us," Harry said.

"Okay, okay. Now what?" Ted asked.

"I think we're done here. Charles has to fine-tune things. Let's see what the girls have going on," Jack suggested.

"I really think this is going to work," Annie said, her eyes sparkling. "There's not one thing Jellicoe can take issue with. It was his dumb luck to move into a place full of Red Hatters. We did so good on short notice, I think we should all go upstairs and have a drink of something to celebrate how wonderful it is when we all work together. And then we can call it a night."

Hank Jellicoe fixed his breakfast, a hearty one made from Egg Beaters and pancake batter that he'd set out on the counter to thaw the night before. He had precooked turkey bacon he warmed up in the oven and fresh-baked blueberry muffins that he mixed from a package. A strong pot of dark coffee was brewing. With a breakfast like that under his belt, he could handle anything that came his way. And the other reason he always liked to eat hearty in the morning was to fortify himself for any and all news he might see when he went online.

He stood at his back door and looked out into the yard. The end of summer, everything was straggly and already turning brown from lack of rain. Like he gave two hoots in hell about the yard or the lack of rain. At best he'd be here a few more days and then . . . *Then what?* he asked himself. "Move on to another safe house."

His policy was never to stay longer than a week in any one place, but he might have to stay longer this time until he could figure out what direction he was going to go in.

He didn't know why, but he felt as safe as a baby in its mother's womb. Maybe it had something to do with pretending to be a woman. For the first time in a long time, he thought about his mother. She'd been a kind, pleasant woman who had loved him, nurtured him, fed him well, made sure he brushed his teeth and said his prayers every night on his knees. He wondered what she would think of him now if she were still alive. Mothers, it was said, loved unconditionally. He shook his head to clear his thoughts. No more waltzing down Memory Lane for him.

Jellicoe wolfed down his food, cleared up the kitchen, and turned on his computer. The first thing he did was pull up the *Post* online. His eyes almost popped out of his head as he read column after column. Son of a fucking bitch! Just when he was feeling safe for the moment. He frowned and went back and read the article again. Maybe he was safe. He got up, walked over to the kitchen counter, where he'd stacked all the crappy junk the mailman pushed through the slot on the door.

He found the weekly newsletter. He reached for the phone and called the clubhouse. A quivery-sounding voice said she was Helen Wasserman and what could she do to help him. Jellicoe cleared his throat, identified himself as Bertha Tolliver, and asked what time the festivities started on Sunday.

"Twelve noon. Sharp. Bertha, I certainly hope you plan on attending. You're on our books, but you never come to any events. Do you need assistance? If you do, we'll be glad to provide help. We help one another, so don't ever be shy about asking for help. So, can I mark you down for attending? Can you see yourself driving that little sports car? It is the buzz of this place this morning. We are going to have such a record turnout this month."

"Absolutely," Jellicoe said in his fake female voice. He

broke the connection and stared at the phone. Nothing screamed at him. It was what it was. He was still safe.

Jellicoe went back to reading the news online. A big bunch of nothing was going on in the world. He went back to the front page and printed it out. Before the end of the day, he would dissect the entire article, memorize it, then make the decision to leave or stay. His instincts hadn't deserted him yet.

With nothing else to occupy his time other than television and the twenty-four-hour news channels and their constant rehash of events, he decided to check out the Red Hat Society. He read everything there was to read, checked and printed out what he could from the RHS Web site. By evening he would have it all memorized.

As he read through the write-ups, he knew, just knew, his mother would have been a member if she were still alive. Not so his wife Louise. No, not Louise. He started to think then about his wife and where she'd gone and taken their daughter. Where was the infamous diary she'd turned over to the CIA? He was never sure in his own mind that she'd just upped and handed it over, then disappeared, but that was the story he was told and the story he'd had to live with. Their way of keeping him in line.

Now he was in a melancholy mood, and he didn't like it one bit, but he also knew he had to let his mind go through the motions before he could move on to other things.

He supposed if he had any regrets, it was that he never got to see what his daughter looked like as an adult. Those growing years . . . those were just a blur. He didn't know if she was into scraped knees, pigtails, bikes, and roller skates. Or was she a priss like her mother and played with dolls and had tea parties? He'd told Louise he wasn't father material with the kind of work he did, but did she listen? No, she did not. She wanted a kid, and that was the end of it. Where the hell was she? How had she aged? Did the girl, Christ, he couldn't even remember what the hell her name was, look like him or Louise?

He wondered if he would have felt differently then and now if Louise had given birth to a son. Probably not. Kids just had a habit of getting in the way. Kids belonged to their mothers.

No, Louise would want no part of wearing a Red Hat or belonging to any kind of society where the women wore red and purple.

"Crap."

Hours later, when he was ready to retire for the night, he'd memorized every single detail from the *Post* and from what he'd read online. His last conscious thought before falling asleep was that he was safe from the Red Hat ladies.

The next few days were filled with whirlwind activities as the Sisters coordinated every single detail of Sunday's event. Maggie kept a story running every day, with pictures of the Red Hat Ladies. She also kept a running tally on the front page of the women eager to sign up with the RHS. Orders online for one-of-a-kind red hats hit an all-time high. The stores that carried hats said they were flying off the shelves.

"Well, aren't we lucky that Alexis is making ours? A pity we won't be able to take part in the parade," Annie grumbled. "The last time I wore a hat was when my mother put a bonnet on me; I was ten months old. That was a lifetime ago. There should have been a few hats in between, don't you think, Myra?"

"Look at it this way. You have those rhinestone cowgirl

boots. Everyone comments on them, and you don't wear a hat indoors. Are you getting the point, Annie?"

Annie sniffed. "Still, I should have worn a hat someplace."

"I wouldn't worry about it, dear. In less than twenty-four hours, it will all be over. I can't remember the last time I was this excited."

"Myra, you look like you're embalmed. Where's the excitement? Oh, you're pulling my leg. I wish you'd tell me when you do that. Maybe you aren't excited, but I am. I want to get my hands around that man's neck and just *squeeze* until the light leaves his eyes and he collapses to the floor. Have we decided how we're going to go in yet?"

"Charles, more or less at this moment, thinks through the back. His thinking is that Hank will be glued to the front part of the house to watch what's going on. I think I agree. He's going to be watching for *us*. That's not to say he won't have the back end booby-trapped. We're probably going to end up going in on the fly, but at least we'll be dressed for the part."

Annie's cell rang. She looked down. "Hello, Maggie. Do you have news? Phase Two is totally sold out. Suddenly seniors from all over want to move here to where all the fun is going on. By here, you mean the retirement village," Annie repeated for Myra's benefit. "All the news crews will be there. The ladies will love that, I'm sure. Such wonderful news coverage for such a fun group. Actually, dear, we are beyond excited. Myra can hardly contain herself. You didn't say, Maggie, are you coming out or are you planning a special edition?"

Annie listened, and said, "That's a good idea. A whole insert dedicated to the RHS. Every senior in the area will thank you. Wish us luck, dear."

Annie broke the connection. "She does wish us luck. A whole section. That's dynamite, Myra. Especially with the capture of Hank Jellicoe and if the RHS are the ones who take credit for his capture. I am so all atwitter. I hope I can sleep tonight. Do you think you're going to be able to sleep, Myra?"

"Not if you keep jabbering at me. Let's go over this one more time, Annie. I know the girls said they had it down pat when they left. The part that worries me is getting him out of the house and out to the road. One of the substations said earlier that all traffic was going to be banned from either going in or out until the parade was over. They're expecting thousands of people. How did it all mushroom so fast?"

"We put Maggie on it is how it happened." Annie laughed. "Come along, friend, we have to try to get some sleep. We've got to be dressed and out of here by ten o'clock. Then, bright and early Tuesday morning, no matter what happens tomorrow, we are out of here and headed back to Vegas to put the finishing touches on Kathryn's surprise party."

"I am so looking forward to that." Myra smiled.

"Me, too," Annie said throwing her arm around Myra's shoulder. "There's nothing like a good party to perk a person up. It's called *living!*"

Sunday dawned clear and bright. The humidity for some reason had deserted the area and the temperature was a pleasing seventy-three degrees. A perfect day to dress up and take part in a parade.

The Sisters and their counterparts were a caravan of their own. State police, the sheriff and his deputies, and police from the neighboring towns were out in full force.

Bert whipped his way to the front of the line, showed his FBI credentials, and whizzed through the now-open barricade, his convoy right behind him. Everywhere they looked, there were red and purple balloons. They drove to Yellow Squash Road and parked their cars. Then they separated and inched their way to Acorn Drive, where they waited in little groups. Their small group didn't stand out in any way whatsoever; the streets were congested with residents, rubberneckers, and people from outside the village, meandering around, taking in the scenery and observing all the activity associated with the festivities. The noise was incredible.

"I can see that little bit of blue on the hood of his car, so he's still in there," Espinosa said, clicking away furiously with his camera.

Jack looked down at his watch. "Oh, Jesus, whose idea was that band?" he asked as he could hear the members tuning up.

"Maggie's. You know, to kick it off." At Jack's blank look, Ted said, "So the ladies can strut their stuff. This *is* about them, you know. You know Maggie, she doesn't miss a trick."

"Yeah, yeah, good idea. What are they going to play?"

Ted let loose with a loud guffaw. "Maggie gave them two choices, along with the promise of new band uniforms if they could play 'Pretty Woman' and 'Cherry Pink and Apple Blossom White.' I imagine it will be somewhere in the middle or a combination of both. Who the hell knows? They're kids. You get what you get. And when it comes right down to it, it's the noise that counts."

"This thing sure did grow legs at the speed of light. Jellicoe must be having a shit fit inside that house as he tries to figure out if this is a setup or not," Jack said, his gaze going in all directions. "That bastard might try to go out the back if he gets spooked. That's what's worrying me right now."

"Relax, Jack. It ain't gonna happen. This thing is too big, too organized for him to think we could pull this off in just a matter of days. You know how he is with strategy, details, and setting up parameters and flanks and all that shit. He's staying put," Ted insisted.

Jack looked at his watch again, then over at the girls, who were wandering around like they had nothing on their minds, their floppy red hats shielding their faces, their flowing purple dresses sweeping the ground. Jack whistled sharply and held up his two fingers. "Get in place!"

The sound of a bullhorn, then the sharp blast of an air horn shattered the noisy Sunday afternoon. The high school band made some off-key noises, then swung into their own rendition of "Pretty Woman" as the Red Hatters fell in line and started marching to the beat of the music.

It was a blinding sea of red and purple as the ladies smiled and waved as cameras clicked and video was shot, making it impossible to carry on a conversation. So Jack used hand signals to get everyone in place.

"What if he tries to go out the front door?" Espinosa asked.

Jack pointed to Harry, who was on his belly snaking his way along the side of the house. If the door opened, all he had to do was lunge for Jellicoe's ankles and bring him to the ground.

The Sisters crept forward, single file, Bert, Jack, Ted, and Espinosa off to the side. It was Bert who was to kick down the door so the others could rush inside. They'd rehearsed this move so many times back at Pinewood, Bert felt he could do it in his sleep.

With the door being six small panes of glass on the top and less-than-sturdy wood on the bottom, he knew the weakest point and kicked with all of his 220 pounds. The door shattered, and the Sisters rushed in, Yoko in the lead. She was the air as she literally breezed through the house and nailed Jellicoe just as he was approaching the kicked-in front door. She whirled and kicked it shut a nanosecond after Harry barreled through.

They were on him like a swarm of locusts, each of them taking out eighteen months of their hatred and vengeance on the man who, they believed, had ruined their lives. The boys could only watch in horror and thank God they weren't the recipient of the Sisters' vengeance. When they were done, Henry, call me Hank, Jellicoe was a bloody mess. To his credit, he hadn't made a sound during the ugly beating. His teeth were scattered everywhere, one ear was hanging by a thin strip of skin. His face was a bloody pulp, his eyes swollen shut. Blood dripped from every part of his body.

Jack kicked at the figure on the floor. "But you girls promised to leave something for us to work over. There's nothing left."

"We lied, Jack," Nikki said. "This was our fight. It's over now. Alexis, where's the duct tape?"

"Right here," Alexis responded, and she pulled several rolls from her bright red bag and tossed one after the other in Nikki's direction.

"Work it, Kathryn. Ankles, knees, and don't forget his dick. If you have to, twist that sucker right off," Nikki shouted. "Come on, come on, we need to move faster. Yoko, where's the dress? Get it out and put it on him. Who has the hat? Someone start up that damn car out there! Move, people!"

Jack and Harry moved closer to each other. Safety in

numbers, as the loves of their lives did what no one else could do. Harry's eyes shone with admiration. Jack had to admit he felt a thrill of excitement. He did love a forceful woman.

Annie raced through the broken kitchen door and out to the carport, where she raised the doors that closed in the front of the carport, then hopped in the car. No keys! She raced back inside. "No keys!" The high school band swung into a blaring version that almost sounded like "Cherry Pink and Apple Blossom White." She supposed they'd earned the new band uniforms.

"Bert, we don't have time to look for them. Hot-wire it," Jack bellowed.

Bert raced out of the house.

"Has he said anything?" Myra asked as she looked down at her bloody hands.

"I think Kathryn might have smashed his windpipe when she swung her arm. No, Myra, he hasn't said a single thing," Yoko gurgled with happiness.

"Who has the diary?"

"It's in my bag," Alexis said.

"Hey, he's good to go then!" Nikki said. "Let's get this show on the road."

They moved like clockwork, the way they always did when they were on a mission.

"No fingerprints to tie us here!" Annie shouted.

The girls as one held up their latex-glove-covered hands.

"You know what to do. We'll meet you there. The road is clear. We did good, girls!" Myra said.

Their destination: the headquarters of the Federal Bureau of Investigation in Washington, D.C.

The entire crew arrived, to no fanfare, on a Sunday afternoon. Once again, they worked in sync, the Sisters calling out instructions, the boys doing their bidding. It was

Bert who called in to headquarters and asked for Director Yantzy. When he came on the phone, Bert said, "Director, someone delivered a package to me and asked me to deliver it to you. It's waiting for you out front. Come and get it. You can thank me later."

The Sisters stood on the periphery and watched as Jack and Bert duct-taped Henry, call me Hank, Jellicoe to the plate-glass door of the FBI building. Louise Jellicoe's diary was taped to his chest. "Just so you know, you son of a bitch, this is your wife's diary. She kept a copy. Yeah, the vigilantes found her, and she's got a great life. Suck on that one, you bastard!"

Jack reached up to adjust the red-feathered hat to a rakish angle. "That purple dress drapes beautifully," Myra said.

"You got it, Espinosa?"

"I do, and it's on its way. The only thing missing is a sign that says he's Hank Jellicoe."

Harry let loose with what Jack called his smoke bombs, and the group disappeared just as the door to the FBI Building opened.

"What the hell. . . . Well, well, well, if it isn't Henry Jellicoe. It is you, isn't it, Hank? You are Hank Jellicoe, right? Well, lookie here, you're all dressed up with nowhere to go. I like that hat. Boys, do you like Mr. Jellicoe's hat? *Tsk-tsk-tsk*. That dress would probably bring out the color of your eyes if you could open them," Yantzy said as he stared off across the pavilion through the waning smoke.

Director Yantzy offered up a crisp salute. "Ladies, I do admire your style," Yantzy muttered under his breath as he motioned for his agents to peel Jellicoe off the door. "No need to be gentle, but we should call a doctor. Well, when we get him upstairs, we can call a doctor. Or not."

Yantzy's lead agent turned to look at his boss. "Do we know who . . . delivered him to us?"

"I do believe the clue is in his attire. Those Red Hat ladies are having a day of it today. Don't you read the papers?" Yantzy shrugged. "Hey, you wanted an answer, and it's the best one I can think of. At the moment. It's a damn good thing those schmucks from the *Post* aren't here. Jesus, can you imagine what that paper would do with a picture of this asshole duct-taped to the front door of the FBI building?"

The agent shuddered at the thought. "What's that book taped to his chest?"

"I don't know, but I suspect that it's the answer to all my prayers." Under his breath, he murmured, "Ladies, I am forever in your debt."

"And they say Monday mornings are dull," Annie said as she opened the paper Maggie had hand-delivered. Everyone had a copy. The Sisters' comments were ripe, lusty, and bawdy as they pored over the luscious picture of Hank Jellicoe duct-taped to the door of the Hoover Building.

Director Yantzy is giving all the credit to the Red Hat ladies for apprehending the notorious terrorist or mercenary or whatever you want to call Jellicoe. He said the FBI is going to give a special commendation to their corporate headquarters. I just love, love, love it!"

"Girls, do you feel vindicated now? Do you think you can put those eighteen months behind you and get on with your lives at last?" Myra asked.

The Sisters looked at one another and smiled. "We can," they said as one.

Harry swooned. Jack went limp, and Bert froze in place. Ted looked at Maggie and winked. She did not return the wink. Espinosa hopped from one foot to the other as he waited for Alexis to look at him. When she smiled, he grinned from ear to ear.

The world was suddenly right side up for everyone.

Charles had the last word. "You did good, ladies and gentlemen. I'm proud of you."

"Then let's drink to that!" Annie said.

Epilogue

"**I** have to say, Kathryn, driving cross-country was an experience I will never forget," Bert announced as he gathered his things to hop down from the cab in the truck. "I can't wait to get cleaned up and take you to dinner to celebrate your birthday. Are you excited?"

"About turning forty? I don't think so. I've been trying to get up the nerve to ask you if we could do it tomorrow. I'm beat, Bert. I just want a nice hot shower, some warm delicious food, and a soft bed. With you in that bed. If you want to give me the perfect birthday present, that's what I want. Please!"

Murphy let loose with a loud bark as much as to say he wanted the same thing as his mistress. Bert hopped down, and Murphy leapt to the ground.

They were in the underground garage, where staff were approaching to unload the slot machines from the back of the eighteen-wheeler.

Bert panicked. His instructions were crystal clear. No matter what, he was to deliver Kathryn to the party room on the fourth floor. They were to use the service elevator, so Kathryn would not see that the casino was empty even though the bells and whistles could be heard periodically. His panic dissipated when a member of the staff approached Kathryn and said that Miss de Silva wanted to see her on the fourth floor as soon as she arrived.

Kathryn sighed. "Can it possibly wait till morning?" One look at the petrified expression on the staff member's face told her it could not wait. Murphy barked again as Kathryn signed off on the manifest. "Okay, okay, I am going to the fourth floor. I don't know what could be so damn important I can't take a shower first," she mumbled as she led Murphy to the elevator.

"You know Annie when she gets a bee in her bonnet. She wants it an hour ago. We are two hours late, Kathryn. I think she just wants to make sure you're okay. In other words, she's being motherly."

"Yeah, yeah, yeah," Kathryn said, leaning back against the wall of the elevator. She closed her eyes. "So, did you really enjoy the trip, or are you just saying that to make me feel good because it's my birthday?"

"I wouldn't do that, Kathryn. I did enjoy the trip. I don't think I could do it every day or even every week, but I do have a new appreciation of why you like what you do. I'm apologizing here. I won't say another word about your driving your rig. If that's what you want to do, I'm okay with it."

Kathryn's eyes snapped open at the same moment the elevator door slid open. "Really, Bert?"

Bert grinned. "Really, Kathryn."

Murphy raced down the hall to the banquet room. "Hmm, wonder how he knew which room it was. Guess he picked up Annie's scent. Come on, Bert, let's get this over with, so I can hit the shower."

Bert opened the door.

"SURPRISE!"

Kathryn sagged against Bert as tears flooded her eyes. She swiped at them with the back of her hand. Annie slapped a flute of champagne into her hand. "Happy birthday, darling girl!"

And then they were all crushing against her, hugging her, slapping her on the back. The laughter and the happiness was so real, Kathryn felt light-headed. These people were her family, each and every person in this banquet room. It was a moment in time she would never forget. Ever.

"So, we managed to surprise you?" Myra said.

"You certainly did. I think I'm shocked beyond belief. However did you manage all of this?" Kathryn said, waving her arms about.

Myra looked at Annie, and said, "This woman is relentless. She worked tirelessly to pull this off. We were so worried something would delay you, the truck would break down, whatever, and Bert just kept sending texts giving us the timetable. We've been waiting for hours. We aren't complaining, so don't think we are. Annie just wanted to make it as perfect for you as she could. She actually closed the casino for today and tonight."

"Oh, my God! You did all that for me?" More tears flowed as Kathryn wrapped her arms around Annie in a fierce bear hug. "It's beautiful. I just love balloons!"

"We had a lot left over from the Red Hat parade." Annie laughed.

"I love the ice sculpture! That's a pretty big forty. And a Cristal champagne fountain! It looks like all my favorite foods. Oh, Annie, Myra, everyone, this is so wonderful! And the best part is, suddenly I'm not tired. I feel like dancing. Who knew turning forty could be so wonderful?"

The two older women watched as Kathryn and Bert took to the dance floor. Kathryn's uniform of well-worn flannel shirt, no matter what the weather, equally worn jeans, and her Timberland boots did not look out of place.

What seemed like a long time later, the dance band trooped out of the banquet room, and the bell rang for dinner. Bert led Kathryn, as the guest of honor, to the gorgeous buffet table. The ice sculpture gleamed in the candlelight. The array of food was overwhelming, but Kathryn did her best to heap her plate with a little of everything.

The guests were seated. Annie and Myra, the evening's hostesses, stood up and proposed a toast to the birthday girl. The chefs, the waiters, waitresses, and stewards discreetly withdrew, virtually sealing off the room. And then just as they wound down from the birthday song, the last seat at the long table was filled.

A hush came over the room as Kathryn looked down the table at the last guest to arrive. She felt a lump in her throat as she gripped the edges of the table.

The uninvited, poorly dressed guest stood and looked down the long table. "I desperately find myself in need of your help, ladies and gentlemen." The poorly dressed guest reached up and yanked at her raggedy wig.

Shocked speechless, the guests could only stare at the uninvited guest. "No one knows I'm here except the Secret Service I traveled with. I'll be back at 1600 Pennsylvania Avenue before the sun comes up, and my PDB arrives at my door. I just have time for a yes or no, ladies and gentlemen."

Either the group didn't hear the words or they were still shocked speechless, because every hand in the room shot in the air. President Connor smiled. "Thank you. It looks like a lovely party; I wish I could stay, but I can't." She fixed her gaze on Lizzie Fox and said, "Call me for the details."

President Connor walked down the length of the table, held out her arms, and hugged Kathryn. "Happy birthday, Kathryn. How wonderful it must be to have so many friends to do something this magnificent for you."

And then she was gone, the crazy-looking wig riding high on her head as her security surrounded her to lead her from the room.

Kathryn took a huge gulp of air. "Well, guys, that was one hell of a present!"

"Party time!" Annie bellowed.

"We can talk about . . . our visitor in the morning," Myra said.

"Happy birthday!" greetings rocked the banquet room.

"And you wanted to take a shower and go to bed," Bert hissed in Kathryn's ear.

"Yeah"—she giggled—"can you believe that?"

"You gonna marry me, Kathryn?"

Kathryn thought about the question. "Ya know what, Bert? I just might."